NOT AFTER EVERY- thing

NOT AFTER EVERY- THING

MICHELLE LEVY

DIAL BOOKS
an imprint of Penguin Group (USA) LLC

DIAL BOOKS

Published by the Penguin Group
Penguin Group (USA) LLC
375 Hudson Street New York, New York 10014

USA/Canada/UK/Ireland/Australia/New Zealand/India/South Africa/China
penguin.com
A Penguin Random House Company

Library of Congress Cataloging-in-Publication Data
Levy, Michelle.
Not after everything / Michelle Levy.
pages cm
Summary: "After his mom kills herself, Tyler shuts out the world—until falling in love
with Jordyn helps him find his way toward a hopeful future"—Provided by publisher.
ISBN 978-0-8037-4158-4 (hardback)
[1. Suicide—Fiction. 2. Grief—Fiction. 3. Love—Fiction.] I. Title.
PZ7.1.L49No 2015
[Fic]—dc23   2014044862

Printed in the United States of America

1 3 5 7 9 10 8 6 4 2

Designed by Maya Tatsukawa
Text set in Calisto MT Std

FOR ARLENE AND FRANK LEVY:
the most supportive parents a creative soul could ever
hope for. Thank you for always believing in me.

ONE

A thick, pink-polished fingernail strikes the edge of my desk—two succinct taps—and I look up from my poetic masterpiece, right into Mrs. Hickenlooper's eyes. They bulge like her three hefty chins are trying to choke the life out of her.

"Am I boring you, Mr. Blackwell?"

I return to scratching the letter S into the top left corner of my notebook. "I assume that's rhetorical."

Muffled laughter from the class. Mrs. Hickenlooper's bulbous eyes narrow—no easy feat.

"Out." She juts her talon in the direction of the door, as if I'm too stupid to locate it myself.

I feel another sarcastic remark bubbling up, but I swallow it back as I casually finish the last of my scratching.

There.

Now F-U-C-K T-H-I-S will be visible in the top margin of at least the next thirty sheets of notebook paper. I know it isn't particularly clever or imaginative, but I smile all the same. Then I calmly collect my belongings and stroll out of AP macroeconomics, unsure how, exactly, being forced to leave all *this* is a punishment. She expects me to report to the guidance counselor's office like she has the last three times, but of course I won't.

I drift down the mostly empty hallways until . . . I don't know, whatever. Truthfully, I kind of hope the asshole hall monitor will find me and dole out some sort of actual punishment.

"'S up, Tyler?" one of my old teammates says as I pass the gym. Before, I would have taken my frustrations out on the weights. Now it just seems so stupid. I nod a greeting to Ted and continue walking.

Time's not the same as it used to be, and suddenly the hallways are filled with people I used to be able to stand. I never even heard the bell. I have AP chem now, but it doesn't really matter if I show up. Mr. Waters wouldn't dare fail me. Even crusty Mrs. Hickenlooper will probably still give me an A. I wish she wouldn't. I wish they would all stop tiptoeing around me just because my mom offed herself over the summer.

A firm hand grips my shoulder, forcing a jolt of adrenaline through me.

"Jeez, man. Relax."

Marcus.

His girlfriend clings to his arm like if she let go, he'd instantly find another chick to hook up with. In all fairness, he probably would. Marcus isn't picky. Well, that's not entirely true. Marcus, much to the chagrin of his mother and the entire African American female population of our school, only likes white girls. Preferably blondes, although this one—number twelve, I think?—is a rare brunette. Probably because she has huge tits. I make the mistake of looking at her face. She stares back at me with that infuriatingly caring look. If people knew how that face really made me feel, they'd be more careful. One of these days the wrong person is going to look at me like that, and I will seriously lose my shit.

"Baby," Marcus says to poor unsuspecting number twelve, "I'll meet you after gym by my locker, 'kay?"

After a disgustingly public tongue bath, Twelve finally leaves.

"Yo, Tyler, where you headed?" Marcus yells down the hall after me.

"AP chem," I say, not stopping.

"I got English," he says, catching up.

Marcus was my best friend, but now . . . I don't know. It's just kind of awkward. I mean, I guess we mostly only ever talked football. But football just doesn't seem all that important in the grand scheme of things. Not to me. Not anymore.

"Well, I'll see you in gym," Marcus says, slowing until he's fallen behind me.

When I reach the lab, I hesitate by the door. Do I really need to be here? The first week of school is always pointless, but the first week of your senior year when you could feasibly fail everything and still get into a state school seems even more pointless. I've always done well in school. Not because I needed to prove something or impress my parents or whatever. I just like it. I actually like learning.

The guys give me shit about my grades, but I don't care. Especially when Coach contacted Stanford about a football scholarship. The scout came toward the end of the season last year when I was totally on my game, and they flew my mom and me out to visit the campus, where they offered me a National Letter of Intent. I signed without batting an eye. A Pac-12 school with an Ivy League–level education for practically free? Um, hell yeah. It's not that I'm all that great a player, but I'm fast as hell. Plus with my 2340 SATs and 4.3 GPA, let's just say the admissions department was happy to offer me a football scholarship. And a scholarship is the only way I'd ever get any kind of college education, let alone one at freaking Stanford.

The second bell rings. Class is about to start. Mr. Waters makes eye contact with me out in the hallway. Damn. Too late to turn and run.

Running is the only thing that brings me any release these days. Thank god for gym. I'm in a groove, way ahead of the others. That is, until Marcus catches up with me, practically killing himself in the process.

"Man, you're on fire," he gasps, like he's not used to the mile-high altitude, when he's lived in Denver his whole life.

I nod, trying not to let the interruption slow my pace.

"You coming to practice today?"

I haven't been to practice since early summer. Since I found my mom in a tub of her own blood. A few weeks before school started, I told Coach, Marcus, and a few others who were in Coach's office, that I wouldn't be back this year because I had to work, that I wouldn't have the time. Coach told me to "take as long as you need," like he thought I didn't really mean it. But I did. And I wish Marcus would stop hounding me about it.

"Gotta work." I push myself harder, setting my quads on fire. It feels good.

I make it a few laps without thinking about anything, but then I'm about to lap the rest of the class, so I slow my pace, keep my distance. Marcus slows down until he's running next to me again.

"So what, are you, like, quitting?" he asks. I can barely understand him, he's breathing so hard.

"What can I say? My dad's a prick. I gotta work."

"What about your scholarship?"

"I guess I'm not going to college."

Marcus stumbles, but recovers and catches up to me again.

"Look, that was my mom's plan, and she didn't have the guts to see it through, so why the hell should I?"

He ignores my tone and presses on. "Well, what are you going to do?"

"No fucking clue." I don't wait for a reply. I push myself again, weaving through the others, focused, until all I can hear are my feet hitting the asphalt, my steady breathing, and the beat of my heart pounding in my head.

○ ○ ○

"Um . . . Uh . . . You want ham and cheese?" the chubby, middle-aged woman asks her tween daughter, who couldn't look more horrified about being in public with her totally uncool mom. She grunts what I think is meant to be a "Yes" and goes back to texting.

"Six-inch or foot-long?" I ask.

Roger glances over at me from the register. I have somehow managed to not meet his high standards of sandwich artistry yet again.

"Let's do a foot-long. Then we can share it," the mom says. The girl snorts her annoyance.

"What kind of bread would you—"

"Wheat," the girl says, the *duh* implicit.

I pull out one of the older pieces of wheat, one that's dry and extra-crunchy.

"Can you cut it now?" the girl says. "I don't want her fatty mayo near my half."

I do as told. The daughter goes back to texting, not even looking up as she orders me to add toppings, like she has eyes on the top of her head. Every time her mother asks for a topping she doesn't approve of, the daughter sighs heavily.

Roger grabs the sandwiches from my hands the second I finish stuffing them into the bag and rings them up. He's aggressively polite to everyone, including me, even though I'm pretty sure he hates my guts. It makes me want to punch him, just to see how he'd react if confronted with any unpleasantness.

It's not like I'm dying to spend all my free time working at Subway, but it was the first job I found after my dad informed me that if I wanted to continue driving my crappy car or, you know, eating, I would have to figure shit out for myself. I don't think he cares that technically he's responsible for me until my eighteenth birthday, which is exactly 217 days away.

The second I turn eighteen, I plan to get the fuck outta Dodge. I will leave this godforsaken place behind and never look back. Screw graduation. Everyone knows the ceremony is really only for the parents. And that would require parents who A) are alive, or B) give a shit.

This year was supposed to be about maintaining my GPA and keeping the Stanford people happy so I didn't lose the scholarship, and then I could be on my way to a better life. I was going to take my mom far away from my prick father, show her that she didn't have to live the way she did. I don't know exactly what I had planned to do—get an MBA and work my way up the corporate ladder at some Fortune 500 company? Maybe. But whatever. She selfishly took that away from me. I'd been doing it all for her anyway. So now what?

"Ty? You want to take your break? I can hold down the fort," Roger says. It takes every ounce of restraint for me not to choke him for calling me Ty. Only my girlfriend calls me that, and the only reason I don't choke her is 'cause she's a girl.

I must look sad or something. I try to hold that shit in for when I'm alone—it makes people uncomfortable.

Shit. Brett's black 3 Series Beemer's parked at the Conoco. But my tank's on E, so I don't have a choice—I won't make it home if I don't stop.

I park at the pump farthest from Brett. It doesn't keep him from spotting me.

Brett's the new running back. He should be grateful I'm no longer playing, but for some reason he hates me. I suspect it has something to do with Sheila.

Brett shakes his blond hair out of his eyes and greets me with a raised middle finger. Then he bends to say something to the passenger or passengers—his windows are so tinted, you can never tell who's inside—before throwing his head back and making a face like he's having an orgasm. Apparently this is him laughing. What is it about BMWs? Do they make you an asshole or are you already an asshole and that's why you have a BMW?

The back door on the driver's side flies open and Sheila sprints toward me at full speed.

I really don't have the energy.

I rub my hand across the back of my neck and wait for the attack.

"Ty, baby!" She launches herself into my arms, and I turn my head just before her lips assault mine; they land at my ear instead. I pretend to be distracted by something on the pump screen as I slide her off of me.

She traces her finger over the letters of my stupid Subway hat. "Did you just get off?"

I nod.

"Wanna do it again?" she says suggestively.

I manage a small smile.

"That's better." She nuzzles into me, gently scratching the

back of my neck with her acrylic nails. It doesn't feel as good as it used to. "You smell yummy," she says. "I haven't had bread in forever."

"Perks of the job," I say, probably a little too sarcastically. I used to love the smell of freshly baked bread. At this point, let's just say it's lost its appeal.

"Sheila!" Cara, one of the other cheerleaders, calls.

"Hang on, bitch." Sheila flips her brown hair all dramatically. "Say the word and I'm yours."

The gas pump clicks, so I turn to finish my business. "Sorry. It's just . . . It's been a long day."

"Your loss." She grabs my ass and snakes under my arm, shoving her tongue in my mouth while I attempt to tear off the receipt. Then she bounces back to her friends. "See you tomorrow, baby!" she sings as she climbs back into the Beemer. There's a symphony of giggling from inside. I wonder just how many girls are actually in there.

Brett grins at me like he's beaten me at something as they drive past. I hate that guy.

It takes my car three tries before finally starting, and then it dies again. It doesn't want to go home either. I halfheartedly pound the steering wheel and try again. It finally starts.

A giant pickup honks angrily as it passes me on the way home. I'm going ten under the speed limit. I'm in no hurry. If I get there after 10:30, there's a good chance my dad'll be locked away in his room. Hopefully passed out. He's always been an asshole, but it's gotten exponentially worse since Mom. It's the nights he's in that in-between state that I have to worry about—

where he's not sober enough to be depressed, and not drunk enough to be numb. I just never know what I'll get. He's like Schrödinger's cat. Except instead of both dead and alive, he's both passed-out drunk and not drunk enough until I open the front door and find out for myself.

I sit in the car staring up at the window above the garage. The light is on in the guest room. As if we need a guest room. Mom was an only child, and Dad's alienated everyone who'd ever want to visit. It's also the room Mom used as her office. There's a crappy rolltop desk that she squeezed between the bed and the window. She had to push the bed out of the way to get a chair back there when she used it. I'm surprised my dad hasn't hawked the thing yet. He got rid of its contents along with everything else as soon as he could. People think it's because he couldn't handle the reminders, but I'm convinced he just wanted extra cash for booze.

There's no movement in the window—maybe he passed out and forgot to turn the light off.

I strangle the steering wheel and let out a silent scream. Then I go in.

Captain comes running to the door the second he hears my feet hit the porch. At least someone's happy to see me.

"Hey, buddy." I lean down and let Captain lick my chin while I give him some pats. If you didn't know him, you might think he was threatening me, baring his teeth and all, but his tail's wagging so fast, he almost throws himself off balance. His teeth are just too big for his mouth, so he looks like he's aggressive when he's excited. I like to think he's smiling.

"Who's a good boy? Who's a good boy?"

Captain tilts his head like he's trying to understand me. He's an Australian shepherd mix but looks mostly Aussie, only with a long, thick tail. He's brown and white, and he has one black leg and a black patch over his brown eye, which offsets his light blue one. Hence the name: "Captain Jack Sparrow." Even though Jack Sparrow didn't have an eye patch or a peg leg. Mom named him. He was the only pirate she could think of. And she loved Johnny Depp.

"Should I give you two some privacy?" Dad thinks he's hilarious when he's in that in-between, not-quite-drunk condition. I do not. "At least I know you won't go knocking the dog up. Just do something about his hair all over the goddamn floor first, that's all I ask. Or are you testing me to see if I'll make good on my word?" Dad loves to threaten to get rid of Captain. It's all talk. He's too lazy to actually follow through.

I slowly get up and start past him toward the closet, leaving my backpack on the living room floor.

"Where the fuck are you going?" He grabs my arm. My muscles flex involuntarily. I know he'll take this as a challenge and immediately wish I could take it back.

He shoves me as hard as he can. I reach out to catch myself but I'm not positioned right and I fall into the closet. My head hits the doorframe on the way down. These are the nights I resent my mother most.

"Answer me." Dad kicks the back of my leg. It's not meant to hurt so much as humiliate. And that he has done.

"I'm getting the vacuum for all the goddamn dog hair," I mumble as I pull myself up and remove the vacuum from the closet.

He smacks the spot on my head where it hit the doorframe. "Wanna say that again?"

I shake my head. My face is on fire and I'm torqued inside from how much I just want to go off on him. At six feet, 210, I have a few inches and about fifty pounds on him. I could do serious damage. And he knows it. Sometimes I wonder if that's what he really wants.

He snorts at me and turns back out of the room. I think we're done, but then just before he reaches the stairs, he kicks Captain in the ribs hard enough for him to let out a high-pitched yelp. I lunge at Dad without thinking. Knowing how I'd react before I did, he easily steps out of the way, and then, using my own momentum, shoves me so that I almost land on Captain.

When I look back at him, he stares me down with a smug smile. He knows I won't try anything else. Asshole.

When I finally hear his bedroom door shut, I feed Captain, vacuum the floors, and lock myself away in my cellar.

Okay, my room's not a cellar. It's a converted basement. With scratchy industrial carpet the color of old oatmeal, and shitty, scratched-up wood paneling halfway up the walls with white drywall above it covered in small holes because I use it as a corkboard. The focal point of the room is a mattress sitting only on the box spring, which I hate, being as tall as I am. And there's a do-it-yourself-quality bathroom next to the wall of bars hung with clothes that would normally be hidden behind the doors of an actual closet.

It's not great but it's mine. Mom let me put a lock on the door when I turned sixteen, like it's my own private apartment or something. Dad hates that. He thinks I'm hiding stuff. Which I am. Only not stuff he would be interested in.

I pull some loose paneling from the far corner and feel along the floor until my hand makes contact with a metal box. I carefully pull the box out and take it to my bed.

Captain jumps up and circles about five times before finally settling in next to me.

I take off the key I always wear on a chain around my neck and unlock the box, like I do every night. Then I pull out the plastic divider holding my secret emergency fund and set it aside.

Six photos stare back at me.

Mom on her wedding day—I cut Dad out of that one.

One of her when she was my age; she was so beautiful: long, shiny dark brown hair and light brown eyes that are full of life. She looks happy. I look a lot like her.

The two of us in Halloween costumes: She's a black cat and I'm a ninja. I think I was ten.

One I remember taking when she finally went back to school. She was getting in her car and I raced out after her with the camera and said, "First day of school! My baby's all grown up." And she laughed. She's mid-laugh in the photo.

The two of us hiking my favorite running path up in the foothills near Red Rocks. Captain was all muddy and jumping on her. Again she's laughing.

And the last one: just the two of us at an awkward angle, slightly out of focus because she's holding the camera out in front of us. We're lounging on the couch after school let out last June. Dad wasn't home and we were watching a *Die Hard* marathon and eating popcorn. She made a big deal about taking that picture of the two of us because it would probably be the last time we'd ever be like that. I was getting too old, she said, and soon I would think it was lame to hang out with my mom. I'm practically rolling my eyes in the picture, but Mom's smiling away.

That's part of what makes it hurt so much. I just never saw it coming.

I set the photos aside and reach for the one last thing Mom ever left me. And no, it's not a note. She couldn't even be bothered to leave an explanation. Oh, no—can't give Tyler closure. Can't leave him a note telling him I'm sorry. Nope. The only thing left of hers is the razor blade that ended her life. Nothing flashy, nothing special. Just a little silver rectangular straight-razor replacement blade.

I don't know why I grabbed it. I'm not even sure if it really is *the* blade or just one of the others in its pack of ten or whatever. The protective plastic container was on the edge of the tub, which, in the chaos of pulling her out and trying to stop the bleeding while dialing 911, I stepped on, scattering all the others in the mess of blood on the floor. It still had her blood on it. I wish now that I hadn't cleaned it off. I know that sounds morbid, but it's all I have of her.

I run my finger along the blade lightly enough so it doesn't cut me. It's still sharp. Probably its only use was to tear through the flesh of her wrists.

Exsanguination.

That's the term the EMT used. It sounds so much better than: "She slit her damn wrists and bled out."

TWO

I'm intercepted by the school guidance counselor before I even make it to first period. I follow her bouncing yellow ponytail to her little office area, past all the pitying looks from the office staff.

Mrs. Ortiz sits across from me, her head tilted caringly to one side, her eyes practically welling up. My stomach churns. I think my sausage and eggs might make a reappearance all over her desk. The thought forces the side of my mouth to pull up.

"How are you, Tyler?"

"'Full of vexation come I,'" I mumble.

A look of confusion briefly overtakes her look of pity.

"*A Midsummer Night's Dream*? It's really good. You should totally read it. It's by some British guy."

She smiles, tolerating me. And then presses on. "Are you seeking help?"

As if you're in any position to help, lady. I shrug.

"Tyler, honey"—her pity-face is back—"it's okay to ask for help. I can recommend—"

"I already have a shrink."

She tilts her head the other way. She doesn't believe me.

"David Adelstein," I say.

She pulls her eyebrows together like she's deep in thought, like all shrinks, therapists, and fucking high school guidance counselors know each other and she's trying to place him.

"I would give you his number, but . . ." *You'd have to torture it out of me.*

She straightens in her chair. She's obviously annoyed but trying to keep her concerned-for-a-student-whose-mom-killed-herself face.

"I understand Mrs. Hickenlooper asked you to leave class yesterday."

I nod.

"Would you like to elaborate?"

"Can't say that I would."

Her jaw clenches ever so slightly. "Well, with your, um, situation, we're willing to be a little more lenient than usual, but please try not to push your luck."

"Understood," I say, like *sir, yes sir.*

"Tyler, why don't you tell me a little about what happened with . . . you know. Maybe it'll help me understand how to better help you." She has the stupid caring look in her eyes again.

"My mom killed herself. I don't know what more you want to know."

"Where were you when she . . . ?"

Jesus. She can't even say the words. "Football. Summer training."

"How did you find out?"

"My dad." This is a lie. But I'll never tell her that I came home from training to grab my knee brace and some Advil but I was out of Advil and went up to Mom's bathroom to grab some when I found her floating lifeless and naked in a tub of pink water, blood still trickling from one wrist to the giant puddle of red on the floor. Nor will I tell her that I scooped my mom out of the tub and tried to revive her. That she was still warm. That the bath water was still steaming. That if I had come home five minutes, or three, or who knows how many minutes earlier, I might have stopped her, saved her. Only one other person knows all this: Dr. Adelstein. Only a handful of other people even know that I found her: the EMTs, the cops, the social worker, and Dad. I can't take the way people treat me now, and if everyone knew I found her, they'd treat me . . . Well, I'd probably just have to kill myself.

Mrs. Ortiz has been talking while I've been zoning out, but I'm done pretending to listen.

"Good talk," I say, standing. "This was definitely not a waste of time." I'm already halfway out the door when she calls after me to stop in tomorrow to "touch base."

Yeah. I'll be sure to do that.

Coach is walking toward me, and it's too late to pretend I don't see him. Not that I'm avoiding him. Okay, maybe I'm avoiding him a little.

"Blackwell." He slaps his hand on my shoulder.

"Coach."

"We sure missed you this summer. McPhearson's not half the running back you are. You been keeping up on your running?"

"Yes, sir," I say as enthusiastically as I can muster.

"Good, good. You just let me know when you're ready, okay? Is there anything I can . . . ?" He trails off awkwardly.

"Nope. I'm good. Thanks."

"All right then." He pats my shoulder again and steps aside so I can get to class. I don't have to look back to know he's watching me. I can feel it.

"There you are!" Sheila calls down the hall just before lunch, pretending to be upset because I did or didn't do . . . something. There's no escaping her. So I walk toward the herd of short skirts staring into their phones.

"You didn't text me back, mister." She pouts. She actually pouts. She's developed this affinity for drama lately. I can't stand it.

"I was in class." I lean down and kiss her neck, and all is forgiven.

"I mean last night." She scratches the back of my neck with one hand and rests the other on my chest. All I can focus on is her ridiculous puke-green nail polish. It looks like fungus. "Hello?" She taps a putrid nail against my pec.

"My dad," I say as way of explanation.

"I'm so sorry, baby." She places her palm against my cheek

and it almost makes me feel better for a fraction of a fraction of a second. Until I see her glance at the girls next to us to check if they're watching, to make sure they see just how tragic her boyfriend is and how wonderful she is to take care of him.

I wave her off, hoping she'll drop it before I say something I shouldn't.

She does.

"You working tonight?"

I shake my head.

"You wanna meet up at my house after practice? My mom's got a dinner meeting, and you know my dad's clueless."

"Sure." I could use a good distraction. As long as she doesn't expect me to talk about everything and get all emotional and shit. She keeps trying, and I get that that's what a girlfriend does, but it's not going to happen.

"Great. I'll wait for you since your practice usually goes longer than ours."

I open my mouth to remind her that I'm not going to practice, but decide I don't feel like a pep talk, so I kiss her instead. No matter how many times I tell her, she won't let it drop. I wish I knew if it was because she cares about me or because she's worried about the social ramifications of not dating a football player her senior year.

"Shee, come on. We're going to lose our table if we don't go." This from the other brunette girl who used to date Marcus—Nine, I think. She playfully tugs at Sheila's dark hair until she pulls away from me. "Hey, Tyler," Nine says, "where's Marcus?"

"Do I look like his keeper?"

Nine giggles. And then she and Sheila turn toward the cafeteria.

Sheila whips around when she sees I'm not following. "Aren't you coming?"

"Not hungry," I say.

I actually am hungry; I just need to not be around Sheila and her friends. I don't bother going back to class after downing my Chipotle—I decide my time will be better spent reading at Starbucks. Plus I don't want another run-in with Marcus about practice, especially because I know Sheila told him I wasn't working tonight.

The parking lot has pretty much cleared by the time I return to school. I head toward the chanting-in-unison coming from the upper gym—our gym has two levels, the smaller upper gym for stuff like volleyball and cheerleading, and the larger main gym on the lower level for the real sports. I make myself comfortable on the ground, leaning my back against the wall to wait for Sheila. A few stragglers walk by; I keep my head down so none of them has the urge to strike up a conversation. I'm pretty safe—it's mostly drama and band geeks. None of them would ever bother talking to me.

"Hey, Tyler. You weren't in chem today," a tinny male voice says.

Apparently I was wrong.

I look up to see a skinny guy with glasses—Jeff maybe?—walking toward me with some Asian goth chick. She drops her pencil and it rolls across the floor coming to a rest when it hits my leg. I hold the pencil out for the girl, who grabs it without bothering to say thank you.

The skinny guy stares, still waiting for me to say something about skipping class, but when he realizes his goth friend has kept walking, he runs to catch up with her. I hear him whisper something about being rude and doesn't she know my mom just died and crap.

"That doesn't give him carte blanche on assholedom," she says. He shushes her and glances back at me to see if I heard. I laugh to myself.

The gym door hits my foot, so I pull myself up. Sheila practically runs into me as the cheer herd stampedes out of the gym.

"Ty? What are you doing here? I was just coming to find you."

"Mission accomplished."

"Is everything okay?" She rests her hands on my shoulders and looks at me with intense concern.

"Everything's fine. Let's go." I take her bag from her and turn toward the exit before she can play up the "I'm with tragedy boy" thing even more.

As we navigate our way to the parking lot, I can feel how much she wants to ask me about practice, but she knows it'll just cause a fight. And that wouldn't look good for her.

"Where's your car?" I ask.

"Let's just take yours. You can stop by and pick me up in the morning."

"Fine."

Sheila cranks the stereo and flips through the stations to find a song she likes. Landing on some irritating pop song, she leans out the window and sings at the top of her lungs at passing drivers. I almost laugh. When we first started hanging out in tenth grade, I had some stupid argument with Coach and she couldn't stand that I was in a bad mood, so she blasted the pop station and scream-sang at the other drivers, getting a variety of reactions, all of which made me laugh. God, we're completely different people now. Sometimes I feel like we don't even like each other anymore. But I guess it's safe. It's comfortable. For both of us. Plus, sex.

Her dad's home, but as she said, he's totally clueless. He's parked in front of his computer and barely grunts an acknowledgment as we pass him on the way to her bedroom.

Before I know it, we're rolling around on her flowery comforter, my hands threaded in her silky hair, her hands brushing up my chest, pulling off my shirt, throwing it over my head to the floor. Then she rolls me over so she's on top and pulls her cheer uniform over her head. I'm still not used to how thin she's gotten. When we first hooked up, there was more to her. She was a little softer in all the right places and I liked it. I know it's a cheerleader thing to be skinnier than the next girl, but it really doesn't do it for me. I swear my tits are bigger than hers; I don't even know why she bothers wearing a bra anymore. Except she's not for long. The thing pops off and she's holding my hands against her perfectly bronzed chest— no tan lines, of course. She groans and grinds her pelvis against me and she goes to kiss me. I'm trying to get into it, but then

I begin thinking about how I shouldn't have to try—I never used to. She kisses my neck and sucks at my earlobes. This gets me into it a little more. She moans and rubs against me. And moans. And rubs.

Despite everything that's going on, I'm really not aroused. I mean, yeah, I'm hard, but that's just a physiological side effect of dry humping.

"It's okay, baby. Don't think about anything. I'll make you feel better," she breathes in my ear. I respond by grabbing her ass and grinding into her harder. She groans and kisses me again. This time it's a light brush against my lips. Against my chin, my neck, my chest.

Her hand plunges under my waistband and she grabs me. "You want me to kiss it?" she says in this goddamn baby voice I've told her I can't stand. I practically go flaccid right then, but her stroking continues and my dick has a mind of its own.

She raises her eyebrows, waiting for an answer.

"If you want."

She sits up, glaring. "You really don't care if I suck you off or not?"

I shrug.

She shoves me as she rolls off and goes to retrieve our clothes from the floor. "I'm not going to do it if you don't want it. You think I'm, like, dying to put your dick in my mouth?"

"Hey, don't get all pissy. You offered."

My shirt hits me in the face. I pull it on as I head out the door.

THREE

Dad trashed the kitchen before he passed out last night, and now I'm stuck cleaning all the shit off the burner before I can make myself a decent breakfast. At least he turned off the stove.

I would normally keep the noise down—no use poking the sleeping bear and all that—but his car's not in the driveway. Which means I have to take him to the bus before school. I need to wake him up in the least confrontational manner, hence all the excessive pot-banging.

Dad finally stumbles out of his room looking like he hasn't combed his hair, and I'm pretty sure he slept in the clothes he wore yesterday and didn't bother changing. I ignore the barrage of inventive names he mumbles at me as he snatches the bacon and egg sandwich I made for him out of my hands and heads to my car. He's still pretty drunk from the night before. This will be a fun drive.

With all the booze wafting from his pores, it smells like I soaked my seats in a bottle of whisky. He's unusually quiet. This makes me more anxious than if he were ranting at me the whole way. Silence means he's thinking, and nothing good ever comes from that.

I think we'll make it all the way to the park-and-ride without speaking, but about five blocks before my turn, he's finally managed to put his thoughts together.

"You know? She never wanted a kid." He's watching me, waiting for a reaction. I can feel it. "Everything was kind of perfect before you came along and fucked it up."

He's said these things before. I refuse to play into it.

"You hear me? She'd still be here if it weren't for you. I'm sure of it."

I tighten my fingers around the steering wheel imagining it's his neck.

"She was going to be a big-shot lawyer. But then she had to worry about taking care of an ugly little bastard."

I consider informing him that they were, in fact, married, thus, I was not technically a bastard, but that'd just give him ammunition.

"You think you're so fucking smart, don't you? You got everything figured out." He laughs bitterly. "You don't know shit. You never know when an ugly little bastard might pop out and ruin your life."

"Well, at least I've provided you with a valid excuse for becoming a raging, psychotic drunk," I mutter.

My cheekbone feels like it's exploded and my ear starts to

ring. I swerve and practically hit a blue minivan that lays on its horn. I didn't even see his hand move.

"You trying to kill me too, you little prick?" he asks.

I focus on the throbbing in my temple and block out his vitriol. When I reach the park-and-ride, I slam on the brakes so hard, his head almost hits the dash. Unfortunately, his reflexes aren't as slow as I had hoped—his hands stop his head from making contact.

"You better watch yourself," he says. Then he gets out and staggers to the bench, leaving the door open. His boss has the patience of a saint. Or maybe Dad's got something on him. Or just maybe when your face is buried beneath a welding helmet no one gives a shit.

I shove my foot down on the accelerator. The sudden forward movement slams the passenger door shut. I'm shaking, I'm so pissed. Punching the dashboard helps a little.

I reach school late and have to park way in the back of the lot. About halfway to the entrance, I reach for my phone in my pocket out of habit. It's not there. It's probably in the car, but I'm almost all the way to the door. Screw it.

All my morning classes are as pointless as ever. I seriously consider not coming anymore. I almost have all the credits I need for a diploma. The only reason I didn't graduate last year was because I was short a gym credit and an elective credit. So this year I was going to pad my GPA and play football so I'd be sure to impress Stanford. But that scholarship's probably off the table now that I'm not playing, so why the hell am I here?

○ ○ ○

"Where were you?" Sheila shoves me from behind just outside the cafeteria at lunch.

I turn, taking a deep breath. "What?"

"Where were you this morning?" Her eyes and nose are red. She's been crying. And it's because of something I did. But I have no clue what.

"Good thing I called Shee before school," Cara, the one friend of Sheila's I can actually stand, chimes in.

"Shit." I remember now and I feel like an asshole. "Sheila, I'm sorry. My dad left his car at work so he could get trashed last night, and I had to take him to the bus this morning."

Sheila used to live down the street from me and has been witness to several blowups on the front lawn with my very drunk dad and my very hysterical mom and me. So her look of pity doesn't bother me as much as the others. At least she has a frame of reference.

She hurries over and wraps her sun-kissed arms around my neck. I pick her up and kiss the side of her head. "Sorry I forgot," I whisper.

I can feel her forgive me with her whole body before she says, "No. I'm sorry. If I had known . . . It sucks that you always have to deal with his crap. I'm here if you need to talk."

And then she looks up at me with bated breath, like I'll just start pouring my heart out right here in the fucking hall. In front of all these fucking people so she can make sure they all know how great she is for being there for me.

○ ○ ○

Roger's assisting one of the regulars—a man with a disgusting beard that always has something stuck in it. It physically sickens me to watch Roger's level of ass-kissery today, so I head to the back room to chop some more damn onions.

Somehow I must have zoned out, because I'm stunned back to life when Roger snaps his fingers in front of my nose.

"I know you're going through a really tough time right now, Ty, but I need you to focus, m'kay?" He's leaning so close that I have no choice but to breathe in his rancid garlic breath. "Julie's out there working the rush alone. D'ya think you can rally it up and give her a hand?"

I nod, because if I say anything, it'll involve too many swear words, and then I head out to help Julie with the "rush." There are two people chatting in line behind the old man that Julie's currently helping.

I put my brilliant sandwich-making skills to use, and Julie, who might be more uptight than Roger, if that's even possible, rings them up. When she's finished, she sighs passive aggressively in my direction. I'm left to stare at the bearded man eating at one of the tables, while Julie takes her break and Roger makes a personal call. Too bad our storefront faces east; from out back we have an almost unobstructed view of the mountains, and even from this side I can tell there's a pretty spectacular sunset going on.

I'm checking the time on my phone when Julie comes back out.

"You can't be on your phone in front of customers," she says in this infuriatingly condescending voice.

"Don't get your panties in a wad. I was just checking the fucking time."

Her eyes widen and her face turns tomato red, swear to god. She spins around and storms into the back.

Once the bearded man clears out, Roger comes around the corner, his face plagued with concern.

"Tyler, I'm gonna need you to follow me to the back and apologize to Julie, then I'm gonna send Julie home, and you'll close up alone tonight. Okay?"

Jesus.

When Julie comes into view, her face is splotchy, her eyes are red, and she's sniffling.

"You can't be serious," I mutter, but not quietly enough.

"Now that's enough of that," Roger says in his *manager* voice.

"You see?" Julie says through a sob.

"Please apologize, Tyler," Roger says.

"For what exactly?"

"Tyler . . ."

"No, really. I have no clue what I've done tonight that warrants an apology. I was checking the time on my phone when Julie had a fit for no reason."

"Tyler . . ."

"This is ridiculous. There is no earthly reason she should be crying over something like this."

"She says you directed offensive language at her."

"Offensive language? Seriously?"

Julie sniffles and wipes her eyes all dramatically and I can't do it anymore. I snap.

"You want offensive? How about this, Roger? A fucking monkey could do this job, and you treat it like we're curing cancer or something. And you should seriously consider seeing someone about removing that stick up your ass."

"That's it. You—"

"And you." I turn to Julie. "You seriously need to get laid and soon, otherwise you better be sure to get the number of his ass-stick-removal guy."

"Tyler!" Roger looks like his head might explode.

"Don't worry. I'm fucking out!" I slam the back door open and make my break for freedom. I was right. The mountains look fucking amazing.

It doesn't hit me until the middle of the night that I actually needed that goddamn job.

FOUR

Dr. Dave doesn't put up with my bullshit. That's the only reason I come back. At first it was because it was mandated by Social Services, but now I actually don't hate his freaking guts. Sometimes he even offers good advice. But not today.

"How did you feel after leaving like that?"

I glare at him. I hate it when he's like this. "I told you. I didn't have a choice."

"You felt you didn't have a choice?" He tosses his yellow legal pad and pencil on the coffee table and leans forward, resting his elbows on his knees. He's in his we're-just-a-couple-of-pals-having-a-talk mode.

I learned early on that if I don't speak but maintain eye contact, Dr. Dave will usually change the subject. He's probably in his late twenties but he only looks a few years older than me. I'm much bigger than he is, and I'm pretty sure I remind him of the guys that bullied him when he was in high school.

"We always have a choice, Tyler. You didn't have to swear in front of Julie, so what do you think made you choose to do it?"

I just stare.

He shifts. Makes a big show of checking his imaginary watch.

I stare.

He runs a hand through his dark hair and down the back of his neck. He tilts his head slightly and stares back.

I continue to stare.

His lips lift at one side. He raises his eyebrows slightly. He crosses his arms.

I stare.

"We can do this all day if you want, Tyler."

I stare.

"We can talk about something else if you like. Football? Your dad?" The smile in his voice makes me want to punch him. "Or we can just sit here for another"—he checks his pretend watch again—"forty-two minutes and stare at each other."

"Are you coming on to me, Doc?"

"Is that what your dad does? Deflect with humor?"

My hand balls into a fist before I can even think.

"Okay." He motions toward my fist with a tip of his head, then picks up his notebook and scribbles something down.

Screw him. I swallow hard, deciding that football is the lesser of the two evils. "Marcus keeps bugging me about football. But I don't miss it. I mean, I should miss it, shouldn't I?"

"Should you?"

"Can we not do the psychobabble answering questions with questions bullshit today?"

"Is there anything you do miss about it?"

I trace the edge of the leather cushion with my middle finger. "No."

"Nothing?"

I shake my head.

"Not the rush of adrenaline before a game?"

"Not even that."

"The camaraderie with the team?" He's being sarcastic. He knows how I feel about most of the guys on the team.

I manage to smile. "I never thought I'd be one of those people, you know? Those people who don't know what the hell they want to do with their life. Those people who don't have a *thing*. But here I am. I am thing-less."

"Or maybe you just haven't found your thing. You have time. That's what college is for."

"I'm not doing the whole college thing."

"Why not?"

"That was my mom's—"

"Bullshit."

"What?"

"I said that's bullshit. You wouldn't have busted your ass as much as you did if it wasn't something you also wanted. I've seen how your eyes light up when you talk about Stanford."

"Well, without football, there's no way Stanford will still want me. And I can't do football, because I need a job to make money to spend on frivolous things like socks. And food."

"Food?" He leans forward looking a little alarmed.

Shit. "I'm exaggerating. You know what I mean."

I know I should tell Dr. Dave everything, but unfortunately, he's obligated to go to the authorities about stuff like that.

"I could try to talk to your dad about—"

"Yeah, that's not happening. He wouldn't talk to you anyway."

"All right, fine." He holds his hands up in defeat. "Tyler, you say Stanford wouldn't want you without football, but I think you're wrong about that. I think you *know* you're wrong about that."

"Grades and SAT scores only go so far, Doc. And even if they'd still take me, I can't afford it. Academic scholarships don't come close to football scholarships, which speaks volumes about the state of our country, wouldn't you agree?"

"Then check out other schools. Stanford isn't your only option."

"And then what?"

"And then you go to school. You meet girls. You have lots of sex. You figure out what you want to do. You enjoy life."

"What the hell kind of shrink are you? Telling me to go have lots of sex?"

"The kind that wishes he had that option when he was in your shoes. So, on behalf of all the schlubby Jewish boys who couldn't get girls to give them the time of day, go have fun. Be safe, but have fun."

"And by fun you mean . . ."

"I mean sex," Dr. Dave says.

"Do they know you give this kind of advice?"

He shrugs. "But it's good advice, am I right?"

I laugh. This is why I come here.

"So what's your plan for this week?" he asks.

"No clue. I guess I have to find another job, so I'll probably head to the mall or something."

"That's good. Now, what about the journaling? How's that going?"

"Dear Diary, today Sheila wore green nail polish, and it made me feel sad."

"You make fun, but I think it might be helpful. You don't have to write about your girlfriend. You don't even have to write about yourself. You know what? I have an idea." He heads over to the cabinet behind his desk. "While you're out looking for a job, I want you to watch some people interact and write about it. Specifically what their interaction evokes in you. Do you pity them? Envy them? I think this could be good. Let's reconnect you with your feelings." He sits back down and tosses a spiral notebook to me. It's black with a big yellow smiley face on the front.

"Did you seriously just say that? Reconnect me with my feelings? That may be the shrinkiest thing I've ever heard."

"That may be the shrinkiest thing I've ever said, but I still want you to do it."

"And is there some significance to this?" I hold up the notebook, smiley face out.

He grins. "It was on sale."

"That asshole boss of yours called. Said something about your final paycheck. You get fired or something?" Dad sounds exhausted. He's lying on the couch with a beer resting on his chest and about five empties lined up on the floor. The TV's off, but he stares at it like he's watching a riveting episode of *CSI*. There's a wadded-up ball of tissues on the floor. I really hope he wasn't just watching porn.

He blows his nose and tosses the used tissue next to all the others. Oh. He's sick. Perfect.

I turn back toward the kitchen. "I think there's some NyQuil—"

"Did you? Get fired?" he interrupts, still staring at the blank screen.

"I quit." Not that it's any of his business.

"I'm not paying for any of your shit."

"Yes. You've made that perfectly clear. I'll go get the NyQuil."

"I don't need NyQuil, I need whisky." He tries to get up and trips on one of the empty beer bottles on the floor. I grab him just before he falls into the glass coffee table, and am rewarded with a chest full of beer. Great. Now I need to shower. Unlikely I'll get a job smelling like him.

"Jesus, Dad. Sit down. I'll get it."

When I return with a glass of Jack (and the NyQuil), he's lying on the couch again, with his back to me. He's shaking; I think he might be crying and I seriously can't deal. So I set the glass on the coffee table and go back up to the kitchen for the bottle. I leave it for him next to the glass, and hear him murmur something about "that stupid fucking lock" as I let myself into my room.

Once I'm safely in my dungeon, I pull my shirt over my

head, throwing it into the hamper on my way to the bathroom. I twist the shower knob all the way up, and I stare at myself in the mirror, gripping the countertop like if I let go I'll evaporate into the steam. It would be nice to just sort of fade away like that. I wonder if that's what Mom thought.

The mall. Kill me now.

Not only is it filled with stupid people, but it's also filled with stupid people I have the misfortune of knowing. And now I'm slogging through this hell looking for a reason to make coming here a regular thing. I only make it to the Colorado-ski-chalet-themed food court before I decide having a job here is absolutely not an option. Some of the guys from the team and their girlfriends sit around the hearth of the giant fireplace in front of Sbarro. Brett's brother works there and likes to give his older brother's cool friends free stuff so they'll like him. It makes me sad for Brett's brother that he wants so desperately to fit in with a bunch of worthless assholes.

I hide behind a large Mormon family to sneak past the guys from the team and head for my car.

I drive around aimlessly, stopping at a few places to fill out applications: a bagel place, a dry cleaner claiming to be "Denver's best," and Home Depot. I'm kind of rooting for the Home Depot job. At least I probably wouldn't see people from school. Plus it's next to a Taco Bell, and that's a place I can still afford.

I'm practically out of the sprawl of suburbia when I consciously realize where I'm driving. I've never been here before. It's not that it's far from home; it's just the opposite direction from anywhere I ever go. It's a new subdivision and things are still under construction. But there's one strip mall. Sorry, not a strip mall. An "outdoor shopping experience," according to the sign. This place, the stores under construction—it's clearly trying to resemble an upscale mountain town. Telluride, maybe? There are a few boutiques you'd normally find in a mall and several chain restaurants, or at least they will be once they're finished. So far the only active businesses appear to be a Pilates place, a barber with an old-timey pole in front, a cafe that looks like it might actually be locally owned, and, of course, a Starbucks. At the end of one of the streets, around the corner from the Starbucks, is a photography studio with a HELP WANTED sign in the window. I decide to parallel park along the fake street and explore further.

The chime of the door alerts an empty waiting area to my presence.

"Hello?" I call to the back.

I'm pretty sure the place is completely deserted until I hear something clatter against the ground, followed by a string of curse words.

"Hello?" I call again. "Is everything okay back there?"

A bearded man who looks like he should be hunting in the mountains and living off of whatever he kills comes out from behind a red curtain that separates the waiting area from the picture-taking area—the, uh, studio, I guess.

"You here for senior pictures? My girl will be back in a few to schedule times if you don't mind waiting." Grizzly Adams gestures for me to wait on one of the velvet couches against the wall, which is filled with dozens of framed photos of kids, families, and dogs.

"No. I'm, um . . . are you still hiring?" I nod toward the HELP WANTED sign in the window.

Grizzly Adams straightens up and a huge smile spreads across his face. At least I think it's a smile; it's hard to tell under all the gray facial hair. He thrusts his hand out at me. "Henry," he says, his eyes going from my worn sneakers to my jeans to my button-down shirt that's a little too tight in the arms to my eyes. "I could use some muscle around here."

"Tyler," I say, shaking his giant paw. "Tyler Blackwell."

"Well, Tyler Blackwell, what do you have to offer this fine establishment?"

"I . . . What would you need me to do?"

"Oh. I guess we need phones answered, uh, computer stuff, like scheduling, I think. My girl takes care of all that. She's the one who needs help, really. Can't do everything herself. She's getting us some coffee right now. Oh, getting coffee, that's another skill we need."

"Um, well, I can definitely do that." Is this a job interview?

Henry runs a hand over his beard and nods his head. Neither of us speaks for a very long, very awkward minute.

"Do I need to fill out an application or something?" I ask.

Henry waves his hand. "Nah. I like you. Let's do this. If you fuck up, I can always fire you." He pats my shoulder in a fatherly way and turns back to the studio. "Follow me."

The back studio is basically just a massive warehouse filled with tons of very expensive-looking lights and stands and rolls of material, backdrops probably. The setup is currently a black backdrop with a black table. The camera is mounted above the table, pointing straight down, wired up to a laptop.

"Shooting a jewelry advertisement for a friend," Henry says, adjusting one of the lights as he twists his head toward the monitor. A rainbow dot moves across his chest, and I wonder if he's shooting diamonds.

The door chimes, followed immediately by the voice of a girl. "I have your venti Caramel Macchiato with extra whip—" She stops when she sees me. And here I thought I'd escape run-ins with anyone from school. But no, it's the goth chick from the other day.

"Thank you, my dear. You can take down the HELP WANTED sign. I hired Tyler Blackwell," Henry says as he raises the large white cup to his lips.

The goth chick is not happy. She stares at me like she wants to rip my throat out, like the vampire she wishes she was.

"Don't be rude. Say hello." Henry nudges her.

"Hello." Her voice is like ice slipped into your jock.

Henry takes another sip and leans down to kiss her on the cheek. "Thanks for the coffee. I gotta get back to work. Show him the ropes? And figure out a schedule or whatever you need to do."

And he's back to adjusting lights again.

Goth pushes past me toward the front. I guess I should follow?

"So, do I need to fill out paperwork or something?" I ask.

"Yeah. An application," she says coldly, entering the circle of shiny concrete countertop that sits atop crisp white cabinets. She slams the divider back in place before I can follow. After digging around in a cabinet, she finally finds what she's looking for, slaps it onto the concrete countertop, and shoves it in my direction.

"Um, Henry kind of told me I didn't need to fill out—"

She slams a pen down on top of the paper and glares at me so hard I can hear it. Then she stomps back to the other side of the counter and clicks at the computer like it's done something to offend her.

I oblige and fill out the unnecessary paperwork, occasionally glancing up, trying to figure out the connection between her and Henry. He couldn't be her father or maybe her grandfather, could he? I mean, she's Asian. Although in all fairness, she could be half Asian. Actually now that I really look at her, she's definitely half Asian. She might even be pretty without all that shit on her face. She's—oh, shit. Heat shoots through my body as strong as a solar flare. I just figured out why she hates me. I *know* her.

"Jordyn?" I ask.

Her back straightens. She doesn't turn around. "You *just* figure that out?"

Here's the thing: Jordyn and I used to be friends. Until middle school, when her parents split up. We started having play dates when we were in second grade because my mom and her mom met at a back-to-school thing, and occasionally her mom would drive me home after school. Jordyn was pretty cool for a girl. She was smart and liked reading. Plus she had a trampoline in her backyard. But we lost touch after she moved.

"I thought you went to East Ridge," I say.

"I've been at Ridge Gate since our sophomore year." She sounds pissed.

"Really?"

She turns to face me now, cocking her head to the side. "We've even spoken."

"We have?" I desperately search my brain for a memory of this supposed conversation.

She stalks toward me and I'm suddenly very happy about the counter being between us. "You really don't remember?"

I shake my head. "You mean the other day?" She can't possibly count that as a conversation; she didn't even acknowledge me.

She shakes her head in disgust and grabs the application off the counter, crumpling it up and throwing it in the trash. "Just go."

I take about four steps before Henry comes strutting out from behind the red curtain.

"What'd you figure out? Because I think I need Tyler tomorrow for the Hightower family. There's about fourteen of them, and I'll need help with the setup. Actually, why don't you come at nine and Jordyn'll give you a tutorial on the books and all that crap. The Hightowers are scheduled for noon, so that'll give us plenty of setup time."

I look to Jordyn to try to figure out what to say, but she stares at the floor. I can still see the steam pouring out of her ears, so I know I should tell him it's not a good fit for me or something. But I really need the job.

"Don't be late, Tyler Blackwell." Henry dismisses me with a heavy pat on the shoulder.

"I won't."

Jordyn finally makes eye contact with me. She looks like I've just killed her cat and she's plotting a very elaborate and very painful revenge. This should be fun.

FIVE

I arrive early on Sunday for my first official day on the job, unsure what to expect besides outright hatred from Jordyn.

She shows up at ten till nine, wearing a long black skirt with this black leather motorcycle jacket even though it's already eighty degrees out, and walks past me to the door like I'm not there. As soon as she's unlocked it, I open it, trying to be nice. She makes a disgusted sound at the back of her throat. It's a don't-even-try-to-act-like-you're-a-decent-person-'cause-I'm-onto-you sound. I hold the door for her anyway.

"So . . . paperwork?" I ask.

She sets her bag on the counter and places her hands on either side of it, looking at me. "You better be serious about this," she says, "because Henry's my family and I won't have you—"

"Look, I didn't even know you had anything to do with this. I didn't even know you were *you*. I'm not doing this to ruin your perfect little life."

"How Tyler Blackwell of you," she says.

I'll be surprised if I make it through the day.

Jordyn spends the morning explaining every detail of the appointment software she's incredibly proud of writing. It's so easy that even my dad in his drunkest state could use it, but Jordyn insists on treating me like I have the IQ of a monkey.

After she's satisfied that I'm not a total idiot, we move on to the paperwork.

"Bring your birth certificate with you tomo—"

I place my birth certificate and driver's license on the counter. "Do you want me to make a copy? Or maybe you should explain how a copier works, because I'm obviously a complete tool."

She rolls her eyes as she heads into the back. I assume that's my cue to follow.

The copier is packed into a claustrophobic "kitchen" behind the studio space. I expect Jordyn to give me a lecture about copier safety or something, but instead she goes to the fridge and pours herself a glass of orange juice.

I open the copier, place my birth certificate and license on the glass, and hit START.

Nothing.

I read the little bluish screen; everything seems in order, so I push START again.

Again nothing.

Well, damn. I just played right into that, didn't I.

Sure enough, when I turn, she's wearing a shit-eating grin so big, I have to remind myself how much I need this job.

She shoves me out of the way, punches in some numbers, and hits START. This time the floor beneath my feet vibrates as the copier roars to life. When it spits out the sheet, Jordyn snatches it and shoves it into my chest. "The code's 10086, douchebag."

I follow her back to the front, where I have the privilege of filling out all my paperwork as she gloats. The most messed-up thing is that it's kind of nice to interact with someone who doesn't pussyfoot around my shit.

"What?" Jordyn snaps at me.

I didn't realize I was staring. "Nothing. It's just . . . What happened to you?"

Her dark, purple-rimmed eyes narrow. She takes a breath and parts her dark red lips to, I'm sure, tell me off—

The little door chime rings. Henry hums an atonal melody as he passes us, heading through the red curtain.

Jordyn and I stare each other down until the air in the room is so thick, I'm surprised it's breathable.

"Tyler Blackwell, I need your muscles back here!" Henry's voice booms from behind the curtain, declaring our staring contest a draw. I feel the corners of my mouth twitch up, then I shrug and saunter back to help my *actual* boss. I'm almost surprised nothing comes flying at the back of my head.

Henry explains the technical aspects of lighting and staging as I move various couches in and out of the studio until he "feels" which one is perfect for the Hightowers. I try my best to follow along but find myself distracted by Jordyn. I can see her up front. She's on the phone, obviously talking about me. She keeps glaring back at me past the curtain and gesturing my way.

The door chimes again, announcing the arrival of a herd of denim-clad blond people. Jordyn quickly hangs up and becomes this bubbly, animated freak, which is hysterical in contrast to her vampiric appearance. "Mrs. Hightower. It's so lovely to meet you in person."

Jordyn, in her long black skirt and black shirt with billowing translucent sleeves, with her purple-rimmed eyes, and lips such a dark shade of red they're almost black, rounds the counter to greet the woman with a handshake.

Mrs. Hightower looks horrified at the sight of this little half-Malaysian vampire, but she doesn't want to be rude, so she offers Jordyn the tips of her fingers—the fuck-you of handshakes. If this offends Jordyn, she doesn't let it show.

"Have a seat. Henry will be with you shortly. He's just putting some finishing touches on the backdrop."

Mrs. Hightower opens her mouth to say something, but changes her mind.

"Why don't you head out and see if anyone wants a drink or something. And close the curtain, will you?" Henry instructs me.

After I struggle with the curtain for an uncomfortable moment, Jordyn comes to my aid, but not without an air of smug superiority. How was I supposed to know there's a trick to unsticking the curtain involving some choreographed arm twist?

"Can I get anyone a refreshment?" I ask the room.

Mrs. Hightower perks up. "Hello there, dear. I'm Helena. What's your name?"

"Tyler."

"What a lovely name. Tyler, do you think you can do me a little favor?"

I glance at Jordyn expecting her to be seething at me for overstepping, but she just smiles at Mrs. Hightower.

Mrs. Hightower places her hand on my arm and gets real close, lowering her voice. "I was told that we would get a few options for the backdrop. But the girl tells me it's already set up."

I know Jordyn can hear this. I can't believe how well she's holding it together. I mean, *I* want to tell this lady where she can stick it.

"Um. I can find out for you," I say, looking over at Jordyn for help. She pretends she's busy at the computer. "Can I get you some water in the meantime?"

"That would be wonderful. Thanks so much," says Mrs. Hightower.

"How many?" I turn toward the room full of blond kids of various ages who are just *sitting* there. Not one of them is on a cell phone or playing a video game. It's creepy.

When two of the younger and one of the older kids raise their hands in unison, I decide that they are, in fact, the Children of the Corn. They're probably going to kill us all by the end of the session. I glance at Jordyn, who happens to be looking at me, and she stifles a laugh.

"I'll be right back," I say.

"I'll give you a hand," Jordyn adds. "Children of the fucking Corn," she mutters, following me into the kitchen.

"Right?" I say a little louder than I should.

She's smiling and I'm almost laughing and I'm reminded of when we used to be friends a million years ago.

"And what's with asking me about stuff when she's been talking to you on the phone?"

"It's the makeup. Some people are small-minded."

"Well, then why don't you—"

"Don't." She gives me an unreadable look, grabs an armful of waters from the fridge, and pushes past me, ignoring my offer to help.

I give up.

"The mom is out there asking about backdrops," I say to Henry as he fiddles with the flash umbrellas. "She says she wanted a choice."

"She asked *you,* did she?" he says, mostly to himself with a bit of a chuckle. "Tell 'em I'm ready for 'em. They can ask me directly."

I nod and head back out to get the family. The door chimes once again, and the tired-looking, gray-haired husband enters with their two freshly groomed chocolate Labs wearing denim handkerchiefs around their necks. Why not?

"Good timing," I say. "Henry's ready for you. Right this way." I hold the curtain back and gesture for everyone to enter.

"Oh, thank you, Tyler. You've been such a help," Mrs. Hightower says. The unnerving children—there are six of them—get up without making a noise and head back behind the curtain. The oldest, a girl close to my age, offers a vacant smile as she passes. The dad sighs, following with the two dogs.

Henry arranges the Hightowers so they look like the perfection I imagine they strive to present at all times. Then he clicks away while Jordyn and I stand back and watch.

I say quietly, "I didn't mean to tell you that you should change the way—"

"It's fine." Jordyn heads over to Henry, producing a handkerchief from her pocket. Henry takes it with a warm smile and mops his forehead. And suddenly, I need a sugar fix.

Jordyn enters the kitchen as I pull a Coke from the fridge and gestures for me to toss it over. I do.

"You and Henry seem close." I kick the fridge closed and pop my can open. "He's your stepdad?"

"He and my mom aren't married."

"Oh. I just assumed."

"Everyone does. My mom just kind of lost all faith in marriage after the divorce, you know? And Henry doesn't really care either way. Even with a fifteen-year age difference, they just . . . work."

"What about your dad? Or if that's too—"

"No, it's fine. Do you remember him? He was having an affair and he married his mistress, like, as soon as the ink dried. She looks eerily like my mom even. I guess he has a thing for pretty, petite white women. The crazy thing is that she and my mom are really close now."

"Seriously?"

"Yep."

"How does that work?"

"My mom's happy. My dad set her free so she'd be able to find love, so she's grateful. They're friends too."

"Your divorced parents are friends."

"Mmm-hmm." She sips her Coke.

"You get two families, and I don't even have one."

I can tell my attempt at a joke has failed when Jordyn's face drains of all color. Well, more than usual.

"I'm sorry, I didn't mean . . ." she says.

"It's . . . fine." I try to sound as "no big deal" as I can. I really wasn't trying to make her feel bad.

After an awkward pause where neither of us knows what to do, I head back out to the studio. Just in time to receive instructions about which couch and backdrop to use for the next setup.

"Can you handle that while I do the outdoor shots?" Henry asks.

I nod.

"Jordyn, bring the reflectors," Henry bellows.

She scoots past me to grab several gold and silver things that look like the shades you put in the car to keep the sun out. She purposefully doesn't look at me. Damn it. The one person who didn't tiptoe is tiptoeing. What the hell was I thinking?

Henry and the others return shortly, and then the Hightowers take turns changing clothes in the small dressing room. They're going to do a Christmas photo to send to all their friends and family. That's something my mom always wanted to do but my dad never allowed. He said we weren't a family, we were a punishment. As if he blamed us instead of the alcohol for ruining his life—her for getting pregnant, and me for not being aborted or stillborn. It used to really hurt when he said shit like that, and I'd try my best to hide that I was crying, but my stupid little snotty nose and red eyes always gave me away and he'd call me a pussy, until I finally realized he wasn't ever going to stop, and I learned to turn my hurt into anger and eventually aggression and use it on the field. Mom never figured out how to manage it, and it finally killed her.

Once the Hightowers' session is over, Henry sends me to Starbucks for all of us. His treat.

The oldest Child of the Corn, the last to finish changing out of her Christmas outfit, is headed outside, so I hold the door open. I didn't really notice her, aside from the creepy, vacant smile she flashed earlier. But now that she's changed into jeans and a button-down shirt that's straining against her ample chest, I realize she's hot. As we round the corner toward Starbucks, she steps in my path, pulls a marker out of her purse, takes my hand, and writes her number across my palm. Then she takes my index finger in her mouth and *sucks* on it. I glance around to make sure her family isn't seeing this, because I'm pretty sure they'd press charges.

"Call me," she says, raising her eyebrows, before heading toward her mother's voice coming from around the corner.

She's hot in that all-American, girl-next-door kind of way. And if that little finger-sucking display is any indication of how fun she might be, perhaps I *will* call her. I glance down at the ink on my hand. Ali. With a heart above the *i*.

"Thanks for getting the door," I grunt as Jordyn watches me struggle with the coffees. I set the drinks on the counter, hand hers over, and go to take Henry his, when she grabs my hand and flips it over.

"Ali? There's no Ali at this Starbucks."

I smirk. "Hightower."

"Too bad you have a girlfriend," she says.

"So?" I pull my hand away and take Henry his coffee.

Jordyn doesn't really talk to me for the rest of the day. Whatever.

SIX

Monday, at lunch, I spot Sheila gesturing wildly as a few cheer-leaders giggle, following her into the cafeteria, and I suddenly have an overwhelming need to be anywhere but here.

One of the guys I'm sitting with is in the middle of a boring retelling about his weekend hookup when I grab the remainder of my sandwich and throw my bag over my shoulder, slipping through the crowd, hoping to make it out before Sheila spots me and makes a scene.

I head upstairs. The art students have staked their claim on the locker bay with the benches. So I head down the back stairs that dump me out near the auditorium lobby. It's empty, so I go all the way to the far end and resume my lunch in peace.

"Are you kidding me?"

I look up to find Jordyn snarling at me with a slice of pizza in one hand and a Coke in the other. She's wearing that stupid leather jacket again. Should I remind her that it's still August?

"What, are you stalking me now, Tyler?"

"Don't flatter yourself, sweetheart." *Sweetheart? Jesus.*

"Like you didn't know I eat here every day."

"Why would I?" I take another bite of my sandwich and a swig of iced tea as I think about where I might find someplace to be alone outside.

"You can leave anytime now," Jordyn says. She shifts on the bench. "Seriously, Tyler. I'm not in the mood. You can't really be that much of a dick."

Oh, but I can. I had every intention of leaving, but she just said the magic words. The disdain in her voice, her words, her body language—

I make a show of throwing my legs up on the bench and crossing them at the ankles as I casually take another bite. "There's room. I promise not to bite."

"You're such an asshole."

"Well, which is it? Am I an asshole or am I a dick? Please choose one part of the anatomy and stick to it."

"Frankly, I'm not sure either is strong enough. Mother-fucker is more like it."

She says this without batting an eye. Calling a guy whose mother just killed herself a motherfucker? Bold. Move. If anyone else had said that, they undoubtedly would have backpedaled, but not Jordyn. Even if she realizes how messed up it is, she's not backing down.

"Thanks," I say. And I mean it.

"Fuck you, Tyler," she says, and then she goes to find somewhere else to eat.

I laugh, to which she raises her hand, giving me the finger around her unopened can of Coke, not bothering to turn around as I watch her walk away.

She should've just stayed. I'm done in three more bites. I gather my stuff and chug the rest of my drink, then head toward my car to listen to music and wait out the rest of lunch.

Jordyn groans as I approach the one trash can in the deserted lobby area. Well, it's not really the lobby anymore; at this point it's the upper gym hallway. Jordyn's just settling in on the top step of a small flight that leads down to the band room.

"Jesus, Tyler. Just leave me alone," she whimpers. Then she grabs her shit and heads back over to her usual spot.

I'm grinning for real for the first time in as long as I can remember when I spot Sheila. I maintain eye contact as I walk past her toward the parking lot. I expect her to follow, but she doesn't. She's probably pissed I didn't eat with her.

"What the eff, Ty? Did you really skip lunch with me to eat with that goth freak?" Sheila greets me at the doors as I head back in for wonderful Mrs. Hickenlooper's class.

There's no sense defending myself.

"Well?" she says, looking around to make sure people are watching. The smile on her face clearly implies: "I caught you. I dare you to deny it."

I lean against the wall and cock my head to the side. But I don't say anything.

Her expression goes from pissed to embarrassed to concerned in the span of about four seconds. She brushes her shiny light brown hair over her right shoulder, running her fingers through it, then glances around at the onlookers, trying to figure out a way to turn this around. "Ty," she says loud enough so her fans don't have to strain their ears, "I think what hurts the most is that I'm here for you and you just—"

I slip around her and head to class mid-sentence. I can't do it. I'm done.

"This conversation is not over!" she yells as I round the corner.

Oh, but how wrong she is. The conversation is most definitely over. And I think we are too.

And in that second, all I feel is relief.

On Tuesday I consider staking my claim on Jordyn's spot again, but I kind of don't even feel like dealing with her. No, today's an alone day. I head to my car and blast some music while I eat my crappy sandwich. I seriously need to get groceries, but I'm low on funds. I could tap into my secret stash, but I sort of have a little pact with myself about that.

Maybe I should bring up the whole money thing at work tonight. I probably won't get paid for another two weeks—I mean, that's how Subway was. And I definitely won't last that long. Plus I'm low on dog food. It's one thing for me to go hungry, but I won't let Captain starve.

"Tyler, wait up, man!" Marcus runs to catch me in the parking lot as I head back in after lunch. "You wanna grab some grub tonight after practice?"

He always has to throw in something about practice. "Working tonight, but tomorrow maybe?"

"I heard you got fired."

"Where'd you hear that?" I hold the door open, letting Marcus lead the way.

"Kyle."

"Where'd he hear that?"

"Mindy."

Who the hell is Mindy?

He gives me a chin-thrust, then turns and runs down the hall toward his next class just as the two-minute warning bell rings. "I'll hit you up later about tomorrow," he calls.

Just as I think I'm in the clear, Coach rounds the corner. A smile spreads across his face. "Blackwell, just the person I was hoping I'd run into." He falls in next to me on my way to class.

Great.

"How are you doing?" I can tell he's being sincere, but he's just so uncomfortable that it sounds forced.

"Same ol', same ol'," I say.

"That's good. Maybe I'll see you at the game this Friday? I know the team would love it if you came."

"I'd love to, Coach. But unfortunately, I'm scheduled to work this Friday." My face hurts from the effort of trying to pretend to give a shit.

"That's too bad. Maybe the next one, then." His walking slows even though he's trying so hard to hide his disappointment.

"Yeah, sure. Next game."

o o o

I get to the studio three minutes late that night expecting some kind of lecture from Jordyn about punctuality, but it appears I've beaten her.

Henry pokes his head out from behind the red curtain. "Oh good. You can help me test this new lens." He disappears back behind the curtain. "Today'd be nice."

I follow.

"Sit." He points at a box in the center of the black backdrop.

I eye the box.

He grunts as he looks at my clothes. "Not ideal, but I guess I don't have a choice."

I cross my arms over my chest in an attempt to cover my threadbare T-shirt and glance toward the front, hoping Jordyn will hurry up and get here already. He can experiment on her.

"Jordyn's off today. Just you an' me." Henry grins. "Now, get over there and uncross your damn arms."

The flash goes off a few times and I wince. Then I take my seat and smile awkwardly.

"The hell kinda face is that? Just smile like a normal person. Boy, I feel bad for the poor sucker who took your senior photos. It probably took him several hundred shots before he got a decent one, am I right?"

I look at the ground, then back toward the front. Henry doesn't need to know I'll be one of those poor, pathetic seniors whose photo in the yearbook will be the same generic picture everyone has taken at registration. As if I could afford a few hundred bucks for some photographs. And what would I do with them even if I could? The only person who'd want one is dead.

He steps out from behind the camera and sighs. I know from the sound that he gets it.

"Tell you what. I'm getting a new lighting kit this weekend and I'll need to test it out. If you bring a couple of 'outfits,' we'll see if we can't figure something out."

I stare at the ground a little longer. Until I hear him shuffle back behind the camera. "Well, you don't have to be so damn emotional about it. Just try not to smile like a serial killer."

I laugh. Jordyn has no idea how lucky she is.

SEVEN

"I got another job," I explain to Marcus, yet again, as I search for any sign of our server. I'd really like something to keep my hands busy, plus I'm thirsty.

"Yeah?" Marcus slides his cardboard coaster in circles. I can tell he doesn't believe me.

"I'm working for this photographer down off Santa Fe."

"Can I get you two gentlemen a soda?" A perky little redhead sidles up to our table. "Or an appetizer?"

"I'll take a phone number," Marcus says, all white teeth, turning on his charm.

"Just water for me," I say.

The server flashes me a thank-you smile.

"And a Coke along with that number," Marcus calls after her.

The server doesn't stop. Marcus scratches the back of his neck, ducking his head.

"Ah, man," Marcus says, cracking his back, changing the subject. "This season's brutal. You don't even know. Everything's gone to shit since you quit."

"I'm sure you're exaggerating. But thanks for the guilt trip anyway." I eye the door. If this is where this conversation is headed, I'll be leaving before I get my water.

"It's just . . . football was, like, your life, man. How can you just throw it—"

"I'm not. I . . ." I take a breath and try to relax my hand. It's curled into a fist under the table. My memory flashes to pink water, pale skin, blood. "I told you. I have to work."

"Tyler, you—"

"Ready to order?" The server. Thankfully. She sets our drinks in front of us.

"Yeah, I'll have the chicken quesadilla," I say. If I order, I won't be as tempted to storm out.

"For dinner?" Marcus scoffs. "You gotta eat more than an appetizer."

I could kill him for saying this in front of someone. He doesn't realize I'm already stretching my limited funds by ordering that. I give him a look like *Let it go.*

"Well, I'll have the southwest jalapeno burger, medium rare, with fries. And bring us an appetizer sampler too please," Marcus says. He's being appealingly regular after getting shut down. It's refreshing.

My stomach grips at the sound of a big, juicy burger. I think about giving in and tapping into my hidden funds. No. I can't do it. I can have some ramen when I get home if I'm still hungry. Who am I kidding? Of course I'll still be hungry.

After the server leaves, Marcus shifts awkwardly before finally speaking. "You didn't order that because of money, did you?"

I can feel my face flush. I hate talking money with Marcus. His family's loaded. He doesn't get it.

"Dude. You know I got this, right?" he says. "Just order a meal already. I'll get the chick back here." He waves at the server, who's just getting ready to type our order into the screen.

"Marcus, don't. You're not buying my dinner. This isn't a goddamn date."

He ignores me and when the server reaches our table he says, "Cancel the quesadilla and make that two jalapeno burgers. And another Coke."

My face is burning. I stare intently at the effervescence coming off the top of his Coke.

"Sure thing," she says, heading back toward the monitor.

"You're not exaggerating when you talk about your dad making you work, are you?" All Marcus's usual bravado is gone. This is as close to a serious conversation as we've had since . . . And it's in the middle of a goddamn Applebee's.

I shake my head.

"Tyler." He sighs. "I just thought you were making excuses because football made you . . . whatever. If it's just because you gotta work, I'm sure Coach can figure something out with your boss."

I glance at the door again.

"Talk to me, man," he says, leaning in.

"I don't know what you want me to say, Marcus. You have no idea what it's like to have to go to a full day of school and then work enough to pay for your gas, groceries, clothes, fucking toilet paper even, because your dad's a total prick who hates looking at your stupid fucking face because it reminds him of his wife who killed herself. You can't possibly understand how, every time you think about football, all you can focus on is how you'll never see your mom's face in the crowd cheering you on. You can't possibly understand how it is to be faced with the rest of your miserable fucking life without one person who gives a shit what you'll make of yourself."

I take a deep breath and try to shake it off. "Can we talk about something else? Who are you screwing this week?"

Marcus meets my eyes, and for a second I see pity, but he pulls it together and tells me about Twelve.

"I think you've got the right idea, not being tied down to one girl," I say.

"Dude. Sheila's awesome. What are you even talking about?"

"I don't know. I feel like she's, I don't know, not the same anymore."

"Well, duh. People change." He nods to me as he takes a giant gulp of Coke.

"I know. I get that I've probably changed more than most. But I think maybe we're just not good together anymore."

"Well, don't do anything stupid until you've really thought about it. Sheila's been good to you. She deserves at least that."

I sigh. "You're right. And I do know she's been good to me." Until my mom died and she didn't know how to act anymore. But I can't tell him that.

After what might be the best burger I've ever had in my pathetic life, Marcus picks up the check without a word. I don't fight it because A) I really can't afford it, and B) that burger was freaking delicious.

EIGHT

It's Friday, and Sheila's scheduled a "face-to-face" with me for tonight. She does this occasionally. She'll talk about how I need to appreciate her more and she knows I'm going through a lot and she's trying, but I need to try harder and then we'll have makeup sex and things will just go right back to how they were.

As soon as I round the corner by the auditorium lobby area, a wad of tinfoil hits me on the chin.

"You've got good aim for a chick," I say, bending over to pick up the trash.

"*For a chick?* You really do think the world revolves around you, don't you?" Jordyn glares at me.

"Most of the time it does."

"Why are you here?"

I head to the bench farthest from her and make myself comfortable. "Eating lunch," I say around a huge bite of my pathetic sandwich. I had to use the last of the sliced turkey for dinner and the remaining roast beef was barely enough for half a sandwich today, so it's mostly mayo, mustard, and lettuce. I can barely taste the meat.

"Look, Tyler, I don't really have much of a choice where I eat. I don't have a place in our little social hierarchy. I don't have a table I'm welcome at in the cafeteria. This is my only option." She sighs heavily. "You know, you didn't used to be such an asshole."

"I thought I was a motherfucker." I grin at her before taking another bite.

She gives me the finger. Then she plugs some earbuds into her phone and turns her back to me.

"How original," I say.

She gives me the finger again, and turns up her music so loud, I can hear it leaking out of her earbuds.

There's no point in saying another word because I know she won't hear me. But my presence alone is enough to drive her crazy, and that works for me.

After I finish my sandwich, I head to the drinking fountain at the other end of the lobby. As I gulp the water, I glance back down the long space to see Jordyn still pouting with her back to where I was sitting. She doesn't even know I'm not there anymore. I could leave and she'd probably still be pouting for another half hour because she's too damn stubborn to simply turn and see that I've left. I can't help but laugh.

Somehow she must've heard me, because she glares back at where I was, only to realize I'm no longer there. But she's also finished eating and now she has to pass me to dispose of her trash. So, of course, I step in her way, forcing her to acknowledge me. She throws her trash straight at my head and says, "Fuck you!" loud enough for the few students in the hallway by the gym to turn toward us. She's really left me no choice. I pull the cord of her earbuds and say, "No thanks," before heading to the door.

I so badly want to turn and see her reaction, but it would ruin the moment. Better to just watch the people around me cracking up. But when I get to my car and think about those people laughing at her and how she was just complaining about our school's social hierarchy and not having a place . . .

I bury the thought and get in.

Sheila's waiting for me at the entrance to the parking lot after school.

I take her bag and head toward her car. I can feel her eyes on me for the entire walk. I can feel her willing me to apologize. And I can't for the life of me remember what it is I've done.

"So . . . I'm sorry, Sheila," I say as soon as we're both settled in the car, hoping a blanket apology will suffice. After she still doesn't speak, I finally make eye contact.

She raises her eyebrows. "For . . . ?"

I rack my brain. What the hell did I do? I honestly can't remember. "For being an asshole?"

She grunts in frustration. "Jesus! You don't even remember why I'm mad, do you?"

"Sheila, I have a lot on my plate at the moment."

"You had time enough to chat up that goth freak."

Oh, that's right. She's mad because she thinks I had lunch with Jordyn. "Really? You're still mad about that?"

"Still? It just happened!"

"On Monday!" My voice is a little louder than it needs to be. I take a deep breath before continuing. "First of all, I don't feel like I owe you an explanation and—"

"You don't feel like you owe me an explanation? I'm your freaking girlfriend!"

"And second of all, I didn't have lunch *with* the goth freak. I had lunch in her spot. She had lunch elsewhere."

"Then why did I see you talking to her?"

"You saw her yelling at me. That does not qualify as a conversation."

"Whatever."

I stare at her, wondering if this is really how it ends.

"You know what? I can't do this anymore. This is way too much work. I don't think we actually even like each other anymore. I think we're only still together because you don't want to be the girl who dumped the guy with the dead mom. So now you don't have to. I think this is it for us." I offer her a half-hearted smile as I open the car door. "See you around, I guess."

I'm parked two rows over, facing Sheila's car, and I see her crying into her phone as I start the engine. I should probably feel bad as I watch her cry, but all I feel is free.

The only thing I'm regretting as I put the car in reverse is that I could've really used a good lay tonight. I should have waited to break up with her until after the makeup sex. But that would make me even more of a prick than I already am.

Dad's not home. If he was going to come home after work, he'd already be here, so it looks like I'm free for the night.

Captain keeps looking at his leash, but I don't feel like going for a run. And for the first time in a long time, I don't feel like being alone. I wonder what Dr. Dave will have to say about *that* tomorrow.

Too bad he's my psychiatrist. I think he'd be cool to go hang out with.

Man, what's wrong with me that I'm thinking about hanging out with my shrink socially?

I pull out my phone and scroll through my contacts. I guess I could see what Marcus is up to, but it probably involves Twelve, and there's nothing lonelier than being a third wheel. That's when I come across Ali Heart-over-the-*i* Hightower.

Why not? I send her a text:

Hey, it's Tyler. Remember me from the photo shoot? Just wondering if you're busy tonight?

My phone chimes almost immediately.

Of course I remember u!!! :) I can get out of my plans if u wanna hang.

I text her my address.

<3 I'm coming now . . . And maybe later? ;)

Whoa. Marcus would love her.

Ali doesn't expect much conversation. She's made it pretty clear this is a booty call, which is an entirely new experience for me. I pop in one of the Christian Bale Batman movies to create the illusion we're going to do something other than just have sex. It makes me feel a little less sleazy. Before the plot even gets going she's got her shirt off and her hand down my pants.

She's very flexible. And very vocal. Very. I find myself wishing I'd closed the window. But then she takes my body to places I didn't know existed and so what if the neighbors hear.

She doesn't linger when we're done. She just kisses me and gets dressed and swears she's not normally like this. Then she leaves. The movie's not even over.

And now I feel even lonelier than I did before.

NINE

"I broke up with Sheila," I say to Dr. Dave as soon as he takes his seat.

"This is a good thing?"

"I feel pretty freaking good. I met this chick last week at my new job and she, uh, *consoled* me last night."

Dr. Dave flips open his notebook and writes as he talks. "You got a new job?"

"Yeah. With this cool mountain-man photographer."

"This is good, Tyler."

"The only problem is this chick from school works there. We sort of used to be friends. And then she moved away after sixth grade and gothed out and now she hates me because I didn't recognize her."

"What's her name?"

"Jordyn." I crane my neck to see what he's writing in his little notepad. "*Y-N*," I correct him.

He adjusts the notepad so I can't see it and then grins at me. "Consoled, huh?"

I shrug like it's no big deal.

"Show-off."

"You're just jealous," I say.

"You're not wrong. I would have killed for that when I was your age." He laughs. "So you think it's okay to shit where you eat?"

"What?"

"How long before you get fired for having sex with this Jordyn?"

"Oh, god. No. It wasn't with Jordyn." I cringe. "The girl was a client."

He raises his hands in a gesture of surrender. "Sorry. I assumed."

"Jesus."

"This reaction is a bit extreme, no?" He's laughing at me.

"Please change the subject," I beg.

"Fine." He flips the page in his notebook. "Let's talk about your dad."

"Nice try." I laugh now. I've told him that my dad's an asshole and that's all there is to say, but he's always trying to get me to "explore my anger toward my father."

"Let's talk about football then."

"You're a real piece of work, Doc."

We settle on the subject of Sheila. He's proud of me for finally letting her off the hook. He thinks I was being a prick to her. And I guess I kind of was.

○ ○ ○

Jordyn shows up to the studio a minute after me wearing a particularly terrifying scowl, and, of course, that goddamn leather jacket. When she passes me to unlock the door, I see the origin of her extremely bad mood. The word *slut* is written across her back in giant white letters. That totally sucks. She probably even paid for that jacket herself, unlike most of the privileged assholes we go to school with.

She lets the door slam on me. I don't take it personally. I'd be that pissed if someone did that to something I obviously love.

She checks the voicemail, scribbling the messages so hard, the pen goes through the paper a few times, and then she growls because she has to listen to the message again. When she's finally done, she slams the headset down—it's probably broken. I mentally map out the nearest office supply store because I will surely be tasked with finding a replacement.

I kind of hover nearby but keep my distance. I'm afraid to step into the circular counter area for fear she'll, like, hit me or something.

Plus I feel completely useless when she's here. She doesn't let me do anything. She's made it abundantly clear that she knows I'll just mess things up and she'll have more work to do.

I head to the kitchen and clean a coffee mug. It's literally the only task I can find.

When I return to the front, I decide to brave the counter area. I need to check the schedule so I can anticipate what furniture Henry will want moved.

I go to the computer I'm allowed to use—the one Jordyn

doesn't—and see that we don't have anyone scheduled until two p.m. Why did they have me come in so early? Not that I'm complaining. I need the money.

I decide to make a coffee run, mostly just to get out of the suffocating awkwardness. I have twenty bucks in my wallet. Twenty bucks that will have to last me the rest of the week. I really need to ask when I'll get my check.

I order a black coffee and when the barista asks if that's all, I find myself ordering a tall white chocolate mocha, Jordyn's drink of choice. It's more than I wanted to spend, but I'll just snack on whatever's in the kitchen for lunch and live on ramen and beans this week.

I set the coffee next to Jordyn, who clasps her sketchpad to her chest like it contains top secret military codes or something, and head back to my computer. She doesn't thank me, not that I expected her to, but she does drink it.

I waste time on the Internet reading about how screwed up the world is, until I notice that Jordyn's not attempting to murder her keyboard anymore.

Taking a deep breath, I brave it. "So what happened?"

Nothing.

I go over to examine the jacket, now hanging on the back of her stool. "Damn. What is this? Permanent marker?"

"Try oil-based paint marker."

"Shit." The leather is old and worn-in and the white paint has worked its way deep into the pores. "Who would do this?"

She jumps up from the stool and gets in my face fast. "Basically, you did this!"

I stagger back. She's small but very scary.

"Your little cheerleader bitch did this because you were talking to me! So the way I see it, you owe me a fucking jacket! Too bad it's irreplaceable!" She storms off toward the kitchen. "ASSHOLE!"

Shit. Sheila did this? Because she thought I was talking to Jordyn?

I pull the jacket off the stool and really look at it. The label is in Italian. It's the smoothest leather I've ever touched. It must've been really expensive.

I could kill Sheila. Who does that? Who does something this mean to a complete stranger?

I have to sit down. I'm shaky and I'm starting to feel sick.

Why did I have to mess with Jordyn at school? I should have just left her alone. But I had to push her buttons. I had to get her to treat me . . . I don't know. I'm such a selfish prick.

And the really messed-up thing is that it feels nice, her being angry at me, me feeling bad. It feels good.

I know what I need to do. I need to replace it. And there's only one way I can possibly make that happen: Dip into my emergency funds. I've got close to a thousand dollars stashed away in the box with Mom's pictures.

I look behind me, then write down all the information on the tag and tuck it into my pocket just before Jordyn returns.

I want to apologize. I want to tell her my plan. But I know she doesn't even want to hear the sound of my voice right now.

I head to the kitchen in search of "lunch." A Coke, an apple, a yogurt, and a handful of chips. I eat over the sink.

And even though Henry told me to help myself to anything in the kitchen, I jump like I'm doing something bad every time I hear a noise.

Henry should be here soon and then I'll have a purpose or at least a distraction. I just hope Jordyn doesn't tell him to fire me. I haven't heard back from any of the other places I applied. I'll be so screwed if I lose this job.

When the door chimes, I head into the studio.

Henry greets me with his usual shoulder pat and asks how I'm doing. I lie and tell him I'm good.

"Did you bring the clothes I asked you to bring?" he asks.

"They're in my car."

"Go get 'em so I can see what we have to work with." He heads to his storage closet and punches in a code—this is where he keeps all his cameras and lenses.

"You really don't have to do this, you know. I mean, it's nice of you to offer, but . . ."

"I told you. I need to test the new kit. You're doing *me* the favor. Now, go get your stuff and don't make me ask you again."

I feel like such an asshole.

Jordyn's face contorts in confusion when I return from my car with my clothes. I can tell she wants to ask, but she's still too pissed.

I hope she doesn't come investigate while he's taking pictures.

Henry smiles widely. "You remembered about the blue, I see."

I nod. But actually I didn't remember him saying anything about blue. I just like blue.

"Start with the blue shirt."

I shrug, pull my T-shirt off, and put the blue shirt on.

"Yep. Looks good, but did you dig it out of the bottom of your hamper or what? We've got an iron back in the kitchen."

I feel my face get hot. I'm not sure how to tell him that the one time I tried ironing after my mom died, I ruined my shirt. It's not that I don't know how to use an iron, it's that . . . Okay, whatever, I don't know how to use an iron.

All of this must be transparent on my face, because Henry bellows, "Jordyn! Help us a minute?"

Great.

She stomps out from the front and awaits instructions, making sure to only acknowledge Henry.

"It seems this poor boy here needs a lesson in ironing. Maybe you can educate him while I set the lights?"

"Why?"

"I'm testing out the new kit, and my friend Tyler Blackwell here doesn't have any senior pictures. I can't allow him to use those generic crap pictures in the yearbook. So he's doing me a favor letting me test my new toys, and I'm doing him a favor so he doesn't look back twenty years from now and curse himself for not getting real pictures."

I didn't think Jordyn could look like she hated me more than she did with the jacket thing, but I was wrong. If she were able to make my head explode from one simple look, I would be blissfully out of my misery.

Jordyn makes a gross throaty noise but she doesn't decline or question his request. She glares at me the entire way to the kitchen. Before I can overthink it, I find myself following.

Jordyn shoves me into the cabinet to get me out of her way. She retrieves the iron from the nearby closet. Then she slams the iron onto the ironing board and throws the cord at me. I catch it, much to her disappointment, and I search around until I locate the nearest outlet.

The moments until the iron is hot are spent in awkward, silent hostility. I'm afraid to look at her. Occasionally Henry grunts or makes an excited noise in between clicks from the next room.

I see Jordyn shuffle closer to the iron in my peripheral vision so I finally look up. She gives me a look that says, *Well?*

Apparently the iron is ready. I turn toward the studio to get the rest of my clothes, but her voice stops me. "You didn't think to get your stuff while you sat here staring at the floor for the last five minutes?"

"I just . . . I . . ."

"Oh. I forgot I'm dealing with a football player." She turns back toward the iron.

As soon as my shirt is unbuttoned, I playfully throw it at the back of her head, hoping I might snap her out of her bad mood. She grabs blindly, somehow managing to catch the shirt before it falls to the floor. Then she turns to glare at me, but when she sees my state of undress, her cheeks and ears turn the faintest shade of pink, and as she attempts to lay my shirt the proper way on the ironing board, the material slips through her fingers. Her discomposure is killing me and I'm trying so hard not to laugh. At least she doesn't seem to be pissed at me anymore.

After retrieving the rest of my stuff, I get uncomfortably close to her so I can see what she's doing. I'm sure I'll be expected to take it from here.

"Do you mind?" She elbows at me not meaning to make contact, but she hits me in the stomach, which I flex. (What? It's instinct.) Her ears flare red again when she realizes I'm still shirtless. Her whole body stiffens and I have to bite my cheek to keep from laughing. But I *am* kind of regretting not putting on another shirt now. I mean, she does have a hot iron in her hands, and my bare chest might make an awfully tempting target.

I take a few steps back and clear my throat. "You gonna show me how to do this, or do you just want to play maid today?"

She sets the iron on its end and gestures for me to take it, meeting my eyes with the best "fuck you" glare I've ever seen.

I pick it up and await instructions.

"Oh, please. You really expect me to believe you've never ironed before?" she says.

"I didn't say that."

"It was implied."

"I told Henry I suck at it. And that's true." I set down the iron and go to get my evidence.

She quickly picks up the iron and places it on its end, looking at me exasperatedly as I hold up a white shirt to show her the triangular scorch mark on the back near the left armpit.

She slowly shakes her head at me.

"So you see why I might be a little gun-shy?" I say.

"Well, maybe if you didn't set the iron on the fabric and walk off, you wouldn't have a stupid-looking burn on your armpit. And you obviously don't learn from your mistakes." She glances at the iron she just picked up.

And now I feel like an idiot.

I scoot past her back to the ironing board and accidentally brush against her, taking absolutely no pleasure this time when my nakedness makes her bristle. It's just not fun anymore. When I finish, I make a show of setting the iron on its end.

"You're not finished." Jordyn grabs my arm. I tense, partially because I'm uncomfortable having her touch me while I'm still half naked . . . but mostly because I'm . . . not.

"You really think I'm ready to tackle buttons?" I gesture at my white shirt for emphasis, hoping she didn't sense my temporary lapse in judgment.

"Oh my god. You're such a *guy*. It's not rocket science. Here." She pushes me out of the way and picks up the iron. Then she gently brushes the pointy tip between the buttons. The clacking of iron hitting plastic makes me nervous.

"Won't the buttons melt?" I don't think she understands just how much I can't afford a new shirt.

"Only if you set the iron on them and walk away." She bugs her eyes out at me, and I laugh.

When I finish the blue shirt, I pull it over my shoulders and quickly button it, feeling a huge sense of relief that I'm no longer half naked—I should have just grabbed another shirt to begin with.

I think Jordyn will leave me to finish the other shirt alone, but instead she pulls herself up onto the counter and watches me. She obviously doesn't trust me not to start a fire or something.

But I must do okay, because she doesn't intervene. She doesn't even make any comments about what a moron I am. When I finish that shirt and go to hang it back on the hanger, she's examining the suit and the tie.

"I think you're done. This looks okay. Actually, it looks like it's never been worn."

"Just the one time," I say, mostly to myself. But she hears. And she gets it.

"Don't go thinking we're friends or anything. And don't think I'm not still pissed at you. Because I'm pretty sure I'll resent you forever for the jacket." She hops off the counter and heads back to man her station.

I smile watching her walk away.

Henry positions me in my newly pressed blue shirt against a plain white backdrop, then against the black one. Then he has me change into the suit. The pants are only a little too big on me now. Not enough that anyone but me will notice.

As I replace the blue shirt with the white one, Henry chuckles, pointing to the iron burn on the back near my armpit. "And that's with help?"

"No, that's from before. I told you I wasn't very good at it,"

I say, pulling the tie around my neck. I've never been particularly good at tying a tie either.

"Looks like you need some help again," Henry says.

Oh, god, please don't make Jordyn help me with this. But it's Henry who walks over and pulls the tie out of my hands. He places it around his neck, quickly and expertly ties it, and loops it back over my head.

"Didn't your old man ever teach you how to properly tie a damn tie?"

"He's not really a tie kind of guy," I say.

"Do I look like a tie kind of guy to you?"

I smile. "Good point."

When he finishes, he fixes my collar and brushes my shirt across my shoulders. And I can't look at him for a sec. Jordyn has no idea how good she has it. What I wouldn't have given for my mom to have left my dad to find a guy like Henry who could teach me to do things like tie a goddamn necktie.

"Jordyn! Can you set up the big fan out here?" Henry bellows.

"I can do it," I offer.

"We're trying to get you not to sweat through that suit."

Jordyn is back through the curtain and pulling the big fan across the room in no time. It's on wheels, so I don't feel so bad.

"Thanks, kiddo. The lights are already fighting the AC. It's gonna be unbearable this afternoon."

Jordyn plugs in the fan and turns it on.

"Okay, Tyler Blackwell, let's get you situated." Henry pats a podium-type thing. Or is it a column? Whatever it is, it's black.

The backdrop is dark gray and there's a circle of lighter gray in the center thanks to Henry's keen eye for lighting.

He has me lean one elbow on the colopodium. I do as told, but I feel like such a douchebag. Especially because Jordyn's watching.

Henry snaps and snaps and snaps whether I'm ready or not. I vow that I will never make fun of models again. Okay, in all fairness, I probably will, but I'll admit that their job's not as easy as it seems.

"Well, Hank, it looks like you actually made a good investment for once," Jordyn teases Henry.

"You shut up over there." Henry chuckles.

"I'm just saying not all of your purchases are well thought out."

"Hank?" I ask.

"She knows it drives me crazy." Henry shakes his head. His smile not only reaches his eyes, but it reaches across the expanse of the room. I can actually feel it from where I stand.

Jordyn's smile is as big as his.

And all of a sudden it kind of kills me knowing that I will never, ever have that—the kind of unconditional love only a parent can give—ever again.

"There you go, GQ," Henry says. "Give me that model pout."

When we finish with this setup, Henry tells me to change back into my normal clothes. Then he takes a few more shots of me in my gray T-shirt. He has me sit on a metal stool in the center of a backdrop the color of faded, weathered wood.

"I really can't thank you enough for this, Henry."

"Don't thank me yet. We gotta go look at the results first." He pops out the memory card and tells me to have Jordyn load it and let us know when it's ready.

I do this on my way to take my stuff back out to my car. She doesn't look up from her computer or say a word as she snatches the memory card from my hand and plugs it in. When I return, she's on the phone rearranging the schedule for tomorrow. I peek around the screen, checking if my photos are loaded yet. She swats at me like I'm an annoying fly, but I manage to see the screen anyway. It's just her precious scheduling system, so I head back to where Henry is and wait.

Unfortunately the door chimes and we'll have to wait till after the session to see if Henry was able to capture anything other than my inner douchiness.

The next clients are a new family: young mother, young father, and very little baby. They tell Henry that they want to do something really arty, like, with them all tastefully naked. Henry shoots me a look that they don't see and I'm forced to cough in order to cover a laugh.

The wife asks that the "girl" help them, instead of me. She's uncomfortable being naked with another man in the room. I guess Henry doesn't count.

Jordyn still doesn't look up at me when I tell her what's going on with the family. I expect her to laugh with me when I explain about the tasteful nakedness. But she's all business.

As I waste time checking Instagram—like I care that Justin Ramos had an orgasmic shake at Smashburger or that Gwynnie Yang posted another duck-face pic—I feel the pull of Jordyn's computer taunting me with the evidence of my humiliation. I can just peek, right? Or, better yet, I could erase the ones that make me look like a complete tool. There's no way Henry kept count of all the pictures he took. He'll never know.

I listen carefully for footsteps as I inch toward Jordyn's side of the circular counter and bump the mouse. The screensaver vanishes. Then I understand that Jordyn's not avoiding me because she's embarrassed. It's because she's back on the jacket. The screen is on eBay—she's found something similar but not exactly like hers. The auction ends next Saturday at midnight. She's put in a bid for $150 and another person has just outbid her by one dollar. One of *those*. The "buy it now" price is $600. I wonder how much she paid for the ruined one. I feel the leather again; so smooth until you reach the white *slut,* then it's rough and cracked. I scrape at it with a fingernail, but it's useless. It's fucked.

I think I hear shuffling right on the other side of the curtain and I freeze, trying to remember how to put the screensaver—alternating photos of Jordyn's mom, Henry, and Jordyn on vacation—back up so she doesn't see me snooping. Then I hear Henry ask Jordyn to move something, and her voice answers from the other side of the room. I hurry and write down the details of the auction so I can find it, then I click on a few things until I figure out the screensaver, and breathe a sigh of relief when Jordyn's mom's face nuzzled into the side of Henry's neck pops up.

When the Tasteful-Nakeds finish, Henry informs me that

we'll have to wait till next time to check out my photos. They have family game night over at Jordyn's dad's place.

Well, I have no reason to be jealous, because I get to go home and play "How Drunk Are You?" with my dad. We have family game night every night.

TEN

On Thursday, when I exit the gym after last period, I'm faced with a horde of cheerleaders. They're in the hall, spewing insults at a pitch I'm convinced only other teenage girls can hear well enough to decipher.

"Who the hell do you think you are?"

"Sheila was too good for you anyway!"

"Asshole!"

And various other, more imaginative insults fly at me while I stand there, blocking the gym exit for those who had the misfortune of following me out of the locker rooms.

I stare past Sheila's friends, trying to wait it out without making the situation any worse. The reactions on the faces of passersby are fairly amusing, ranging from uncomfortable to annoyed to absolutely horrified for me. Truth is, I'm enjoying how completely normal it all feels. It takes every ounce of self-control not to smile.

"What the—" Sheila pushes her way through the mayhem.

"What the hell are you guys doing? Have you lost your freaking minds?"

"We were helping," Julia, a junior who loves it when people call her mini-Sheila, says.

"How exactly is this helping?" Sheila turns on the others. "What's the matter with you? His mother *died*. Have a little compassion. Jesus."

"He can't use that excuse forever." Julia pouts.

"Seriously? It's his *mom,* not an excuse!"

Julia's posture withers under the intensity of Sheila's glare.

"Okay, people, move it along," Sheila says. "Show's over."

I step out of the gym so the rest of my classmates can finally get around me. "Thanks," I say.

"I didn't tell them to do that." She nods toward the girls, now waiting in a clump down the hall.

"I know."

"Just so we're clear."

"Crystal."

We stand there a minute. It's awkward as hell. I can't look at her for more than a fraction of a second at a time.

"Look," Sheila sighs, "it's not like a few days ago I wasn't saying all the things they were just saying. I mean, the way you strung me along was pretty shitty."

"You're absolutely right." I lean back against the wall, then take a deep breath and push on. "It's just . . . After my mom, things between us started to feel so . . . strained. I know you wanted to help, but you didn't really know how to help me, and I could tell it frustrated the hell out of you. And—I don't know.

It made me pull away. I was sure you were going to break up with me as soon as it was, like, socially acceptable. I should have ended it then. Given you some space, or your freedom or whatever. But then there were times where we were like the old us, and I thought maybe we'd get through it. Then school started. And then I'm pretty sure you only stayed with me, and would *still* be with me, if I hadn't ended it, just so you could milk the tragedy-boy angle." She makes a face and I say quickly, "Don't deny you didn't love the extra attention, because—"

"How can you even say that, Tyler? Jesus. And you started off so well. But then you had to go and turn into the dick you've been lately. *I'm* pretty sure *you* only stayed with *me* because I'd have sex with you. And now that you're getting it from that goth skank, you—"

"For your information, I *am* having sex with someone, mind-blowing acrobatic sex, but that has nothing to do with breaking up with you, it's just a bonus. And it's not *that goth chick*. Is that why you destroyed her jacket? Because, what the fuck, Sheila? Who even does that?"

"Whatever. I should have let the girls berate you. But you know, you go ahead and keep hiding behind your tragedy. It's obviously worked very well for you this far." She flips around and struts off toward the rest of the herd, all giggling, practically stamping their feet and snorting with glee.

God, I'm glad to be done with her and all her bullshit.

Almost immediately after I enter the studio that night, practically in unison with the door chime, Henry bellows for me.

"I got a last-minute gig," he says as I make my way through the curtain. "I need your help, like, thirty minutes ago. Almost thought about calling Jordyn in, but she's working at the animal shelter tonight and she'd kill me if I made her miss it."

I picture Jordyn wearing her goth getup while holding kittens and almost laugh.

"Didja hear me? Jordyn show you how to handle all the paperwork stuff?"

"Don't worry, Henry. It's under control," I say with a reassuring smile.

"Good. Now get over here and help me with this, would you?" He pats the table sitting in the middle of a setup.

We move the table aside and then I straighten up his mess—the man is a walking tornado; gum wrappers, toothpicks, anything that aids a person who's recently quit smoking, plus various lens caps and cords—and I head back up to the counter just as the client arrives.

A woman with one of the most unfortunate faces I've ever seen—eyes too close together, nose too long, serious lack of a chin, and the kind of buckteeth I didn't know still existed after the advent of orthodontics—enters with her equally ugly son who must be around seven or so. Actually, the ugly son *bounces* in. The kid is either suffering from severe ADHD or he's just done a line of coke.

The woman is wearing pink, and I mean *pink,* lipstick on her buckteeth in addition to her lips. I'm about to inform her of this until she points her bony witch finger at me. "We will be doing four changes of clothes. And each change will require new backgrounds and props. Now, take me to see the props. I'll let you know what works for me."

I smile and say, "You must be Mrs. Hill."

"It's Mrs. *Reynolds*-Hill," she says, like I should know better.

"Of course. Excuse me for one minute." I step behind the curtain.

Henry's setting up the white backdrop.

"Your gig has arrived," I say with a tone that lets him know it will be a fun shoot.

Henry grins. "One of those, huh?"

"She wants to take a look at the props in order to see what works for her."

"Fantastic." He wipes his hand over his beard. "Send her back."

I do. I expect her to take her demon offspring with her, but she does not. The child ricochets across the room and—

"What's your favorite animal?"

"Uh, I don't know, a lion?" I'm trying to check the jacket on eBay. Auction's up to $286 already and I have till Saturday to figure out what to do. I've signed up for an e-mail alert every time someone bids and I just hope to Christ no one opts for the buy it now price.

"Mine's a shark, which is totally better than a stupid lion. What's your favorite color?"

"Black." I press ENTER on my bid of $290. Yeah, I'm one of those guys now too.

"Black's not a color, dumb-ass. You're not very smart for a grown-up." He hops over and picks up every single picture frame we have on display—well, every frame he can reach, anyway, knocking them over and smearing greasy fingerprints all over the glass.

Coke-baby's photo shoot is a total party. The mother complains about everything she can possibly complain about. She even *tsk-tsks* some of Henry's camera angles. I don't know how he remains so cool. I want to grab her by her soccer-mom ponytail and drag her out the door. And the kid? He might be the literal spawn of Satan. I swear his head even does the Linda Blair 180 at one point.

When they finish, the mom tries to argue her way into getting free retouching. I don't know what to do, but Henry hears it from the back and comes up and puts her in her place.

"We outsource the retouching, so we have no say in the pricing. It's all pretty standard. So I guess it depends on how much retouching you want. You don't really have to do any, it's a personal preference kinda thing."

The woman wants to argue more, but Satan's spawn has now started throwing a tantrum about it taking too long and wanting ice cream and shit. Henry smiles as she drags the kid toward the door and tells her he'll see her on Monday to pick out which prints she wants.

"I think that kid might need some major retouching," I say as the door closes.

"I don't even know if I got one shot where he didn't look deranged. Monday'll be fun."

I don't work on Monday. Part of me is relieved and part of me is bummed—I'd kind of like to see her reaction.

"Hold on," Henry says as he pushes the curtain out of his way. He quickly returns with the memory chip. "Plug her in. Let's see what the damage is."

I do as asked. It's not as bad as we thought. Little bastard is actually photogenic. He's one of those kids who's so ugly, he's cute. Damn. I was hoping for a good laugh.

"Oh, that reminds me," Henry says, pulling open the drawers, searching for something. "It's gotta be here somewhere . . ." After a few minutes of rifling, he gives up. "I don't want to mess with Jordyn's system too much. She'll make my life hell."

"What are you looking for?"

"The chip with your pictures on it. Aren't you curious about how they turned out?"

"I forgot all about that," I say. I didn't forget; I just hoped that he had.

"Sure you did," he says with a grin.

Dad's home when Captain and I get back from our run. After school, it was either jerk off in the shower or get out of the house and do something productive. Since the first option would still be there after the second, it was only fair to take Captain for a run.

But now Dad's sitting on the couch, watching some ghost-hunting show, drinking what looks like the last of an entire case of beer, from all the empties on the coffee table and floor. Oh, and a Jack Daniel's bottle is at his feet. I haven't been gone more than two hours. I can tell he's in the in-between state and I brace myself—unfortunately, I can't lock myself away for the night because I'm starving. Fucking biology.

For dinner this evening, I have ramen or ramen to choose from. God, I have to talk to Henry about money tomorrow. The bad thing about ramen, especially at this very moment, is that it requires me to be in the kitchen long enough for Dad to start shit with me. He's down in the family room. Seven stairs and a railing separate us, but we have a clear line of sight on each other. And he can make it up those seven stairs much quicker than one might think possible.

I'm hyperaware of his every movement. Every hair on my body is alive, like it's sensing a shift in the electric currents in case I need to flee the storm before lightning strikes.

I feed Captain by picking the kibbles from the bag with my hand and placing them in the bowl with minimal noise. Dad clears his throat and my jaw snaps shut. I freeze, sure he's heard my teeth hit together and he's going to view it as an opening. He takes a swig of JD right from the bottle and sniffles. As I stir my ramen, I hear Captain descend the stairs, his tags clinking against each other with every step. Dad sighs and I hold my breath, waiting for him to take out his aggression on Captain again, but the flap of the doggie door clacks shut after he's made his way outside. I jump when the flap clacks again and Dad shifts on the couch. I brave looking and see the self-satisfied smile on his face as he scratches Captain's ears and lets Captain lick his face. What is he up to? I mean, he's obviously fucking with me, but what's his endgame?

And now that my ramen's finished and Captain, the traitor, is all taken care of, I have two choices: Sit at the kitchen table and jump every time Dad takes a breath, or retreat to my bedroom to take shelter and wait out the Friday night storm. I choose option two. Now all I have to do is descend those seven stairs with my ramen in hand, balance said ramen as I unlock the door to the basement, lock the door behind me, and I'm home free. But I'm so on edge that I fumble with the keys longer than planned while trying to balance the ramen.

I wait for something to fly at my head—a bottle, a snot-filled, wadded-up napkin, a fork, a knife. He's not picky. But instead, he lets out a low laugh and mumbles something about what a fucking disappointment I am and how I killed my mom, the usual shit, to Captain, who's now curled up in his lap. Once I'm through the door, I calmly close it, and when the lock slides into place, I feel completely drained. Like after an adrenaline rush how your body just wants to shut down. I swear he has a bible that he uses to plot his various methods of torture. Today: psychological warfare. Next up: Who the hell knows?

I try to talk myself out of my nightly ritual because I'm so afraid I won't be able to keep myself from doing something to Mom's pictures after having to deal with Dad's shit, but I just can't. It feels like I'd be insulting her or something. All I feel tonight when I see her face is sad. I almost understand her wanting to escape. But why the hell couldn't she talk to me about it? I could have helped. I would have skipped practice in a heartbeat if she'd asked. Why didn't she just ask? Her depression seemed managed. The lows weren't any worse than usual. Why didn't I sense it coming? Was there something that happened that sent her over the edge? I just wish she'd left me some kind of clue, even like, *Tyler, this is what happened that made me understand there's only one way out. I hope you're smarter than me. I hope you're able to figure out another.*

ELEVEN

"Statistically speaking, twenty percent of all suicides don't leave a note."

"It doesn't matter how many times you throw that statistic crap at me, Doc. I'm never going to stop obsessing."

Dr. Dave has told me this about ten thousand times. Every time he brings it up, I want to punch him in the face. It's one of the only things that makes me hate our mandatory time together.

I don't buy it. I mean, the statistic might be true, but I don't think it applies to my mother. My mom was a planner. She kept a calendar of appointments a year in advance, some of which I've been able to find phone numbers for and cancel. The gynecologist was a fun call to make. Thanks, Mom. This is why the whole "no suicide note" thing doesn't sit well with me. I'm convinced that either my dad found a note that made him sound like the abusive asshole he is and was afraid he would be implicated or some shit and destroyed it, or he actually killed her and made it look like a suicide. But since she was still warm when I found her, and Dad was nowhere nearby, I'm pretty sure it was option number one.

"Well, I still don't think it applies to my mom. Like I've said, she was a planner. It just doesn't . . . fit." My leg is bouncing. My muscles are wound so tight, I'm surprised I'm able to move at all. "Can we please talk about something else?"

"We can talk about whatever you want to talk about, Tyler."

"It creeps me out when you use my name like that, *David*."

He laughs. "I know. I apologize. What do you want to talk about?"

"You know that goth chick who works at the photo place? I kind of did something."

"I knew it. If I were a betting man—"

"If you were a betting man, you'd be totally screwed because I didn't have sex with her."

I give Dr. Dave the rundown about my indirect involvement in the ruining of Jordyn's leather jacket. "The strange part is that I feel like such an asshole about the whole thing. I mean, I think I need to replace the jacket . . . I have an interview with a company that specializes in picking up dog shit for lazy bastards to make some extra cash."

Dr. Dave sits back in his chair and grins. "Why, Tyler Blackwell, I do believe I've earned my first paycheck."

"You were just *hoping* I'd find salvation in the scooping of dog shit?"

"I think it's great that you feel bad."

"You're reveling in the fact that I feel bad? That's pretty messed up, Doc."

"This is huge, Tyler. You've allowed yourself to actually feel. To, you know, give a shit."

"I don't give a shit."

His face beams in triumph but he holds his hands up. "Fair enough. Let's talk about your anger toward your dad."

"Nice try." But I begrudgingly smile at him—gotta admire his determination.

I have to stop at home before the photo studio, so I'm a little late. Really only thirty seconds late, but I feel like I should be there early to show Henry how appreciative I am for the job. I have to wait for Jordyn to come out from the back to open the door for me.

"Sorry I'm late," I say.

She looks at me like I have three heads as she raises the counter divider to our circular work area. I hear the whirr of her computer and hover behind her to see the schedule on her screen.

"You can get into the calendar from your own computer." She sounds annoyed.

"But that would require patience. Plus I wouldn't get my daily dose of up close and personal Jordyn-hate."

She glares at me and I smile bigger. "Ah, yeah." I make a big show of taking in a deep breath. She doesn't strike me as a perfume kind of girl, but there's a hint of something sweet and fresh coming off her. Jasmine maybe? "That's the stuff."

She reaches back and smacks my arm pretty hard. When I laugh, she slaps me again, only this time I grab her wrist and hold it until she turns her full glare on me. After I've fully basked in her hatred, I allow her arm to drop. When I turn back toward my area, I'm thumped across the back of the head. This time she's the one laughing.

Crap. Are we flirting? I have to stop with this. I need her to hate me. Shit. But then why am I trying so hard to fix the jacket thing?

I sneak a peek at the eBay auction. It's up to $452. Fuck me. Also, I see that Jordyn's stopped bidding. Her last bid was $402, and now the two assholes who kept outbidding us by one freaking dollar are outbidding each other by a few at a time.

I know what I have to do. I have no choice. I'll have to pay the "buy it now" price. Six hundred goddamn dollars. I have the wad of cash in my front pocket. I stopped home to grab it out of my emergency funds just in case, and I'll have to go to the bank at lunch to put it on my debit card so I can get the jacket before the auction ends at midnight—if one of the two assholes doesn't "buy it now" first.

Henry enters around lunchtime. We have some senior photos to do this afternoon at 3:00, so I'm not sure why he's here now.

I follow him back to the studio. "Do you need me now, Henry? Because I need to run to the bank and I was hoping to do that at lunch."

"No problem. Actually, that's more than fine. Lunch is on me." Henry digs out his wallet. "I'll have Jordyn call in the order and you can pick it up. You like Chinese?"

I nod. I should probably make a show of telling him he

really doesn't have to pay for my meal, but I'm so hungry and I can't stomach the thought of another lunch of snacks, so I just nod.

"Good. You know that place on the corner of Santa Fe?"

Again, I nod.

"Great." He places three twenties in my hand. "Hurry back. My mouth's watering just thinking about it. Jordyn!" I hurry past her as she pushes through the curtain.

Good thing my bank is pretty close. I head in and deposit $650 into the account. My balance is now a whopping $659. But not for long. After the jacket I'll have enough for a quarter-tank of gas and some more damn ramen. That's about it.

Then I stop and pick up our lunch. The total is over fifty bucks plus tax. I give the lady the whole sixty dollars and head back.

There's so much food. I feel like Henry ordered one of everything from the menu.

When I return, he and Jordyn have set up chairs by Jordyn's end of the counter. She arranges all the containers in a row and hands me a plate, then scoops out piles of fried rice and chow mein. I do the same.

Then we all dig in. And it's so good! I'd forgotten. It's been forever since I've been able to afford good Chinese. Since before . . .

Once we're all too full to continue, Jordyn packs up the leftovers. "You want this for later?" she asks Henry.

"Nah. Your mom's making a roast tonight and we're gone tomorrow. You want it, Tyler?" he asks.

"I'll take it if you don't want it," I say, trying to be as casual as I can, but I'm pretty sure I've failed.

After stashing my delicious dinner in the fridge, I return to a computer screen full of me.

"That's the one." Henry taps a greasy finger against the screen.

Jordyn smacks his hand. "No touching. Use your words."

This gets a gruff chuckle from Henry. "Number forty-seven, then," he says. "Well, Tyler Blackwell? What d'ya think?"

The screen is alight with my face. I'm wearing the blue shirt and a smile I don't even recognize. I wasn't aware I still owned such a smile.

"It's good, but it's not him," Jordyn says. Then, as if the realization that she's just admitted to knowing me hits her, her cheeks turn the slightest shade of pink.

"Why? Because I'm smiling?" I try to make it into a joke.

"Pretty much," she says. "I like this one." She clicks through and stops on a shot where I'm in the suit. I'm not smiling. My focus is off screen, like I'm looking at something. I look . . . I don't know, sad, I guess.

Henry grunts and gets closer to the monitor. "Hmm. It's a good shot, but not for a yearbook. It's sorta depressing, don't you think?"

Jordyn and I make eye contact. I'm begging her not to explain. I don't want Henry to pity me. She nods so slightly, I almost don't see it. Henry certainly misses it.

We finally land on a shot where I'm—well, not really smiling. Maybe smirking? But not in, like, an assholic way. It's the one that all three of us agree is the best for the yearbook. Henry tells me to sleep on it. He has Jordyn e-mail me the top pictures, and then he retreats to the studio.

Back at my computer, I slyly click on the eBay screen. The bidding is up to $521 with eight hours to go till midnight eastern time. I have to get this jacket. I won't be able to stop obsessing until I do.

I hide the screen and glance over at Jordyn. She's looking at the photo of me looking sad again. I can feel heat climb my neck and settle in my cheeks and ears. I clear my throat and she quickly clicks off the picture and turns around to see if she's been caught. I turn back in time for her not to notice. At least I think I do.

Then I hear her shuffle through the curtain and I know this is my chance.

I click to eBay and hit the BUY IT NOW button, quickly entering all my information and hitting CONFIRM.

It's done.

The confirmation screen reads $629, including shipping, and I practically start hyperventilating.

I now have $30 to last me the rest of the week. Or until however long it takes to get paid. I'm totally screwed. But I know I've made the right decision when I turn toward Jordyn's chair and the word *slut* stares back at me.

I close the eBay window for good.

Jordyn must know I caught her looking at the picture of me because she's taking her time in the back. So I sit at her computer and open the file with my name on it. The sad picture comes up again. It really is the most *me* of any of the pictures. Now I remember what I was looking at off screen when Henry took it. I was watching him and Jordyn. They were teasing each other, and I remember thinking how I will never feel that. I will never know that kind of parental love again. It's a photograph of my heart breaking that is now frozen in time for all of eternity. I drag the mouse over the picture and contemplate deleting it.

"Don't you dare." Jordyn is right behind me. I didn't hear her come in.

"It's just so depressing," I say.

She shoves me out of her chair before I can do permanent damage. "It's the most honest thing I've seen in a long time. Not just from you, you know? So don't go reading into it or anything."

"Fair enough."

"Also, it kind of reminds me of your mom." She says this so quiet, I almost don't hear her.

Neither of us says anything for a long moment.

"I'm sorry. I shouldn't have—"

"No, it's fine," I say.

"It just . . . Well . . . never mind." She closes the picture.

"Pull it back up." My voice sounds hoarse. I get close to the screen. "You're right. I see what you mean." A flash of Mom making that same face burns into the back of my eyes. I can't swallow. My eyes sting. Shit, I can't cry, not here.

I feel Jordyn's warm hand on my arm, and I close my eyes, holding everything back.

I open them again and meet her eyes. She says, "I'm really sorry, Tyler." And it's the most sincere anyone's been since my mom died.

I hold Jordyn's gaze. It's comforting. It's intimate. Then the door chimes and we jump apart like we're doing something wrong.

When I turn my attention to the client, I find myself staring into the smiling face of, who else? Ali Heart-over-the-*i*.

TWELVE

"Hey . . . you," Ali says. She can't even remember my name. That would probably make a chick feel cheap, but I'm strangely turned on by it.

"How's it going? Hightower, right?"

"Yeah. Ali." She glides up to the counter, smiling all innocently. I flash back to last weekend and her complete lack of innocence paired with extreme flexibility and I can't stop thinking about maybe doing it all again tonight.

Jordyn clears her throat.

"Did you bring any clothing choices?" she asks Ali. Her tone is pleasant, but there are all sorts of "you asshole" vibes wafting off of her in my direction.

"Yep. My daddy's bringing them in for me," Ali says.

Daddy, huh?

Jordyn aggressively shoulder-checks me as she heads past the curtain. She's informing Henry that his next gig is here just as Mr. Hightower trudges in, carrying, I'm guessing, fourteen changes of clothing.

He greets me with a nod, seeming better rested than he did last time I saw him with his entire brood, but he still seems unhappy. I return his greeting with a smile. Perhaps I should thank him for being distant or absent or whatever it is that makes girls like Ali desperately crave the attention and approval of guys like me.

Jordyn pops back through the curtain. "Henry's all ready for you." Then she takes in the massive wardrobe choices and smiles wider to suppress her annoyance. "We sort of have a four-change maximum. Would you like my help in choosing what'll photograph best?" Jordyn takes the stack of clothes from Ali's dad and slings it over her shoulder.

Ali giggles like she's made a new best friend, and she grabs Jordyn's hand as she races to the back to begin her fashion show.

"You coming, Daddy?"

Mr. Hightower doesn't answer. His eyes have been glued to his phone since the second Jordyn relieved him of his armful. He stiffly sits down on the sofa closest to him with his back to his daughter.

Ali sighs before turning to me. "I'd really love a guy's opinion too."

"Too bad he's color-blind," Jordyn says, daring me to challenge the lie.

I shrug. Jordyn thinks she's cock-blocking me, but I'm grateful I don't have to deal with that fashion shit. The only thing I want to do with Ali's clothing involves removing it.

After about a half hour of Ali squealing and giggling from the back, Jordyn finally returns to the counter. "Henry needs you," she says. And then, as I pass her, she hisses low enough so only I hear, "You totally had sex with her, didn't you?"

"Jealous?" I grin, waggling my eyebrows.

Jordyn makes a disgusted sound as the curtain falls back behind me.

The photo shoot is never-ending. Henry allows Ali to do seven changes. The thing is, the clothes are practically the same. Variations of sweaters, sweet, innocent-looking flowery dresses, and button-down shirts. All in tasteful pastels.

The only thing that makes the shoot go faster is the surreptitious sexting going on between Ali and me while she's changing outfits.

She even sends me a dressing room selfie wearing nothing but lacy white panties.

We agree to meet at my house at 8:00.

After the Hightowers leave, Henry tells me not to worry about cleaning up and to go ahead and go. I really need to talk to him about money, but not in front of Jordyn. And definitely not when she's glaring at me like she is.

"What's your problem?" I ask as we're shutting down our computers.

"Nothing. I just think you're disgusting." She looks at me like I'm the vilest thing she's ever encountered, but her tone is completely flippant. She's using that goddamn *girl* tone like Sheila. That I'll-just-pretend-everything's-fine-until-you-ask-me-the-right-question-then-I'll-rip-your-fucking-face-off tone.

"Well, I guess it's a good thing I don't give a shit what you think." I turn back to my computer, shut it down, and head toward the exit. "Later," I say, throwing the door open.

It's not like I'm forcing Ali to have sex with me—she's the initiator here, not me. So why am I disgusting?

I head to King Soopers on Sunday to plan my rations for the week. I hadn't realized I was nearly out of toilet paper—I'd sneak some from Dad, but he's such a dick that he'd probably notice and get in my face about stealing from him.

So the toilet paper eats into my ration fund way more than I had planned. And that's with the help of crotchety Mrs. Hemlock, whose Sunday paper just might be short a coupon section this week.

I'm pretty much stuck with ramen and tuna for every meal now. I can't even afford bread to make sandwiches. Lunch will be tuna straight from the can.

On my way home, I stop to fill my tank. I don't even have enough to fill it a quarter of the way. I have to get that dog shit job. But even then, I don't know how soon I'll get paid. I'll have to cut down on my driving—to and from work only, which means I'll have no choice. I'll have to do the most dreaded thing a senior in high school can do: Take the mother-fucking bus.

○ ○ ○

Monday morning I head out when I see a freshman neighbor across the street leave for school. It's been so long since I've ridden the bus, I don't even know where the damn stop is.

The corner of the neighboring development is awash in underclassmen. We have the quiet nerds with backpacks twice as thick as they are, twitching with anxiety at the mere possibility of socialization; the skaters, who haven't received the memo that wearing your pants below your ass was never cool; and the band geeks huddled together wearing their letterman jackets, carrying various instrument cases. Why they give letterman jackets to the band is something I will never get.

Apparently we're the last stop on the route, because when our little motley crew gets on the bus, there's not a goddamn seat anywhere in sight. The driver gives me a look when I board, like she's wondering what I did to get my car taken away. A guy I sort of recognize from football training last summer—a sophomore, I think—shoves the guy next to him so he gets up and is forced to squeeze in with two freshmen chicks across the aisle, then he waves me over. The entire way to school he gives commentary on some of my best plays. It's equal parts flattering and painful and it almost makes me miss it, but I don't.

The ride is so much longer and bumpier than I remember, and then comes the worst part: getting off the bus at school as all my former teammates sit around the main entrance waiting for the first bell to ring. Of course it's Brett who sees me after shaking his stupid blond hair out of his eyes, but he smartly pretends he doesn't. For now anyway.

When the final bell rings at the end of the day, I contemplate hanging around until the after-hours bus comes for the underclassmen who have practices or rehearsals, so I can be spared the humiliation again. But in the end, I decide: Screw it. I'll have to do this until I can figure out my financial situation anyway. Might as well embrace the big, bad, yellow limousine.

The guy who runs the dog shit business is working on a yard a few blocks away the next morning, conveniently near my bus stop. I know which house he's at thanks to the clever magnetic sign on the side of the car that reads "Sh*t, Richie!" above his phone number. The sign is in the shape of a steaming pile of dog shit, including three wavy lines above the words, indicating the stench. The owner's name is Rick. Rick is doing this job because he got laid off from his fancy corporate job—he won't elaborate further, which I find a bit fishy—and was unable to get another job for over a year.

"I figured, who likes to pick up dog shit, right? There's gotta be cash in that, right? Well, guess what? I'm doing okay now," he says.

"Well, I'm not sure what exactly qualifies one to clean up dog shit, but I do have a dog. And he does shit. And if I don't want to step in it when I mow the lawn, I am responsible for cleaning up said shit," I say.

"You bein' smart?" He grins at me, narrowing his eyes.

"No, sir. I really need the job." I think about just how much I need the job and I consider playing the "dead mom" card, but he laughs and pats my shoulder.

"You'll do just fine. You start next Monday. I'll work out a schedule over the weekend."

"Do you need me to fill out some paperwork or something?" I ask.

He laughs again. "I'll be paying you cash, unless that doesn't work for you."

"Cash is great. Cash is perfect," I say, shaking his hand vigorously.

He digs into his backseat and pulls out another magnetic "Sh*t, Richie!" sign the size of my forearm. "Don't lose this or it'll come outta your pay. And I expect you to keep it on your car even when you're not working. Gotta advertise." He hands me the magnet.

Fantastic. My very own dog shit sign. Oh, wait, there are two—one for each side of the car.

I get off the bus the next day wondering which is more humiliating, taking the bus or pulling up with "Sh*t, Richie!" signs on my car. I make eye contact with Brett again. This time he watches me instead of looking away. He's up to something. I can feel it. I just have to decide whether or not I care.

Since it's a slow day at the studio, Henry shows me some basic retouching—Jordyn's better at it than he is, so she'll do the real teaching later on. Then I'm finally rewarded with a paycheck on my way out the door. I rip into the envelope the second I get in the car. $344.62 after taxes. I can definitely work with that.

I stop by the bank and deposit it at the ATM. Since it's a

check, I have to wait until Saturday for it to be available but I still feel better knowing it's there. I'll just have to remember to take out the usual fifty dollars I've been putting away in my just-in-case-I-need-to-get-the-fuck-outta-Dodge fund, plus another fifty per week to replenish what I took out for the jacket.

When I get home, Dad's car isn't there, which is always good, but since there's a package waiting for me on the door-step, it's even better. He'd have opened it not caring what kinds of federal laws he was breaking and might have even destroyed it, just as a fuck-you to me. I could have had it delivered to the studio, but I wanted to be the one to give it to Jordyn. Worth the risk.

I dump some food in Captain's dish and I grab a knife to gently slice the package open. The jacket looks as good as in the pictures, but the leather . . . ! It's maybe the nicest leather I've ever felt in my life. Even softer than the old jacket. I hope Jordyn has the sense not to wear it to school again. If someone dares to mess with this one, I will seriously kick the shit out of them.

I can't wait to see Jordyn's face when I give it to her on Saturday.

But as I try to fall asleep I glance back over at the jacket hanging on the folding chair next to my pathetic desk. I can't just give it to her. What was I thinking? That'll be way too awk-ward. I'll have to figure something out.

Wednesday afternoon, Henry's shooting a very talkative little girl who asks a million questions without bothering to wait for any answers.

"Why is *that* light flashing at the same time as *that* one?

"What's that little red light do?

"Why am I stepping on this paper thing? What would you do if I ripped it?

"What's your favorite food?"

I don't know how Henry's doing it, but he actually seems to be enjoying her.

When we finish for the day and I go to shut down my computer, I dig the jacket out from where I stuffed it under the counter and I smooth it across the back of Jordyn's stool. What if she hates it? What if she throws it away? That's $629 dollars I'll never get back.

When Henry ducks through the curtain, I stand in front of the chair blocking the jacket. But he doesn't even glance toward it as he sets the alarm and gives me an impatient look.

It's out of my hands now.

THIRTEEN

I'm waiting for the bus Friday morning when a car pulls up to the corner, a sensible, silver American-made hatchback with dark tinted windows. One of the windows rolls down and I hear my name called over some shitty emo music.

"Tyler. Fucking. Blackwell!" the voice yells again. "Get in before I change my mind."

It's Jordyn.

How the hell did she know I was taking the bus?

"Get. In." She lowers her sunglasses and stares at me until I do as she says. "A senior taking the bus is just sad. Even you don't deserve that kind of humiliation."

I guess she liked the jacket. This is probably the closest thing to a thank-you I'll ever get. I glance in the backseat and see the new jacket carefully laid across her backpack, which is somehow resting on a pile of, I don't know, art supplies maybe? Her car is a disaster. It's almost like Henry was let loose in here. Not at all what I imagined.

After she pulls the car into her usual spot, she kills the engine and says, "Don't think this means I like you now. I still think you're a total asshole." Then she gets out and slams the door, but is smart enough to leave the jacket in the car.

I laugh. It's the most perfect reaction I could have imagined.

I'm in the hallway before lunch when some of the guys from the team round the corner, hanging on Brett's every word.

"How the mighty have fallen," he says under his breath. "I'd kill myself before I had to take the bus."

Only one of the other guys dares to laugh at this, but stops abruptly when he sees me. Then he looks embarrassed.

Everything gets eerily quiet for a second. My back tenses and my fist tightens. It takes every ounce of self-control to walk away. I'm not sure why this sets me off as much as it does, but I'm enjoying this feeling of pure unfiltered rage. Maybe a little too much.

I walk out the door like I'm heading to my car but I don't stop. I don't stop until I've reached my front door. It takes me well over an hour and it's hot as hell out and I'm sweating and reveling in the discomfort. I'm still so amped, even after walking forever with my heavy backpack, that I decide to take Captain for a long run up near Red Rocks. On my favorite path—the one I discovered with Mom. The one we made a tradition to hike every summer.

My feet pound the red dirt and I'm thinking about one of our final games last season when I ran for three touchdowns, including the one that won us the game. I'm smiling, and just as I realize it, I lose my stride. I've reached the tree, our rock. Mom and I used to have picnics up here, staring out at the red rocks, the way they tilt toward the mountains like piles of dust mid-sweep, how a stray tree here and there will find a way to grow out of the most improbable places. The first time we hiked this trail, she said this would be a great place to take a date. But I only ever brought her here. And Captain, who's panting so hard, I'm afraid he'll swallow his tongue or something. I crouch down and pour some water into the collapsible yellow bowl—yet another reminder of Mom. She got so mad at me for running Captain without any way to drink water—we got into a big fight about it, even—and then when I came home from practice the next day, this was sitting on the counter. I'm fighting back tears as Captain finishes his water and we head back down the trail.

When I return, Dad's car is in the driveway.

"You wanna tell me what this is doing in the middle of the goddamn room?" He kicks my backpack at me the second I enter the house. It hits me in the leg and a corner of a book digs into my shin. I try not to flinch but fail. He's just been standing there in the dark waiting for me to walk through the door?

"Sorry. I forgot to throw it in my room before going for a run." I lean down and free Captain from the leash and then grab my bag, starting down the stairs. Dad follows right behind me. I brace myself for what he'll do next, but once we're in the family room, he just flops onto the couch and sighs while I fumble with my keys. It's like he's waiting for me to say something. I notice that there's a serious lack of alcoholic beverages in front of him. Okay . . . ?

"There's some crap for you on the kitchen table." He points the remote at the TV.

Captain looks up at me, waiting for me to open my door, but my curiosity is piqued. I need to feed him anyway, so we head back up the stairs, where I see several bags of groceries on the table next to a large bag of dog food—the kind Captain likes, even. One bag is filled with shampoo, deodorant, toothpaste, and disposable razors. And the other contains a four-pack of toilet paper. The nice kind.

My throat tightens. I look through the railing at Dad, but he just continues scrolling through the channels like nothing's happened.

I feed Captain and throw a frozen burrito in the microwave. It sounds like Dad has decided on some hillbilly show about something no one really cares about. Once Captain's done eating, I load my arms with all my groceries and head for my room.

I pause at my door, staring down at the key in the lock. "Thanks." My voice sounds strangled.

I hear him start to cry. My stomach grips in a small spasm of guilt and I almost turn, but then I wave Captain down the stairs without looking back. If he knows I heard him crying, things will go south very fast.

How did things between us get so messed up? We used to talk. We used to joke, even. Sure he had his alcohol-induced violent episodes, but he wasn't quite as much of . . . Who am I kidding, he was always an asshole. Pathetic that I'm feeling nostalgic for the days when he was slightly less of an abusive dick.

o o o

I tell Dr. Dave about the jacket at my session Saturday morning.

"Well, Tyler, I'm proud of you." He's just over the moon about the jacket thing. "I'm impressed that something affected you enough to do something this thoughtful for someone you claim to dislike so much."

"I never said I didn't like her." I sink back into the cushion.

"You intimated it."

"No, *she* doesn't like *me*."

"If she was kind enough to drive you to school, she obviously doesn't hate you as much as you think." He looks at me. "I wonder, why is it so important to you that she doesn't hate you?"

"It isn't," I say. But then I think about her disappointed face when she found out about Ali.

"You care about her." He's smiling that smug shrink-smile of his. "I'm right aren't I?"

Is he right? "Sorry to burst your bubble, Doc. I don't."

"Why do you think you're afraid to admit that you care?"

"I don't care," I repeat. And I hate that I maybe do. Mostly I hate Jordyn for confusing me in the first place.

"I tried to get your attention yesterday as you bailed on school," Jordyn says when she finally arrives at the studio. She's almost forty minutes late. I guess if your stepdad or whatever is the boss, you get to be forty minutes late without consequence. Never mind the poor employee forced to sit outside waiting for you to open the damn door.

I pull myself to my feet but don't bother looking up from the blog post I'm reading about last night—Marcus had a pretty awesome game. Brett, not so much. Jordyn sighs and sits at her computer, like she's annoyed and waiting for me to ask what's wrong. Not going to happen.

Henry doesn't have anything till 11:00, and then he's booked solid for the rest of the day—four sessions back-to-back. I won't have time for lunch, let alone to think. Thank god.

After I finish reading again about how Brett fumbled what should have been an easy touchdown at the end of the fourth quarter, which led to a turnover, which led to the other team's winning touchdown—go, Falcons!—I get on YouTube and try to alleviate my guilt by watching a series of videos about quantum mechanics. I feel Jordyn studying me, but I ignore it. After the fifth video, I head back to the kitchen to grab a Coke and a snack.

Jordyn enters the kitchen just as I'm taking a huge swig of Coke. I let out the nastiest, loudest belch in the history of belches, blowing the stench her way as I pass her. She grunts and shoves my arm. I wish she'd stop being so damn nice. I head back to the computer and watch yet another video about quantum physics and alternate universes and time-travel and shit. Wouldn't that be something, if that stuff actually existed? I would go back in time, get home from training earlier so I could stop Mom from slitting her wrists, and then I would force her to explain to me how she can be so goddamn selfish.

Henry throws the door open and saunters in, whistling. He's in an annoyingly good mood. Somebody got laid last night.

Henry tries to teach me about lenses and perspective while bombarding me with lighting terminology during the shoots. I'm kind of getting it by the final session. I can tell it bothers Jordyn that he's teaching me, and as petty as it sounds, I'm enjoying that very much.

I've caught her smiling a few times when I crack a joke to Henry, and it makes me want to shove her out to her workstation, where I can't see her stupid face. I want her to go back to being indifferent or, even better, hostile. What the hell was I thinking spending over $600 on some chick I used to be friends with a million years ago? Fuck her for making me feel like I had to do that.

"What's your problem today?" Jordyn asks as we clean up to leave.

"Nothing." I grunt as I lift a light off the stand.

"You're mad at me?" There's an edge to her voice, like she's just daring me to admit it.

"I don't care enough about you to be mad at you," I say, stacking the last light in the closet. I don't wait for a comment. I don't turn to see her reaction. If I act like I don't care, maybe I won't.

She comes up behind me as I walk to my car. "So I see you're driving again. I guess you're not planning on taking the bus this week?"

"Actually, I have another job to do in the mornings now"—I point to the "Sh*t Richie!" sign stuck to the side of my car—"so, no, I won't be taking the bus anymore." I get in my car and start the engine.

"You're welcome. Asshole," I hear her say through my back window that won't roll up all the way.

I wave at her as I drive off.

"Dude, you look like you haven't eaten in a month," Marcus says as he walks up to where I'm waiting with the table pager. He's insisted on treating me to a steak.

I didn't realize it was that obvious. I mean, I've had to adjust my belt a few notches, but I didn't think anyone but me would notice. Thanks, Dad. "I haven't," I say. Marcus thinks I'm joking.

Once we've placed our order, I tell him about Ali Heart-over-the-*i*.

"Dude! She sounds hot."

"I knew you'd like her."

He tries to grab my phone, but I'm too fast. "What, are you just going to call her and say 'Hey, I'm Marcus. I'm friends with Tyler, you know, the guy you hooked up with from the photo place and forgot his name? And anyway, you're totally my type. Wanna hang?'"

"Damn, man. I'd give it a shot. What can she do? Say no? But she could also say yes." He's grinning, waiting for me to put my cell back on the table. I stick it in my pocket instead.

"Not cool. Hook a brotha up."

I'm saved by the server bringing our food. The scent of perfectly cooked prime rib hits me. My stomach pinches and my saliva glands explode. I dig in and it's as good as it smells. My eyes shut involuntarily and I let out a groan.

"I'm flattered that I'm able to affect you this way, but maybe this is not the time or place for noises like that. Perv," Marcus says around a huge bite of steak.

"Can't help it. It's that good." I'm trying to eat slowly. Trying to savor every bite, but I just want to shovel it all into my belly as fast as humanly possible.

"What's up with you lately? You doing okay? I mean, I know I joke about you being hungry, but I'm not sure it's a joke now that I see you inhaling that cow. Your job paying you enough? Maybe your dad—"

I feel my face turn into a vicious scowl. I set my fork down. "I told you my dad won't pay for anything. I wasn't making that up." My words sound detached and staccato.

Marcus sets his fork down too and looks at me, really looks at me. "I'm sorry, man. If there's anything I can—"

"It's not your problem." I wave him off. "Anyway, I have two jobs now. So I'm fine." I pick up my fork and cut another piece of bloody prime rib. "But thanks for offering." I'm not sure he can hear it, but he smiles and nods and then he goes back to his steak.

I tell him about my jobs, leaving out the part about Jordyn working there. I'm not sure he'd even know who she is anyway. He gets a real kick out of the dog shit thing.

"Just wait till you see the signage the guy expects me to keep on my car at all times."

Marcus laughs. He insists I order dessert. "You're teetering dangerously close to hipster-skinny, dude. Unacceptable."

"I promise to up my calories and get back in the gym before

I start wearing ironic T-shirts, glasses, and stupid fucking hats."

"You better," he says. Then he asks the waiter which dessert has the most calories and orders it for me whether I like it or not.

The waiter laughs and assures me that I'll like it. It's everyone's favorite.

"So, homecoming is this weekend . . ." Marcus trails off. "It'd be cool if you came to the game. The team would like it, I mean, I know *I* would like it if you were there."

"I don't know, Marcus."

"I figured. I just thought it was worth a shot," he says with a genuine smile.

"Thanks for understanding."

"Just think about it?"

I sigh. "Okay. I'll think about it." I won't think about it. There's no way I'm going. "Who are you taking to the dance?"

"Haven't decided." Marcus grins. "But if you'd like to give me that chick's number . . ."

"Not going to happen."

"Well, maybe *you* should take her."

"You think *I'm* going to the homecoming dance? Have you lost your damn mind?"

"You can't not be there, dude. You know you'll probably be homecoming king."

"No, I won't. We both know I only got the nomination because everyone feels sorry for me. Plus Sheila's been busy campaigning against me. I should probably thank her for that."

"Sheila's not campaigning against you. Freaking narcissist." Marcus flicks a piece of bread at me.

"You ever think of asking Cara?" I ask.

"Cara? Are you high? That chick knows what I'm all about. I'd love to hit that, but there's no way. She's too smart to fall for my shit. Why?"

"Just trying to figure out who you haven't banged yet."

"Well, yeah. Man, her tits!"

"Right?" I say.

"But yeah, no. There's no way she'd go for me. Unless you know something I don't?" he asks hopefully.

"Sorry, man. You're right. She is too smart for your shit."

FOURTEEN

Dog Shit Rick meets me at the butt crack of dawn on Monday morning. I had to get up so early that Captain didn't want to get out of bed. I had to carry him out of my room so I could lock the door, and he groggily climbed onto the couch and went right back to sleep.

I'm making five dollars per house. So it's a matter of how many houses I can get in. Rick gives me a list of all the Monday clients, which, luckily, are all fairly close together. There are twenty of them and I have an hour and a half before school starts. I don't waste any time. It's not even that bad, except for the one house that has three Great Danes with shits the size of footballs. I wonder if Rick charges them more but pays me the same.

I, amazingly, get all twenty houses done and I'm only ten minutes late for school. Like I care.

Mrs. Ortiz tries to stop me in the hallway. She wants to check in on me. She says that my being late is a blatant cry for help, but I explain that it's just because it was my first day on a new job and I'm still trying to figure out my scheduling. Then I lie and say that we're having a test in calc and I can't miss it, and she lets me go if I promise to stop in at the end of the week. So I do. Promise. Not stop in. Screw that.

At lunch I actually have enough money to buy a pathetic slice of pepperoni pizza and I'm a little too excited about it. Until I see Sheila walking toward me with a purpose.

"I heard you're taking the bus now. You poor, poor thing. Anyway, I'm not here about that, I'm here to make sure you won't be at the homecoming game or the dance this weekend."

"I hadn't planned on it."

"Good." And with that, she turns back to her table.

Really? Well now I'm definitely going. She thinks she can dictate where I can or cannot spend my weekends? Who the fuck does she think she is?

I'm forced to walk past Brett on the way to eat in my car. He shakes his hair out of his eyes and snickers something that involves the word *bus*. What a dick. He's the one guy on the team who should actually be happy I'm gone—I mean, he *is* the running back now. But for some reason he gets off on trying to push my buttons. Whatever. I bet he's going to homecoming with Sheila. Well, good luck to him and his sloppy seconds.

"Haven't seen you at any of the games, Blackwell. Does that boss of yours hate football?" Coach chuckles, trying to cover his disappointment—annoyance?—that I've been avoiding him. "I hope he'll find it in his heart to let you come to the homecoming game this week."

"I will absolutely be there. Wouldn't miss it for the world," I say. And then I feel really bad because of how happy this news makes him. So, of course, I overcompensate. "I've been following the school blog every Saturday. Marcus is having quite a season. And Reece? He's getting better and better. Brigham Young is lucky to have him. Bummed I haven't had a chance to play with him this year." I'm shocked to realize I kind of mean that.

"Yeah. I'd have loved to see what kind of damage we could've done with the two of you. McPhearson's not half the player you are. But don't tell him I said so." He winks, and heads off.

For a second, I feel like such an asshole for missing this season. Then an image of Mom cheering from the bleachers hits me, and— Nope. Coach is the one who should feel like an asshole for trying to make me feel guilty. I don't think I can go to the game.

By Thursday I'm really sick of eating in my car, so when I see Jordyn, I follow her to her usual lunch spot.

"Really?"

"Come on. You totally miss me." I spread out on the bench directly across from her.

"Yes. It's not enough to have to put up with you every weekend; I need to see you every day so you can make me feel like shit. Otherwise I might do something stupid, like feel good."

"I'm flattered that you care that much about me, Jordyn. I had no idea." I place my hand on my chest and flutter my eyelashes.

"Yep. And it must drive you crazy because I know you don't want anyone to care. You just want to push everyone away because you can't stand to have people feel sorry for you. Well, you know what, Tyler? I do feel sorry for you. Your mom left you here and it's fucked up. It's okay to be angry. I'd be. I even understand why you do something kind for me and then just push me away. But I'm not going to pretend, because it's just too exhausting."

My stomach knots in fury.

"And I'm not going to tell you that you can't eat lunch here, because I saw your little encounter with the cheerbitches and I know you don't have anywhere else to go. I know you had to ride the bus and that you have to work two jobs for some mysterious reason, and that sucks. I'm sorry you have to go through all of that. I'm sorry that you feel the need to hook up with some random girl you met at the studio because you're so incredibly empty inside. And I feel privileged that you feel comfortable enough to grace me with your presence. So I'm not going to ask you to leave, because, Tyler, I feel sorry for you."

All the anger I've forced down is starting to bubble to the surface. I feel my heart pounding in my fingertips, my toes, my temples. I need to punch something. And it's not that I'm pissed at her; I'm pissed at me. I'm the one who allowed myself to be vulnerable. But I'm also pissed at her.

Jordyn looks a little uncertain when I stand up and slowly begin to walk toward her. I'm shaking. I look down at my hands, the left is a fist, the right is holding the half-eaten pizza. Before I even register that I've moved, my right hand thrusts out, skimming her hair as I shove the pizza into the glossy gray cinderblock wall behind her. Her eyes are wide. She really thought I was going to hit her. I seriously have to get the fuck out of here before I do something really stupid.

I'm walking briskly to my car when Mrs. Ortiz grabs my arm. Her fingernails dig in as I jerk free. I don't stop. I don't look back.

When I get in the car, I pound my fists against the steering wheel so hard, I hear something snap on the steering column. And I scream at the top of my lungs. I scream. And scream. And fucking scream until my throat hurts and my screams sound like I've swallowed razor blades.

I don't realize I'm crying until I calm down enough to notice that the tears have stained the blue material of my shirt three shades darker where they've landed. Which only makes me angry again. Fuck Jordyn Smith and her insight.

I spot Mrs. Ortiz heading toward my car with the security guard. I get the car started up before she reaches me and drive over the grass median because they're blocking my path.

I end up at Dr. Dave's office pacing the length of the waiting room. A woman close to his age, maybe thirty, watches me while clutching her purse.

When Dr. Dave pops his head out to fetch his next patient,

my waiting room friend, he takes in my red eyes and pacing.

"I'll just see you next week," the woman says, slipping out the door before he can utter a word.

Dr. Dave ushers me into his office and begs me to sit when I start pacing again.

"I can't sit," I say. "If I sit, I'll cry."

"Then you cry. So what?"

I glare at him, but he points to the couch and waits until I finally do as asked. I'm right. The second my butt hits the cushion, the tears start up again.

Dr. Dave slides a Kleenex box across the coffee table and waits for me to get it together. Then he speaks. "What happened?"

I explain about Jordyn. He just listens. Once I've finished, he scoots to the edge of his chair and rests his elbows on his knees, leaning toward me. "You know that holding all this shit in just causes cancer, right?"

I manage a smile.

"It's perfectly normal to feel this way. Frankly, I'm thrilled you feel at all. Your lack of emotions was really starting to freak me out. This I can handle. This I understand. That emotionless thing you've been for the last few months was not okay."

"But it's just so much easier if I turn it all off."

"It's really not. It's like putting a piece of tape on a leaky hose. Sooner or later the tape is going to come unstuck and the water is going to gush out harder because of the buildup."

He's right. I know he's right. But I don't know how to face people when I'm like this. I tell him about Mrs. Ortiz demanding I check in with her. "She'll probably stalk me until I talk to her. I can't do it, Doc."

"Have I mentioned how much I hate high school guidance counselors? I'll take care of it. I'll tell her that it's interfering with my treatment plan. I'll even make up some fake plan and you watch, she'll pretend she's heard of it."

"Thanks, Doc. This is . . . You're . . . Thanks. And I cursed Social Services when they forced me to come here."

"So did I." He's grinning. "And I'm glad I'm able to help. But I think you're wrong about only being able to talk to me. It sounds like this Jordyn could be someone to lean on when I'm not available. She kind of sounds like she might make a pretty good shrink one day."

"I thought you hated that word," I say.

He grins. Shrugs.

When I get to the studio that night, Henry shows me some of his favorite photographs and explains why he likes each of them. His very favorite is not artistic at all. It's a shot of Jordyn and her mom playing mini golf. Jordyn's head is thrown back and her mom is doubled over laughing. You feel like you're part of their moment when you look at it. Like you know what they're laughing at even though there's no way of knowing what was so funny. They probably don't even remember why they were laughing so hard.

"Jordyn told me about your mom," Henry says as I study the photograph.

I'm unsure how to respond.

"Suicides are a fucked-up thing," he says. "My brother shot himself in the face when I was fourteen."

I don't look up. I just study Jordyn and her mom mid-laugh. It feels like he doesn't want me to look at him, but maybe that's my shit.

"I found him with half his cheek smeared across my pillow. We shared a room. Wish I could tell you it gets easier, but I'm not much for lying. I don't expect you to say anything. Just wanted you to know that I get it."

I nod and we sit in silence for a good ten minutes.

Then the family portrait people walk in and Henry and I go about working like nothing has changed. But everything has changed.

FIFTEEN

A female cover of "Tainted Love" blares on my old alarm clock, yanking me from a dream. It had something to do with Jordyn and her mom and that photo Henry showed me of them laughing. I try to remember the details, but the harder I try, the foggier it is. But I remember how I felt. I haven't truly felt it for so long that it takes me a second to recognize it: happiness.

By the time I see Marcus in gym, I've decided that I *am* going to go to the homecoming game after all.

"Dude! That's . . . It means a lot to me, man," Marcus says. Then he slams his locker shut and we head for the gym.

I hurry home after school to feed Captain and get out of the house before Dad gets home to ruin my extremely rare good spirits. I'm sure nothing would set him off more than seeing me happy. Not that I have anything to base this assumption on. It's just a feeling. And I'm not in the mood to tempt fate.

So I'm way early for the big homecoming game. Thankfully there's a Starbucks across the street. Our school doesn't have a proper football field, so the games are always played at this top-of-the-line stadium that acts as home field for all the surrounding schools—all the teams we play—which means no one really has an away game. It gets confusing when it comes to trash-talking.

I sip my coffee and watch the parking lot fill up, waiting till the last minute to head in. I find a place way in the back, sneaking through the crowd with my head down.

I brace myself for that part of me that still longs to be on the field, but by the end of the first quarter, it still hasn't presented itself. I don't get it. I truly thought football was my thing. I look around at everyone in the crowd, cheering and jumping and chanting and laughing with their friends, and I feel nothing. I have nothing. I am nothing. So much for that good mood.

"I thought it was you," Cara, one of Sheila's cheerleader friends—the one I can actually stand—says, smiling down at me. "Don't worry, I didn't tell anyone I saw you." She means she didn't tell Sheila.

"Thanks," I say.

She shoves me so I scoot down and then sits next to me. She's kind of hot. If I made a move on her it would definitely piss Sheila off. She's wearing her cheer uniform, which doesn't do much for her tits, but her legs are completely exposed. Such long, smooth, shapely legs.

She notices me looking. "I know, right?" She rubs at them, embarrassed. "Freaking goose bumps."

"What are you doing up here, anyway? Shouldn't you be screaming at us from down there?" I point to the edge of the field, where most of the other cheerleaders are chanting and clapping in unison.

"Varsity has a halftime dance, so we're off the hook for the first half of the game. Which means I get to watch it with all you commoners." The team scores a touchdown and she jumps up and screams with the rest of the crowd. I clap half-heartedly, still seated.

"Can you believe they're doing this well? Even after Brett's already blown two plays."

I grin at her.

"You're just loving that, aren't you?" Her grin rivals mine. She has a pretty smile.

I shrug. "What can I say?"

"You going to the dance tomorrow? Because, well, you know you're probably going to be crowned homecoming king, right? I mean . . ." She doesn't have to say it. I know she means I'll be getting the sympathy vote.

"Yeah, I don't think I'm going to go."

"Really?" I might be crazy, but I think I hear disappointment in her voice. Is she trying to ask me to go with her or something? She's Sheila's friend. That would be very bad. For both of us. I don't mind pissing Sheila off, but I don't want Cara to suffer Sheila's wrath because of me. But then again, she has a nice rack.

"You really think I should go? You know, with every-thing . . . ?"

"You mean Sheila and Marcus?"

I look at her, puzzled.

Her face goes pale. She looks like she wants to vomit. "Oh, shit. You don't know."

"What don't I know?" My voice is much angrier than I mean for it to be.

She looks around for someone to throw her a rope.

"Just tell me," I say through gritted teeth. I'm unable to look up from my hands, which are once again balled into fists.

She swallows so hard I can hear it, and then takes a deep breath. "They're going to the dance togeth—"

I get up and push past her. I mean, I don't give a shit about Marcus and Sheila. But I. Am. Pissed. I guess it's because Marcus treated me like nothing was up when he could have just been a man and told me.

I'm at the door to the locker room before it even registers that I've walked there. I'm not sure what I plan to say to Marcus. I should just leave. It's not worth it. What do I care if he and Sheila go to homecoming together?

The crowd noise merges into the sounds of halftime as the snare drums of the drum line begin their assault. I'm about to leave, when several players round the corner. I find myself searching for Marcus. If he just sees me like this, he'll know that I know. I'm not exactly hiding my anger.

"Dude! I can't thank you enough for quitting the team," Brett says when he spots me. He struts over to my side, shaking his hair out of his eyes. "Really, I can't thank you enough. I haven't gotten so much pussy—"

His blond head jerks back and to the side and my hand aches. The look on his face is of complete and utter shock. I'm not sure if there are other people in the hallway. I can only see him. And I can only think about how good that punch felt and how I need to do it again.

So I do.

This time, he sort of half blocks it, but not well enough. My fist makes contact with his face, just not as hard. His shocked expression is replaced by rage.

He throws his fist into my ribs and I thrust my elbow into his face. I feel his teeth dig into my forearm. It stings enough to make me pause, and his fist lands hard against my lip and chin. A delicious gush of blood explodes in my mouth like I've bitten into a copper-flavored Starburst. I spit it at him. He winces as blood spatters across his face and his dirty white jersey.

I go to hit him again, but large arms are now pulling me backward.

"What the fuck, Tyler?" Marcus yells, spinning me around.

"Fuck you, Marcus!" I shove him into the wall and head back out to the field, passing Coach, who shouts something, but I don't hear it. The inside of my lip is bleeding pretty badly where Brett's fist forced it into my teeth. I spit the blood onto the sidewalk.

"What the hell are you doing fighting with my players during halftime?" Coach grabs the top of my arm and twists me so I'm facing him. His face is purple and the vein in his neck looks like it might explode. He's right in my face. "I've tried, Tyler. To help you, to give you your space, to get you to talk. I kept thinking you'd come to your senses and come back to us. You've always been stubborn. But this— You start a fight with your replacement?" He pokes his finger into my shoulder each time he emphasizes a word. "You know what? I don't care what you're going through. You get the hell off this field. Don't even think of coming to another game this season, you hear me? And good luck with Stanford."

I shove him away from me. A few of the people nearby gasp. Fuck him. Fuck them all.

Dr. Dave stares at me, deep in thought.

My hand is pretty bruised and I have a small gash across my arm just under my elbow where my skin met Brett's teeth. Otherwise, my face is bruise-free. There's not even any swelling. Is it wrong that I'm kind of disappointed about that?

"He thanked you for quitting the team so he could get your spot," Dr. Dave says, not like it's a question, but like he's saying the words to hear how they sound outside his head.

I kick my legs up on the coffee table. "I think he was even being sincere. It's hard to tell though, the prick is so damn smug all the time."

"So you decided to take your anger toward Marcus and Sheila out on this Brett guy." Again, not really a question.

"And I don't even feel bad about it. It was kind of exciting. Thrilling. I felt alive. Even when he hit me, it was great. It felt good."

Dr. Dave writes something in his notebook and then looks up at me, frowning a little.

"Don't worry, Doc, I'm not going to go all *Fight Club* or anything."

He holds my gaze.

"I swear. I'm not going to go looking for fights. It just felt good in the moment. That's all."

"Okay. Let's go back to what your coach said about Stanford."

"I don't know. It's not like I'm surprised. I didn't think they'd still want me when I can't even play my senior year."

"So you're really not planning on playing at all this year, then."

"Did I ever say anything to make you think otherwise? Or have you not heard a goddam thing I've said this whole entire time?" I pace to the window and peer down into the parking lot.

"You shut down the conversation every time I bring up the subject. I guess I was hoping you would eventually trust me enough to really discuss your options."

I turn and glare at him. "Well, let's discuss, then. I'm not playing fucking football. Satisfied?"

"You feel strongly enough about it to jeopardize Stanford?"

"That fate was sealed the second I found my mom."

Doc doesn't say anything for a minute. On my way back to the couch, I can practically hear the gears in his head turning as he chooses his next words carefully.

"Have they contacted you? Stanford?"

"No. I don't know. My dad wouldn't exactly let me know if they had."

"Is your dad hoping you fail?" he asks.

"I think our time's up."

○ ○ ○

"What's that?" Jordyn asks, poking at my forearm as I situate myself at the computer.

"A gash."

She pokes it harder. "I can see that. What's it from?"

I shrug her off, but she grabs my wrist and examines the bruising and abrasions on my knuckles. "It was from teeth, not that it's any of your business." I yank my wrist away and head to the back for a Coke. That's just what I need, for her to be all judgmental about me fighting.

"I just hope you weren't fighting over that bitch Sheila, because she's so not worth it," she says.

Fuck her. She doesn't know everything.

Henry intercepts me on my way back from the kitchen. He needs help replacing the white backdrop roll. We don't say much as we work, but we don't need to. There's a difference since he told me about his brother, like a connection we share that most people would just not get. I don't know who or what is responsible for our paths crossing, but . . .

"What else do you need for this one?" I ask.

"Not much. This one's easy. A regular. They just like a plain white backdrop with a white stool, or a bench. The mom's been bringing her kid here for about four years. She's raising him on her own. They're very close. They always wear complementary outfits without being obnoxious about it. The boy's about the most polite kid I ever met too. So well behaved. And he worships the hell outta his mom."

I hate them already.

"Jordyn!" Henry calls as he changes a lens.

Jordyn appears through the curtain.

"I think today'd be a good day to fiddle around with the retouching stuff. Tyler needs to learn."

Jordyn looks at me, her face unreadable, and nods. Then she turns back through the curtain.

"Well?" Henry says, not looking up. "Go on. I'm not paying you to stand around drinking Coke."

Jordyn's pulled my chair next to hers. I set the Coke on the counter, take my designated seat, and await further instruction.

"Switch with me. I'm betting you're the kind of person who learns by doing." She gets up and pats the back of her chair, waiting for me to move over.

"Open the file with your name."

I do as told.

"Your choice. Just pick whatever and I'll show you how to improve on the perfection of Henry's photographs. If only the subjects were as perfect as his work."

I choose photo 113. Just because, why not?

The photo that pops up is the one where I look like I'm suffering something fierce.

"Good choice," she says suspiciously. "How'd you remember which one was my favorite?"

"Honestly, I just picked something with the number thirteen in it. I figured my luck is pretty shitty so why not, you know?"

I'm not positive, but I think she might be blushing. I don't get a good look, though, because the door chimes and she jumps up to greet the mother/son dynamic duo of perfection with a hug. The annoying thing is that I see exactly what Henry means about them. They really are the mother/son dynamic duo of perfection. God, I miss my mom. I feel my eyes begin to sting. Shit. I blink furiously until everything's back under control.

After Jordyn delivers the clients to Henry, who greets them with a hearty hello, I hear them catching up on the past year. The son's doing well with his violin lessons; the mother thinks he's a prodigy or something. The mother dated a loser who loved mooching off her until he yelled at the son when he thought she wasn't there. She dumped him. I wish my mother had had the guts to do that. If it had just been the two of us, I think we might've had the kind of relationship these two have. We were close as it was, but when Dad treated her like shit and she just stayed and took it . . . I don't know. It was hard to respect her sometimes.

Jordyn resumes her seat, a smile still plastered on her face, and we get back into our work. I follow all her directions. I'm surprisingly good at the detail work. I even kind of enjoy it.

Time goes faster now that I have something to focus on. Jordyn even lets me try one of the "real" jobs—after making a copy of the original, of course, in case I screw it up so badly, she won't be able to fix it.

When Henry and the mother/son dynamic duo of perfection come back out from behind the curtain, I realize it's been two whole hours. It seriously felt like twenty minutes. Maybe photo retouching will be my thing.

Henry calls Jordyn over to say good-bye and they all start talking about their loving families and everyone's plans for the holidays. I cringe. I mean, the holidays are still a month and a half off, so it hadn't crossed my mind. Now it's like whatever was holding one edge of me to the other breaks. Just fucking snaps. Having to spend the holidays alone or, worse, with my dad . . . Those goddamn tears that were plotting their escape are free. I feel one fall, then another. I keep my head down and escape to the bathroom. But it's taking everything in me to stay quiet, which really pisses me off. I want to wail and scream all of a sudden, like I did when it really hit me that Mom was dead. That wasn't until two days after. I guess I was in shock or something. It was so bad that even my dad didn't bother me. Why the hell do I have to feel like that again?

There's a soft knock.

"You okay?" Jordyn asks.

I can't speak or she'll hear me crying.

"I'm going to Panda Express for lunch. You want anything?"

I can't eat. I remain quiet, sitting on the ground in front of the door.

I can feel that she's still standing there. I don't hear Henry. He might still be talking to their client friends.

Finally Jordyn says, "I'll be back in ten. I'll lock the door so you don't have to worry about watching the front." And then her footsteps retreat. Henry must have left for his on-location gig at three p.m.

I'm alone.

After I finally get my shit together, I pull myself up and dare to look at my reflection. I don't even look like me anymore.

I've lost my football weight, probably a good thirty pounds; I'm getting dangerously close to thin. And I really can't pull off that look with my height. My eyes are sunken in. My skin looks unhealthy; it has that greasy sheen you get when you're really sick. And my hair is in serious need of a cut. Maybe I'll just shave my head.

I tongue at the cut on the inside of my lip. Man, I really went off on Brett at the game. I study my features, trying to see if there's any of my dad in me, any visual confirmation that I'm, like, turning into him. But I look exactly like my mom, she of the prominent genes. Maybe that's why Dad always hated me so much, because he might as well not have played a part in my making. And now he hates me because I'm a constant reminder of her. I find it hard to look at myself for that same reason.

I run my hands under the cold water until they're numb, then I splash the water on my face over and over again, until I feel like I've sort of snapped back into reality.

I have no idea how long I was in there. But when I fumble back through the curtain, Jordyn's finished eating and is now scribbling in her sketchpad with something that looks like chalk but isn't. My chair is now back on my side of the counter. As is a container from Panda Express with the fortune cookie on top and a can of Coke next to it.

Why is she being so nice to me?

And when I go to eat the food, it's exactly what I would have ordered: broccoli beef and orange chicken with fried rice. I can't believe she remembered.

The food's still warm-ish, so I guess I wasn't in there for that long. I finish every last bit of it, and after seriously contemplating licking the sauce from the container, I toss it and reach for the fortune cookie.

It reads: "There is no shame in asking for help." Stupid fortune cookie.

"Thanks for this," I mutter. "What do I owe you?"

"Don't worry about it."

I start to protest, but then I spot that freaking fortune staring up at me and instead I thank her again.

Then I turn my chair, about to ask if there's another photo I can work on, but she turns to face me at the same time.

She speaks first. "Are you okay?"

For some reason, her tone makes me feel like answering. "Honestly, I don't know."

She's quiet for a sec, like she's deciding whether or not to push it. "You know, Tyler, you don't fool me with this 'screw the world' thing you've developed. I know the boy I used to be friends with is still in there somewhere."

I'm not so sure.

SIXTEEN

I should have gone for a run after work.

This is what I think as I pull into the driveway. Next to Dad's car. On a Saturday. Perfect.

Captain greets me with his usual smile. I pat him and listen for any signs of Dad. The TV's off. There's nothing coming from the bedroom. If I didn't know better, I'd think he wasn't home. But I can still *feel* him here. Maybe he's taking a nap or hasn't woken from last night's binge.

I tiptoe to the kitchen to get a glass of water before I lock myself in my room. I run the water till it gets cold and hold the glass under the stream. Out of nowhere a punch lands against my lower back and the glass falls into the sink, shattering.

"I got a call from your coach today. Said you were fighting. How stupid do you have to be?"

I don't know how he does it, but somehow I'm smaller than him when he's like this. I cower against the counter, water still running behind me and I stare at the floor waiting for the next blow.

"Fucking look at me!" He smacks my head as hard as he can. The hollow thunk rings in my ears.

When I look up, he kicks my knee and I have to grip the counter so I don't fall. Shit, it hurts.

"The fuck are you thinking? Fighting?" He's right up in my face, breath ripe with alcohol. I feel my adrenaline spike, my fingers curl. I'm afraid that if I throw a punch, I won't be able to stop until he's dead.

"I learned from the best," I say under my breath as I turn to shut off the water.

I feel his reaction behind me—a flare of heat like from a fire that's just been doused in fuel. I brace myself, but he remains silent and still. Every hair on my body is on end, waiting. But there's nothing. What's he waiting for?

I take a breath and prepare myself to walk past him to my room. But when I turn, he slams his whole body into me, pinning me into the corner of the counter. He takes my head in his hands and slams it into the cabinet. The sound comes first, then the pain. I feel heat spread through my hair. I must be a bit stunned, because he gets in several punches to my stomach and one to my face—reopening my lip wound—before I even understand what's happening. When he goes to grab my head to bash it into the cabinet again, I react without thinking—I shove him as hard as I can. His back hits the fridge. He starts laughing even though I know it had to hurt. Then he rushes me again.

This time I clock him right in the stomach as hard as I can. He doubles over, gasping. "Ungrateful little shit," he breathes. "Shoulda been you who died."

I punch him in the side. "It should have been you! You're the reason she's dead, don't you know that? She couldn't take your neglect and abuse and she didn't know another way out! The wrong parent died!" I scream, and then I deliver another blow to his back.

I'm about to hit him again, but Captain barks, snapping me out of my rage. I spit at Dad doubled over against the fridge. Blood spatters across the back of his tan shirt. Then I head toward my room.

Just as I'm halfway down the stairs, Dad says, "You know? The note she left didn't say anything about me."

I stop dead in my tracks. "There was no note," I say, still facing away from him.

I hear him shuffle behind me. "Wasn't there?"

I turn to face him and I'm met with a full beer bottle to the eye. It knocks me back into the wall and I lose my balance and fall the rest of the way down the stairs. Damn if he doesn't have good aim. I guess I know where my athletic abilities came from.

Blood blinds one eye, throwing off my depth perception. I struggle to get the key in the lock.

I call Captain into my room, lock the door, and head to the bathroom to assess the damage. There's a cut beneath my eyebrow from where the bottle hit and it's gushing pretty bad. Probably needs stitches. Will definitely leave a scar. It's swelling right before my eyes. Then I dig through my dark hair until

I find the source of most of the blood that's ruined my shirt. There's a small gash from the cabinet and it's bleeding almost as much as my eyebrow. Fucking head wounds. And my damn lip again. I spit blood into the sink. He's never gone for my face before—he never went for Mom's either. Too afraid of people asking what happened. Fucking Coach just had to tell him I was in a fight. What better news is there when you want to beat the shit out of your son without anyone questioning the damage?

I wet a small towel, trying to clean off some of the blood. Then I pull out my butterfly bandages—when you live with someone like my dad, you're prepared—and I butterfly the cut just beneath my right eyebrow. I'm not sure how to deal with my head, so I hold the towel on it so I don't keep bleeding everywhere.

I pull out the metal box and sit heavily on my bed. I feel my pulse in my skull as I spread all the pictures of Mom out in front of me.

"Did you or did you not leave a note?" I ask her.

There was so much blood when I found her. After I called 911, I held her naked, wet body and I sat there on the bathroom floor. There was nothing on the counter. Her clothes had been put neatly away because she knew she wouldn't be needing them ever again. The counter was immaculate. The entire house was immaculate, like she didn't want to leave a mess. The only thing in the bathroom besides all her blood was the little plastic box of razors.

But there wasn't a note.

I try to remember every detail of her room. Maybe I overlooked a note somewhere in there. But all I recall is that it was uncharacteristically spotless. If he found a note and has kept it from me all this time . . .

I pick up the photo of her going to school and another memory comes flooding back.

When she got home that day, Dad decided he didn't like her new holier-than-thou college attitude. He beat her so badly, I thought about stealing his car and trying to drive her to the hospital even though I didn't know how to drive.

It was Mom who stopped me from calling 911. She told me they'd take me away from her and she'd die if she didn't have me. Then, after Dad left to drink himself stupid, she had me help her to her bathroom, where she talked me through cleaning her wounds and the art of the butterfly bandage.

The prick gave her a concussion, slamming the back of her head into the wall repeatedly. She had severe bruising on her stomach and back and a broken rib or two, I'm pretty sure, though she never confirmed that with an X-ray. And her arms were black and blue with his handprints from where he held her as he slammed her into the wall and then threw her down the stairs into the family room.

He might have killed her if I hadn't stepped in. I got off with several very sore bruises on my back where I shielded her from him, but none of that mattered as long as I kept him from killing her.

She didn't want to involve any authorities. She was protecting him.

"Look what good that did. *You left* me here with him. Alone. You selfish bitch." I scream at her smiling face before crumpling the photo in my hand and dropping the towel from my head. It's now more red than blue.

I take the razor blade between my thumb and fingers and let it catch the light. Then I turn my wrist over and remember the deep gashes that went up each forearm.

They say it doesn't hurt. That you lose so much blood so fast that you sort of just fall asleep. That doesn't sound so bad.

The pulsing in my head has pretty much stopped. I go to examine the gash again. It's not bleeding too much anymore. And since my hair is dark and thick, it's mostly just a sticky matted mess on my head. So I get in the shower.

I let the water run hot, then I sit in the tub and allow it to wash over me—I'm too tired to stand. The cuts scream their anger, but I don't flinch. After the water runs clear again I reach to the edge of the tub, where my mom's razor-sharp friend now sits.

I pick up the small silver rectangle and turn my wrist over again. I drag the blade over my skin without pressing down. Even this draws blood. And it stings. I place it on my wrist again. All I have to do is press down and it will all end.

But I can't.

I throw the razor across the bathroom and cry in silence until the water runs cold.

SEVENTEEN

I slip out of the house on Monday just as the sun's coming up to avoid another encounter with Dad. I hid in my room all day yesterday. I didn't even open the door to let Captain out. Instead I pulled the screen off of one of the small windows and pushed him up the window well to do his business—not sure why I never thought of that before. And as hungry as I might have been, I figured staying alive was better than eating. Well, I could have eaten from the spare bag of dog food in my room, but I wasn't *that* hungry. So as early as it is this morning, even after hitting McDonald's, I'll get all the houses on my shit list done with time to spare.

I check my face in the rearview mirror. My eyebrow and eyelid are so swollen, I can barely open my right eye, which is a lovely shade of blackish purple. My lip isn't as swollen as it was, but the two vertical cuts, one on the side of my upper lip and one dead center on the lower, look angry and disgusting. I'm not a pretty sight. There's no way I can go to school like this. The poor guy at the drive-thru about had a heart attack when I paid, and it was still pretty dark out.

I pull myself out of the car with a stomachache from eating too much. I'm at the house with the three Great Danes—the one house that truly makes me regret this job. The dogs are pretty cool, though—after you get used to their size and realize they're not going to eat you. But they shit like horses. I'm not kidding. One would be something, but three? It's awful.

I don't know the dogs' names, but the largest of the three, a black-and-white version of Scooby-Doo, is my biggest fan. He comes loping over as soon as I enter the yard. He jumps up, lifting all paws off the ground, to lick at my face. The first time he did it, I saw my life flash before my eyes, but I've almost grown used to it. The other two, both tan, like to jump up and put their paws on my shoulders so they're looking me right in the eye. If the black-and-white one did this, he'd be several inches taller than me. But they really are cool dogs. I kind of want one. As long as someone else cleans up the shit.

After they finally calm down, I get to work. One of the three had diarrhea. Fun stuff. Once I've finished the scooping, I use the hose to rinse off the scooper. The owner of the giant dogs, a tiny little old lady, pops her head out to call them in for breakfast and cringes at the sight of my face. As soon as the dogs are inside, she slams, then locks, the door, and then she's immediately on the phone. That can't be good.

I load my still dripping, but free of shit, tools into the trunk and head to the next address.

This is an easy one compared to the first. I've never seen the dog that lives here, but it's relatively small. And it always uses the same corner of the yard to do its business. I'd like to know how the owner accomplished that. I'd love to teach Captain that trick.

After rinsing off my tools, I head back to my car to find Rick peeling the "Sh*t, Richie!" decal off the driver's side.

He does not look happy.

"I'm running a legitimate business. I can't have people who look up to no good letting themselves into respectable people's yards." He gestures at me with his magnetic decals.

I open my mouth to explain, but he raises his hand. "I don't care. You're done." Then he comes over to snatch the tools from my hand. "I won't be needing your services anymore."

He slaps two twenties in my palm even though I've only earned $35 so far this morning. Does he expect me to give him change?

"You know you shovel shit, right?" I say as I pocket the cash.

He glares at me as he gets into his car. Then he revs his engine to emphasize how pissed he is. His window's down, so I say, "I guess it doesn't matter to you that my prick father is responsible for my beautiful face." His expression turns to one of "Oh, shit" and I immediately wish I hadn't said it. I don't even know *why* I said it. It's kind of a relief, but I'm also terrified. What if he calls the authorities? Dad might actually try to kill me, or I'd end up killing him. Either way, one of us would be dead and the other would be fucked for life.

Rick starts to say something but I cut him off.

"Don't bother. You can take your shitty job."

I get in my car and crank up my stereo so I'm not tempted to hear his apology. Then I throw it into gear and race up the street.

Well, shit. I really needed that money. As soon as my face heals, I'll have to go looking for another second job. With hours that don't conflict with my primary job or school. Right. Screw that Great Dane lady. I'm tempted to leave Captain's shit in a flaming bag on her doorstep, but then I'm worried that one of the Great Danes will run at it and get burned in the process. They don't strike me as particularly smart dogs.

My phone wakes me just after five p.m. I don't even remember falling asleep. Thank god someone woke me up before Dad came home because A) I'm on the couch, B) my bedroom door is wide open, and C) from the pile of junk food wrappers and empty soda cans on the coffee table, it's pretty obvious that I didn't go to school today.

"Hello?" The number is one I don't recognize.

"Hey." The voice sounds worried. "It's Jordyn."

Long pause.

"I got your number from your paperwork," she says. "When you didn't come to school . . . I . . ." She exhales heavily. "I just wanted to make sure you were okay. So, are you?"

"I've been better," I say. "I probably won't be there tomorrow, or maybe for the rest of the week."

"Because of your former football friends?"

"N— Um, not entirely."

"You don't . . . um . . . You want me to let you go?" Jordyn asks.

I sigh. I'm not sure. It is kind of nice to talk to someone. "I got fired today."

"Fired? From the dog shit thing?"

"Yep."

"How does one get fired from picking up dog shit?"

"One would have noticeable bruising from fighting and look, and I quote, 'up to no good.'"

"You're kidding."

"I never kid about dog shit."

She laughs. "Well, we can carpool again. You know, so you don't have to spend money on gas and stuff. If you want."

"So, what? Are we, like, friends now?"

"I'll have to get back to you." I can hear her smile. It almost makes me smile myself. But then I hear a car outside and jump off the couch.

"I gotta go," I say, hanging up. "Captain!" I quickly gather my trash and stand at the door leading down to the basement, frantically signaling with my free hand for the damn dog to move faster. As soon as he's in, I lock the door. Just as the front door slams. Now I'm trapped for the night. And goddamn it if I'm not starving. I wonder if I'd fit through Captain's new window exit. With my luck I'd probably get stuck.

EIGHTEEN

I feel like a complete ass perusing the makeup section at the drugstore, but I can't go to work looking like this.

Yeah, I skipped school again, but now that I have no second job, I can't afford to not go to the studio.

"Can I help you with anything?" a woman asks from behind me as I hold my hand up to the various shades of Cover Girl.

I turn with a sheepish smile, dialing up the ol' Tyler charm.

She's older than me, but not by much—probably just out of college and realizing that a bachelor's degree doesn't mean shit these days.

"I see." She raises an eyebrow. Then she flips her red hair and places her hand on my shoulder. "I hope she was worth it."

"It was a football thing." I shrug with a smile.

I can see she's happy my fight wasn't about a girl. She steps closer and grips my chin with her thumb and forefinger, tilting my face down. Her brows furrow. "I think it might be too dark to cover. And there's not much that'll disguise the swelling, but let's see if we can make it less . . ."

"Disgusting?"

She laughs. "I was going to say obvious, but yeah, that too."

She reaches across me and picks a color I think looks way too tan, and then with the tip of her finger, she dabs a little under my eyebrow, a particularly gruesome part of the bruise.

"Let me know if I'm hurting you," she says.

She kind of is, but I don't say anything.

"Hmm. I don't know. It's sort of helping, I guess . . ." She looks around and then walks off down one of the aisles, returning with a bright pink handheld mirror.

"See?" She hands me the mirror. "It's not as black as it was."

It's true. I just wish there were a way to erase it completely. "Sold," I say. "Thanks for your help."

"No problem. Try not to get into any more fights. Hate to see that pretty face ruined."

"Promise." I smile at her one last time and then I go to pay for my makeup. Like a man.

The cashier, an older woman, rings me up with a scowl. I don't bother trying my charm on her. She can judge away.

In the car, I attempt to mimic what the redhead showed me, but it ends up cakey and streaky. If anything, it's making the damage more obvious. I consider going back in and talking the chick into helping me, but then I notice the time. I must have been standing there for a good twenty minutes.

Screw it. I don't think Henry's the type to get all bent out of shape over a bruise.

o o o

Henry's at the counter playing around with a retouch and doesn't look up from the screen when I come in. He's working on Ali's pictures.

"Grabbing a Coke. You want anything?" I call as I walk through the curtain.

"Stuff'll kill ya," he says. "Bring me one."

I set his Coke on the counter and watch him work, making sure to keep my bruised eyebrow on his far side.

"Is she coming in tonight to go over her pictures?" I ask.

"Tomorrow."

Tension I didn't even realize I was carrying around melts off my shoulders.

"Why? You want to be here when she comes? She is quite a looker. High maintenance, though."

He has no idea.

"Nah. I mean, yeah, she's cute," I say, "but not my type."

"Pull up a chair. Your hovering is making me nervous."

I do.

"So what is your type, then?" he asks.

"Uh, I sort of had this girlfriend for a while until recently. She's a cheerleader. I thought *she* was my type. But now, definitely not."

Henry laughs. "Yeah. I never went through that cheerleader phase. Couldn't ever see what all the fuss was about. Artsy girls. That's where it's at," he says.

"Yeah? I'll have to remember that."

"What happened to your face?"

Shit. I thought he hadn't noticed.

"Stupid fight," I say, trying to make light of it.

"You lost, I take it."

"You should see the other guy." I wonder how bad Dad's nose is. He's been in bar fights, so his boss'll probably just write it off on account of alcohol.

Henry turns to me. He lowers his head, then waits until I turn to face him full on. "You wearing makeup?"

"Yeah," I admit.

He lets out the heartiest, loudest laugh imaginable, pats me on the shoulder, and between fits of laughter, tells me to go wash my damn face.

So I do.

I cringe as I rub the shit off. It doesn't just wipe off, evil stuff. How the hell do girls do this every day? How does Jordyn do it? Her makeup is way more severe than this stuff. I wonder why she started doing that. She doesn't seem like a goth. I've never even seen her talking to any of the other goth kids.

After I finally seem to have removed everything from my face, I head back out.

Henry's in the studio fiddling with one of his cameras now.

"Better?" I ask.

He nods. "I picked the pictures of yours I like. They're up on Jordyn's computer. She tells me you have to have one in by Friday or they'll use that shitty generic one. So if you don't pick, I'll pick for you and have Jordyn send it in. Can't have one of my employees using a picture I didn't take, now can I? How would that look for business?"

"We could take another now. I think I'd like to be remembered this way forever."

He chuckles. "After you pick one, bring the flash drive back here. Then I can show you how to work the printers."

I choose the picture where I'm in my T-shirt, smirking at the camera. It's one of Henry's top choices and I remember Jordyn also liked it. Before I can talk myself out of it, I go to the yearbook website and submit it. Then I head back to Henry and present him with the flash drive.

"Follow me."

Around the corner from the bathroom there's a door I hadn't even noticed. The room beyond it is filled with various intimidating printers. Henry flips the switch on the one closest to the door, then hands me the flash drive and nods toward the laptop on the table.

I pull up the photo marked "T. Blackwell: 134." Henry tries to print a poster-sized version of me, but I manage to talk him out of it, using the wasted paper argument. He settles on a one-sheet 8½ x 11. Not that I have any use for it. What the hell do I need a picture of me for?

The printers are easy enough to figure out. The only tricky part is remembering the settings and which printer is which. Henry says I'll know it inside and out by the end of October. October . . . Maybe now's a good time to ask for more shifts.

My heart speeds up at the thought, but I take a deep breath. "I don't suppose you might need me to work more hours or anything?"

Henry stops what he's doing and turns to face me. "You got money trouble?"

My face flashes hot. And then I find myself explaining about how my dad thinks he shouldn't have to pay for my gas and car insurance and running shoes. I consider explaining about the food and toiletries, but I stop myself.

"Hmm."

"It's okay. I just thought I'd ask."

"I might be able to get you in another day. Especially now that you can help with the printing."

"If it's a hassle, don't worry about it."

"No hassle. Jordyn?" he calls.

My stomach tightens. She's not here, is she?

"Yeah?" She pokes her head in the door.

Shit. When did she get here? I turn to the computer so my back is to her.

"You think we can figure a way to get Tyler some more shifts?"

"Yes!" She seems a little too excited about this. "I'm dying under the load of my classes. You can take three days during the week and I'll cut back to two."

"Well, there you go," Henry says.

"You sure?" I ask, half turning to her.

"I was going to ask you about it yesterday, but then I was so rudely hung up on."

"Sorry about that."

"I'm kidding. Stop taking everything so seriously," she says.

"Tyler's learning how to print. Practically an expert already," Henry announces.

"Good," she says.

"And we were doing the Hightower girl's retouch."

"I've got it from here. Mom's waiting in the car."

"You got a set of my keys?"

"I do."

"Great. See you tonight 'cause I know you'll still be up when we get home, vampire."

She makes a hissing vampire noise and he laughs, pats her head, and heads out.

When she turns back to me, I realize that I've forgotten to hide my face in all their stepfather/daughter love. She's across the room in three strides and holding my chin in her hand to examine the damage. "Jesus, Tyler. What the hell happened? Did you get in an accident or something?"

I jerk my head from her grip and turn away, but she ducks under my arm and gets in front of me. "Seriously. Have you been to the hospital? That looks awful."

"Heads bleed a lot. So they also bruise a lot," I say.

She stares me down till I meet her eyes. Without a word spoken between us, she knows what's happened. I see it as soon as she gets it.

"That son of a bitch."

I have to sit down—this is too big a conversation for standing—but there are no chairs, so I plop down on the floor, resting my back against the wall. She joins me on the side my bruised eyebrow's on.

We don't speak for a while. I feel her examining me.

"I tried to wear makeup tonight," I say.

Then we both laugh.

"I bet Henry got a kick out of that."

"Oh, he did."

"You don't have to tell me what happened. Unless you want to."

"Is that your way of asking what happened?" I turn toward her, my head still leaning against the wall.

She smiles sheepishly.

"Coach called him and told him about the fight at the game."

"What was that fight about anyway?"

"You know Brett McPhearson?"

She nods. "Yeah, with the annoying head tick."

"That's the one. He kind of got my spot when I quit the team."

"As running back?"

"You know what I played?" I ask, amused.

"I'm not a complete loser, you know. I have gone to a few games."

"I seriously can't picture it."

She shoves me with her shoulder and I wince.

"Shit. Did I hurt you?" She's turned her whole body to face me now.

I sigh and then I lift my shirt up to show her my ribs.

"Tyler! You've got to report him."

"No. What I have to do is wait it out till my birthday. If they can't keep him in jail, it'll just make it worse. And I don't know if I can control myself. I might kill him. And if they can keep him, they'll make me go live at some home or something till I'm eighteen." I turn to face her, grabbing her arm. "Seriously, you have to promise you won't tell anyone."

She looks stunned. "Okay."

"I mean it."

"I promise."

I let go of her arm but hold eye contact. I think I can trust her. She rubs her arm where I grabbed, making me feel a little guilty. "Sorry—it's just . . . I can't go to a home. That's way worse than a few bruises."

"I get it."

We sit in silence for a minute until she finally gets the courage to speak again. "Your ribs might be broken. I think you should go to a doctor."

I let out a bitter laugh. "That would require health insurance. Or money."

"Your dad must have health insurance."

"Never said he didn't."

"And his plan covers you."

"No. I was on my mom's plan. When she died, the social worker told him he'd have to make arrangements for me, but as soon as she left, he laughed and said I was on my own and I'd best not get hurt or sick till I could afford it."

"Jesus," she says.

"You don't know the half of it. He won't give me a dime. I have to pay for my food, my shampoo, my gas, my car insurance, my fucking toilet paper."

"He can't do that."

"But he can. If I make a fuss about it, he'll just make things worse for me."

She watches me carefully for a long time. We don't break eye contact. "Well, shit," she finally says.

"Tell me about it."

And suddenly we're like we used to be when we were in fifth grade. Talking and . . . whatever. I'd forgotten how good that feels.

She's going to tell Henry that she needs to not work at all during the week because of school, so I can take all her shifts. She even offers to pay me back for the jacket.

"Absolutely not. It was completely my fault Sheila did that to your old jacket. This was a gift. You just say 'thank you' and appreciate the hell out of it. Also, maybe don't ever wear it to school."

She smiles. She knows I won't back down. "Fine. But we're definitely carpooling to school from now on. And now that I know every time you drive you have to starve, I will not take no for an answer."

"Deal." We shake on it.

It's so strange how much lighter I feel.

NINETEEN

Jordyn convinces me to go to school on Wednesday. She says I look scary and that no one will dare say anything to me about the fight. We agree to carpool today, but I make her pick me up at the corner; I don't want to risk her having a run-in with my dad.

"The swelling's gone down some," she says when I get in.

"I didn't bother to look. There's nothing I can do about it."

She puts the car in park and reaches into the backseat. She struggles with the fastener of her bag and has to practically climb into the back. It's amusing watching her squirm and grunt. If someone were to pass by us they'd get a pretty nice shot of her ass.

"Need some help?" I ask.

"Got it." She sits back down and produces a compact.

"No. No more makeup."

"Shut up. This'll work."

I sigh and allow it. I'll just wash it off when we get to school.

The compact houses something creamy. Jordyn rubs her finger in it and gently dabs it under my eyebrow.

"Hmm." She climbs back to her bag and this time produces . . . lip gloss?

She unscrews the cap and pulls out a wand of oily tan liquid, dabs it on my eyelid, and lightly spreads it with her finger. "There." She lowers the visor so I can see. The bruise is still there but not quite so in-your-face. And it doesn't even look like I'm wearing makeup.

"Thanks," I say. "You're right."

"I'm always right, Tyler. Haven't you realized that by now?" She smirks at me and then shifts into gear.

As we wait in the horrific line to the parking lot I admire her work in the visor mirror again. "You're good with this stuff."

"Thanks."

"But you know you don't need it, right?"

Her ears and cheeks flush pink.

"I mean, wear it if it's your thing, but you have the kind of face that doesn't need makeup. You were always pretty." *Jesus, stop talking*

She taps on the steering wheel. It's awkward as hell now.

"Look, I'm not coming on to you or anything, I'm just stating a fact. You have a nice face," I say.

Then she looks at me and we both start laughing.

We finally reach the entrance to the parking lot—why there's only one entrance is beyond me—and she picks a space toward the back.

"So, you want me to, like, not go in with you, right?" she asks, not looking at me.

"Why? Do you think I'm embarrassed to be seen with you?"

"Aren't you?"

"Not even a little. Besides, you're pretty much my only friend at the moment."

"It's your funeral. Shit. Sorry. I mean—" She looks completely mortified.

I start laughing so hard, my aching head throbs. "That's why I started bugging you at lunch, you know. You're the only person who would dare say something like that to the guy who just buried his mom. Please don't start apologizing for it. It's a figure of speech. I'm not as fragile as everyone's treating me." But then I remember my flirtation with the razor blade in the shower and I feel hot with shame.

"If you say so." She pulls her bag from the backseat and it hits me in the head, right where Dad slammed it into the cabinet.

"Agh!" I feel for blood.

"Shit! I'm so sorry."

"It's okay," I say. And it is. It snapped me out of my shame, at least.

When we walk through the gates of hell, it's unclear if people are staring because of my face or because Jordyn and I are walking together. I can tell the attention makes her uncomfortable, so I tell her I'll see her later and duck into a bathroom.

I go right for the mirror, turning my head side to side to examine the damage.

The makeup blends the really bad parts of the bruise into the less bad parts, but my eye still looks pretty gross and my lip is still swollen. And no matter how much I may want to, I can't even leave school. I'm stuck here until Jordyn wants to go.

The first bell rings. I can hear the panic of people rushing to class. I take one last look at the disaster that is my face, and then turn to confront the masses. Only I don't make it far. A couple of guys from the team enter as I'm reaching for the handle. Jason and Bryce. They play offense. And they're inseparable.

"Dude," Bryce says looking at my eye.

"Shit, man." Jason shoves Bryce out of the way to take his turn gawking. "What the hell happened to you?"

"What the fuck do you think?" I say. They obviously have amazing memories.

Bryce puts his hands up and backs away. "Hey, man. We're cool."

"Come on." Jason taps Bryce on the shoulder and they sneak past me.

I really wish I had my car.

I get a lot of sideways glances in my first few classes, but no one dares to address it.

Until lunch.

I see Sheila searching the cafeteria and I just know she's looking for me. I pay for my shitty pizza and when I turn to leave, Sheila's blocking my way.

"Holy shit!" She gapes at me, as do all the people in our vicinity. "I can't believe Brett was able to do that much damage." Her voice lacks any concern. In fact, she sounds amused.

"Yep," I say. "He has a hell of a left hook." Let them believe this is Brett's doing. At least no one will suspect my dad.

Sheila follows me as I move toward the exit. "That must've seriously hurt."

I ignore her.

She takes my silence as a confirmation. "Good. You deserve it."

And I'm done being at school today. I hate that Brett's going to get credit for my face. Like that asshole needs a bigger ego. I'm about to walk home again, but Jordyn sees me and she knows exactly where I'm headed, so she runs to catch up with me. We walk out to the parking lot together. When we reach her car—she's decided neither of us needs to be there for the rest of the day—I'm smiling with relief.

"I just couldn't be there anymore," I tell her as we drive away. She gets it.

"So . . . what should we do now that we've been freed from the clutches of hell? My treat. No arguing."

"I don't know. Give me some options," I say.

"Hmm. You like to swim?"

Even though it's in a regular old subdivision, Jordyn's dad's house looks like it's right in the middle of the woods. It's this giant A-frame log cabin. The pool is designed to look like it was made by nature, but it only looks more man-made. It's heated, though, and it's a pool and we're ditching, so it's perfect.

Jordyn tells me to change in the guest room—we stopped at my house for my suit on the way over—and meet her in the pool.

It's not exactly warm out—it's officially fall in three days—so I jump into the cool water and gasp and swim over to where the warm water from the elevated hot tub spills into the pool. I splash around for an eternity attempting to amuse myself. What's taking her so long?

But when she finally emerges, I understand. She had to take off all her makeup.

"Now, if you'd looked like this at school, I would have absolutely recognized you, so you really can't hold that against me anymore." In fact, she hasn't changed much. Except now she has curves. I didn't realize she had such impressive, perky breasts under all those layers of black.

"Yeah, yeah. Whatever."

I swim over to her. "Seriously, though. You're kind of hot. I know like six guys that would keel over dead if they saw you right now."

"Sure." She quickly gets in the pool.

"Marcus would be first in line. He likes his blondes, but he's always mused about bagging a girl of the 'Asian persuasion.'"

"Oh, god. Does he really say that shit?" She swims toward the hot waterfall.

"You would cringe if you heard half the shit that comes out of his mouth."

"And why are you friends with him again?"

"I guess I'm not anymore, really." Marcus didn't even

acknowledge me in the hall, so either he's scared that I'm mad about him and Sheila, which I still kind of am, or he's mad that I beat the shit out of Brett and they lost the game. Whatever. I stand up so the hot water can splash down my back.

"I still think you should get that looked at." She points at my ribs.

I wave her off. "They're not broken. Cracked maybe, but they'd just wrap me up and send me on my way with some painkillers I couldn't afford the prescription for anyway."

She lets it go.

The wind kicks up and we both huddle under the hot waterfall.

"Maybe I didn't really think this through," she says sheepishly.

"Hot tub?" I suggest.

"Yes please."

The hot water feels great, but it also makes all my injuries angry. Still, warmth wins out.

She starts laughing out of nowhere.

"What?" I say, wiping at my face like I have a bug on me.

"You know what I just remembered? Brian O'Reilly."

"Aw, man," I say splashing at her, which only makes her laugh harder. "Dude. That asshat attacked me with a squirt gun filled with Nair in sixth grade."

"Is that why you shaved your head?" Now she's laughing so hard, she has to wipe her eyes.

"Shut up."

"I can't believe you never told me that. That's really messed up." Her laughter slowly dissolves into a smile, but the spark remains in her eyes. "You were just beginning to think you were hot shit and he didn't like it."

"I didn't think I was hot shit."

"Oh, but you did. Remember the girls who formed the Tyler Blackwell fan club after they watched you play football?"

"But I didn't, like, tell them to do it."

"Still. You threatened the very nature of the sixth-grade pecking order. Brian had to take you down."

"Now *that* dickhead thought he was the shit."

"You know, it's pretty ironic that you went from being bullied by Brian O'Reilly to becoming Brian O'Reilly."

"What? I didn't become him."

"You did. When I first moved back, you had this gross aura of arrogance. And when I tried to talk to you, you pushed me out of the way and called me a 'fucking goth freak.'"

"I did?"

"Yep."

"Well, shit. I don't want to be Brian O'Reilly."

"If it's any consolation, you're not anymore. But only just recently."

"I'll take it." I run my hands down my face and then back up through my hair, trying to recall when I might have had this encounter with her. I can't believe I was such a douchebag.

We're both quiet awhile. Deep in thought, I guess. Utterly relaxed by the scalding water.

"It sucks about your mom," she says quietly, her head back, eyes closed.

I expect her to say more—the usual "I'm so sorry . . . I can't imagine how you feel . . . You poor thing . . ." But it never comes. She never says another word about it.

TWENTY

"I thought you said you weren't going to go all *Fight Club*." Dr. Dave studies the new bruises that have appeared since I last saw him.

"I didn't start this one, Doc. Brett, I guess to save face after I beat the crap out of him, blindsided me on Monday. I merely defended myself. If I'd responded like I'd wanted, his face would look like this and mine would look the same as last week."

I can tell from his look of utter disapproval that he totally buys this story.

"But I think I might have gained a friend thanks to that asshole. When Jordyn saw this"—I gesture to my face—"we sort of bonded." I tell him how we're carpooling again, how I got fired from the dog shit job, and how Jordyn gave me all her weekday shifts and ditched school with me.

"So now you're friends with Jordyn?" Dr. Dave has completely abandoned his notebook. And his disapproval. He doesn't even call me out on ditching.

"Crazy, right? I mean, I totally thought she'd hate me even more for being some stupid Neanderthal football asshole and fighting again, but then she's ditching school to make sure I'm okay."

"And there's a history there?"

"Yeah. I mean, we were friends until her parents divorced and she and her mom moved away. We tried to stay in touch at first but, well, you know how it goes."

"Well, I think it's good you have someone to talk to. Just don't screw it up by trying to sleep with her."

"Seriously? You think that little of me?"

He flips back in his little notebook. "You want I should show you my notes?"

I hold up my hands. "I know. But in all seriousness, she's too goth for me. I like girls who don't feel the need to hide behind layers and layers of makeup. And the thing is, she's actually a pretty girl without all that stuff. Maybe I should refer her to you."

"Don't you think it's interesting how hiding behind layers bothers you, yet you hide behind your own shit?"

"Whatever." And damn if I didn't walk right into that.

"So, no notebook. I take it you haven't been keeping up on my assignment."

"Not really."

"Okay. Well, do you think you can try to write in it a little this week? Not every day. Say, twice?"

"I'll try." But I probably won't.

o o o

At school the next week, people have stopped blatantly staring at me. The bruising above my eye is at that in-between purple-slash-green phase, and I wear it proudly. My lips are practically healed. The cuts on the upper are gone and the lower is scabbed but not in an overly disgusting way. But my ribs still hurt like hell.

Jordyn and I have taken to leaving campus for lunch every day. Today we're at Wendy's, as I have insisted on treating and she understands my financial situation.

"You remember when our moms met here, like, every day? I'm only just getting over my Wendy's fatigue," Jordyn says as we take our trays to the only free table in the whole place.

"You ever wonder why they lost touch? I mean, I thought they were pretty close, but maybe that's because my mom never had many friends."

"Yeah. I think it's because when my mom met Henry, her life just became all about him. It's like she was missing part of herself and it was him. I've never seen her so happy. Honestly, I didn't know she was so miserable with my dad. She was pretty good at hiding it."

"Right? I had no clue Mom was *that* depressed. I mean, she had depressive episodes from time to time, but it never seemed that bad, you know? She would just seem sadder than usual. It's not like she ever stopped eating or getting out of bed or any of those Lifetime movie symptoms. I wish she'd talked to me about everything. I wish I'd known, like, how much she was hurting. I still have no idea why she did what she did. I mean, I know it was because of Dad, but then why didn't she just leave him? And why now? Why not wait until I'm off at school? Did she just assume I was all set up for the future and that I'd be okay without her this year? Why would she leave me with that asshole? Did she think it would make him stop drinking? That he would get his shit together and be a decent human being? How could she think that, you know? He's a fucking monster. Always has been. Obviously she knew it or she wouldn't have done what she did. God, if she would have just left a goddamn note or something explaining—"

"Wait, wait, wait. She didn't leave a note?"

"Nope." I take a bite of my chicken sandwich, not even tasting it.

"Nothing?"

I shake my head.

"That's seriously fucked up."

"Right?" I take a sip of Coke. "I kind of wondered if my dad killed her and made it look like a suicide, but he was too far away to have been able to—"

She's stopped eating. "How do you know for sure? He could've—"

"I know because she was still warm when I found her." Now I've also stopped eating.

"Shit. Tyler . . ."

"And now there are four people on the entire planet who know that, so . . ."

"I won't say a word. To anyone. You know I won't."

And I do know.

"You think if our moms had kept in touch, we would have kept in touch?" I ask.

"I was thinking about that the other day. And yes. But I don't know if we would have been friends. You were just getting cool and it was pretty obvious I was never going to be cool."

"But we're friends now."

"But, well, I hate to break it to you, but . . . you're not cool anymore." She dips her fry into my chocolate Frosty and pops it into her mouth.

"Hey." I fling a fry at her.

She throws one back but I catch it.

"So, you still do that?"

"Dip my fries? Of course! I was wrong to ever have doubted you on that. It's awesome," she says, dipping another fry.

"Then why didn't you get your own Frosty?" I dip the one I caught and pop it into my mouth.

"'Cause I knew you'd get one."

If you had asked me two weeks ago if I would be hanging out with Jordyn Smith, I would have told you you were high. And now, it's like we've been friends all along. Life is strange.

TWENTY-ONE

Just as my bruise has managed to turn the color of piss, Jordyn and I get to assist Henry at a wedding shoot. He's even letting her take some of the photos.

I'm waiting for them out in front of this venue that looks like a massive Colorado craftsman mansion/castle. Henry had to replace a flash, and Jordyn had to run back to their house to grab a lens he took home, thus our carpool fell apart.

School has been bearable thanks to Jordyn. Sure, there are all kinds of rumors about us floating around, things involving me letting her drink my blood while we have sex and stuff, but we just laugh them off.

I've been able to replenish some of my emergency fund now that Henry's giving me more shifts. More shifts means more responsibilities, but nothing I can't handle. I've even done a few of the retouches from start to finish. Jordyn used to do all the final finishing touches, but she doesn't have to anymore. And when we have downtime, Henry shows me some of his work that doesn't revolve around people staring into the camera. Landscapes and candids of unsuspecting people at various locations who spark his interest. He explains what drew him to each subject and I'm starting to understand composition. Last week he gave me an old DSLR camera to experiment with. I'm still too afraid to show him any of my attempts, though. Most of them are of Captain and stuff around the house—nothing that would mean anything to anyone except me. I did bring the camera along tonight, so we'll see what I come across. Plus wearing it around my neck makes me feel a little more official.

Finally I spot Henry's car and meet him to get his gear. That's my job for the night. I get to follow Henry around with his bags and bags of stuff, just in case something doesn't work or he feels like swapping lenses. The ol' funeral suit is getting a lot of use these days. The belt has to be tightened a little more and the jacket's a little big now, but it's not too noticeable. I hope.

Jordyn pulls into the space next to him. When she steps out of her car wearing an elegant silk dress—and it's not even black, it's the rich dark blue of the sky just before it turns black—I stop dead. Not just because of the dress, but because she's made herself up to look like a normal almost-eighteen-year-old girl. Actually, she looks pretty damn beautiful.

"Shut up," she warns before I have a chance to compliment her.

"Can you believe it?" Henry chuckles.

"I thought she was someone else," I say.

"You guys are so funny." She scowls as she takes a bag from the trunk.

"Allow me, m'lady." I bow to her as I reach for the strap.

She smacks my hand away and shoves past me toward the front door.

Henry and I are both chuckling as we follow.

"I'm amazed she agreed not to wear all that shit on her face," Henry says. "Wish she knew how beautiful she was without it."

"Me too," I say. Then I see Henry smile to himself with a certain gleam in his eye. What's with everyone jumping to conclusions about us? I have to set him straight. "I mean, it would make her life so much easier. The kids at school aren't very nice about it."

"Yeah. I think that's why she does it. To keep everyone at a safe distance," he says. "I'm just glad the two of you are gettin' on so well. It's about time she had a friend."

He says "friend" but "boyfriend" is clearly implied. I'm about to correct him, when the father of the bride introduces himself.

After the most elaborate and expensive wedding ceremony I will ever attend, I follow Henry around so he can switch lenses at will. Right now he's in the middle of the dance floor shooting the couple.

I find myself watching Jordyn. She doesn't look like she's having fun. I have the sudden urge to put my camera to use, when a young guy who was in the wedding party sidles up to her. She's shooting pictures of the cake. I click off some shots as the guy flirts with her until she's finally smiling. I want to hug him for it. And I'm getting it on film! I have actual proof that she can smile! Then another guy, the first guy's friend, joins them. He's a little more ambitious with his flirting. He finds ways to touch her with the ol' "Can I see your camera?" trick.

Henry switches his lens once again and asks me to tell Jordyn to take a break.

I slowly move to where she's talking to the guys. She's still smiling, but I can tell the second guy's hugging the shit out of her.

Her face lights up when she sees me. "Hey."

"I've been ordered to tell you to take a break," I say.

"Great." She hands me the camera and takes the first guy's hand, leading him onto the dance floor, leaving guy number two holding his dick.

"She your sister or something?" guy number two asks.

"Clearly," I say.

"Oh. Cool. Well, your sister's totally hot." He obviously doesn't get sarcasm, or that she's half Malaysian and I am unmistakably not.

I follow his gaze to where Jordyn's dancing and flirting and laughing. She really is beautiful. I hold up the camera she handed me and take a few candids of her and the guy dancing. Was she always this beautiful? I have to talk her into ditching the vampire look for good. She'd have guys lining up around the block. But then I'd have to really start bulking up again in order to ward off the assholes.

Henry waves me back over and, this time, he switches cameras *and* lenses. I wonder what the difference is.

Jordyn taps my shoulder.

"You want your camera back?" I offer her the bag on my shoulder with a grin, wondering when she'll see the shots I took of her.

"Sure, but, actually, do you want to get some air?"

"After you."

The grounds are landscaped to perfection. The focal point is the pergola that I'm sure is used in the outdoor ceremonies. Off to the side is a little man-made waterfall with stone benches surrounding it.

"Why'd you stop dancing with that guy? You looked like you were having fun," I say.

"Did I? I'm not even sure I know what that looks like myself."

"Yeah. You were, like, smiling and everything. It was scary." I sit on the wall next to the waterfall.

She shoves me playfully, sitting herself. "Mike's pretty cool, we used to kind of hang out or whatever but . . ." She kicks her feet out and in, out and in. They don't quite touch the ground. It's adorable.

"But?"

"He always asked me not to look how I normally look when we did stuff where he might run into his friends."

"Henry thinks you do that to keep from getting close to people."

She stares at me, her expression unreadable. Is she going to hit me? Scream at me?

"Well, then why the hell didn't it work on you?" she says with an intensity that cuts me.

"I'm not trying to be a dick," I say. "I'd just really like to understand you."

She takes a deep breath. Stares at her still-kicking feet for a long second. "Okay, fine. It started when I came back from summer break between sixth and seventh grade with boobs. I'd always been happy being a wallflower, but suddenly some of the boys started talking to me. Flirting, even, not that I really knew how to interpret it. Some of the popular girls, one in particular, Jenna McCoy, did not like it. She spread rumors about how I was easy, as if a twelve-year-old could be easy. She and some of the other girls would corner me in the hallways and write 'slut' on my clothes or sometimes on my skin with permanent marker— I'm pretty sure Sheila got the idea for my jacket from someone who went to my middle school."

"Shit." That makes what Sheila did so much worse.

"Yeah. My mom tried to talk to the teachers and the principal about it, but they didn't do much. And Jenna didn't let up until everyone hated me, or feared her too much not to at least pretend to hate me. It was brutal.

"Then one day at lunch, I found myself staring at the goth kids and I thought they looked like they just didn't give a shit, you know? So I went out and bought some makeup and a billowy black shirt that covered my boobs and tried it out the next day. Something else came with the makeup and the clothes, something I didn't expect." She smiles. "Balls."

I laugh. "Balls, huh?"

"Yep." Then her face goes serious again. "When Jenna finally realized I was me one day at lunch, it was more slut-shaming humiliation. But this time I didn't let her get away with it. I threw my tray down, shoved her up against the wall, and got right in her face, swearing I would kill her if she didn't leave me the fuck alone. I think she believed me too, because she did."

Jordyn's quiet. I wait.

"I thought about ditching the look when high school started," she says, "because Jenna was going to a different school and I wouldn't have to worry about her anymore, but . . . I don't know. Maybe I do use it as a way to keep people at arm's length. It's worked pretty well, until you."

I smile and roll my eyes. "I'm really sorry we lost touch. I would have set them all straight. Even that Jenna McCoy."

She bumps my shoulder with hers.

When I turn to smile at her, I notice she's covered in goose bumps. "Shit. I'm such a dick. Here." I pull off my jacket. I think she'll say no because she's such an I-can-take-care-of-myself kind of girl, but instead she pulls it tightly around her shoulders.

"Thanks." We're quiet again awhile after that. Then she says, "I read this study that said twenty percent of all suicides don't leave a note."

I nod. "I know the one. My shrink brings it up constantly."

"That's really messed up."

"What, that I have a shrink?"

She swats at me. "The twenty percent thing, asshole." She's smiling again.

"Yes, yes it is. It would have been nice to have some kind of explanation, since it basically came out of nowhere."

"She really didn't give any indication at all?"

"Not a goddamn thing. She didn't even seem depressed that day. She used to be depressed when I was younger. She thought she hid it from me, telling me she was sick, but I figured it out by about junior high. Though it was never so bad that I thought she'd resort to suicide. And with all the good things that were happening for me last year, she'd been happier than I'd ever seen. We had a lot of fun those months leading up. And she was business as usual right up until I left for practice that morning."

"Wow."

"Yeah, wow." Now her feet have stopped kicking. I'm such an idiot. I should have realized she was cold. "Should we head back in? I'm sure Henry probably needs to switch lenses for the thousandth time tonight."

She gets up and takes my jacket from her shoulders.

"You really look beautiful tonight, you know." I take my jacket from her hands.

She stands there, not looking me in the eyes for more than a second at a time.

"What? It's true. I'm being completely sincere. I, Tyler Blackwell, think you, Jordyn Smith, look quite beautiful without all that shit on your face. But if you feel like you still need it, I promise I won't bring it up again. Shall we?" I hold out my elbow in a gentlemanly fashion, bracing myself for her to slap it away, but she surprises me and takes it.

I glance down at her to be met with a somewhat reluctant and embarrassed smile.

"I'll take your opinion under advisement," she mumbles.

As we walk back into the reception, I smile to myself. Maybe I've managed to get through to her. But I doubt it.

TWENTY-TWO

Jordyn is absent from work the next day. I find myself wishing she were here. Henry's in an unusually bad mood, so I don't dare ask why she isn't. But I'm feeling kind of off.

On my way to the bathroom between retouches, I catch Henry arguing into his cell. I make out something about Jordyn doing something he's less than thrilled with. As horrible as it is, I'm kind of happy about that—not that he's mad at Jordyn, but that they don't have an absolutely perfect relationship.

With Henry's mood, I don't want him to catch me doing something not work related, so I figure I can't take too long to calm myself down. I'm not even sure why I'm so worked up. Maybe I have, like, a Pavlovian response to anger. I splash some cold water on my face and run my wet fingers through my hair, reminding myself that I need this job and that Henry's not my dad and that he would never act like him in a million years.

I open the door to find a very unhappy Henry. "Did you encourage her to rekindle things with that ex of hers?"

"What?" I'm getting a bit of a *Deliverance* vibe off him. I back into the bathroom.

He follows me in. "I saw you two talking at the wedding and then next thing she's dancing with that Mike kid."

How is this my fault? I try to recall our conversation last night, but the walls are closing in and the piss smell of the toilet is making me want to vomit and Henry looks like he's about to rip my head off. *Henry is not like Dad. Henry is not like Dad.*

His phone rings. I think about using the distraction to get the fuck out of here, but once he realizes it's Jordyn on the other end, he stands in the doorway deliberately trapping me.

"Where the hell were you? Your mother was a wreck all night thinking something happened to you."

Henry glares at me as he listens to her response. I feel like I'm on trial for something I have no idea I've done.

"Aslan called us. Said you didn't come home."

His glare intensifies as he listens.

"He is. And he didn't bother saying anything to me about that. He has some serious explaining to do, if you ask me."

I swallow the golf ball in my throat.

"This ain't over," Henry says into the phone before thrusting it at my chest, about knocking the wind out of me. He storms out of the bathroom, slamming the door behind him.

I stare at the phone until I hear Jordyn on the other end telling me to pick it up.

"Um?"

"I'm so sorry, Tyler! I'm so, so, so sorry!"

"What's going on?"

"I told Henry I was with you last night. Will you please, please, please go with it? I'll owe you."

"Are you fucking crazy? He already went on a rant about your ex. I'm not telling him you were with me last night."

"Not like that. I told my mom that I had a little champagne at the reception and that you were taking me home and I begged you not to take me to my dad's house because I didn't want him to see me drunk, so I stayed at your house to sleep it off."

"And this will make them hate me less, how?"

"Please, Tyler?"

"I need this job, Jordyn."

"I swear my mom will calm Henry down. It'll be fine. I'll even tell them Mike tried to make me go home with him, but you intervened, and you can be the hero. Please?"

Of course I'm going to help her, but I'll make her sweat a little first.

"Please?" Her voice has taken on a tone of desperation I didn't think she was capable of.

"Fine."

"Oh, thank you, thank you, thank you, thank—"

"One condition."

"Anything."

"Tell me where you really were," I tease.

"Shut up." I can practically hear her turn red.

"You little slut."

"Really? You're going to call me a slut?" She's back to normal.

"I hope you at least—"

"I'm not an idiot. Of course we used condoms."

"Good for you. But what I was going to say is, I hope you at least enjoyed yourself." My face is starting to hurt from smiling.

"I, um, well, it's really none of your business, but yes I did enjoy myself." I can all but feel the heat from her blush through the phone and it's killing me. I am loving this. Oh, how the tables have turned. "At least, I enjoyed myself until this morning when I remembered how things used to be."

"Well, you want to know something really messed up?"

"Of course."

"I . . . I really miss you here."

She goes silent.

"Henry's really fucking scary when he's angry!"

"Oh, god. Tyler, I really, really owe you. I'm taking you to dinner. Someplace nice. Your choice."

"It's a date."

She's silent again.

"Don't be so literal," I say. "I'll see you at school tomorrow. And I'll start making a list of places I've always wanted to try but didn't have the money."

"Thanks again." She hangs up.

"Anytime," I say to myself.

TWENTY-THREE

I wait for Jordyn at lunch in the usual spot on Monday—we're cooling it on the carpooling since I have a tendency to take off without warning these days. When she rounds the corner and her face isn't caked in all her usual makeup, my stomach drops. She didn't do that because of me, did she?

"Hey," is all I'm able to manage. She's still wearing heavy eye makeup and dark lipstick, but at least her natural skin is on display and not covered in that powdery white chalk stuff.

"You look disappointed. You didn't think I'd listen to you, and now you're annoyed that I did?" She tucks her shiny black hair behind one ear.

"No. It's that I—I'm just surprised you *did* listen. I mean, who am I to tell you to change what you're doing?" I set my pizza slice down on the bench. My appetite is gone.

"Don't flatter yourself. I did this for me. You helped, maybe, a little. The other night— Well, not all people suck as much as

Jenna McCoy, okay?" She sits across from me and lifts her slice to her mouth.

"You look good," I say.

She rolls her eyes and takes a bite of her pizza.

After school Friday, I take Captain for a long run through the greenbelts. I thought about heading for the Red Rocks path, but it gets dark so early now. The paths here are nearer civilization, so the chances of encountering a mountain lion are less likely.

It's not until I hear someone calling my name that I realize I'm not far from Jordyn's house.

I slow my pace and head up the path toward the street.

"You stalking me?" she asks.

"You wish."

"Who's this?"

Captain jumps up on her, tail wagging like crazy, and of course he's smiling. I expect her to freak that he's showing his teeth, but she gets down and allows him to lick her all over her face. It's only then that I realize she's not wearing any makeup. Like, at all. No eyeliner. No lipstick. And she's never looked better. She's wearing jeans and a hoodie under her coat. She's beautiful. How can she cover all that up? What the hell am I thinking? This is *Jordyn*. She's my friend. My *only* friend. I can't screw that up.

"He's smiling," she says, snapping me out of my stupidity.

"That's what I always say. Most people think he's threatening, though. His teeth."

"Nah, he's a good boy. Aren't you?" Captain licks her face again. "What's his name?"

"Captain Jack Sparrow, but we call him Captain."

"Jack Sparrow didn't have an eye patch. Did he, Captain?" Her adorable puppy-talk voice is killing me, it's so cute.

"Mom liked Johnny Depp, so that's the pirate we went with."

"It suits him," she says, sitting on the ground so Captain can worm his way onto her lap. He sits facing me but he looks back and kisses at her every two seconds. She laughs each time. And when she laughs, she's even more beautiful. What is wrong with me?

"Where are you off to?" If she says a date, it might kill me. In fact the idea of that asshat ex of hers getting to have sex with her last week is killing me.

She's waiting for me to say something.

"Sorry, what? I was distracted."

"I'm going to the animal clinic—the shelter where I volun teer. They just took in a hoarder's loot. There were like fifty cats or something ridiculous like that. They've had to put a bunch down because of feline leukemia, but they need me to help out with the ones that are healthy. I get to de-flea and de-worm. What can I say? I lead a glamorous life."

Shit. Why is she so freaking perfect?

This is not going to end well.

I have to stop this line of thinking.

I'm staring. She notices I'm staring. And we hold eye contact for an uncomfortable length of time. Shit. I just know she can tell I'm into her. Now she'll be all awkward, and I've ruined my, like, one friendship. And I didn't even get to have sex with her.

"I gotta run. I'll see you tomorrow," she says, pulling her keys from her pocket. She leans down and gives Captain a good scratch and a kiss on the head. "And just so your human doesn't get jealous," she says to Captain as she reaches up and kisses me on the cheek. And it's the best cheek kiss in the history of cheek kisses. Closer to my lips than a normal cheek kiss and also a bit more lingering. Talk about mixed messages. I am so totally screwed.

I run for another hour, trying to stop picturing Jordyn beneath me, sweaty and naked. When that doesn't work, I head for the shower. I'm pretty sure it's just that I haven't gotten laid in a while. It's just that she's a girl, a not unattractive girl, who's showing interest. Nothing more. I just need to get laid. I'll call Ali Heart-over-the-*i* after my shower. But I don't want Ali, I want Jordyn.

I settle for myself.

I don't notice that Dad's home until he comes down from his room grumbling about "where the fuck have you been hiding."

I'm in the kitchen, and I didn't close my bedroom door because I assumed he was off getting plastered for the night. I can't let him see that I'm worried, or he'll head right for it. But he doesn't go downstairs. He comes into the kitchen and stands right behind me. I'm making some stir-fry-in-a-bag thing.

"Smells good. What are *you* gonna eat?" He laughs. He thinks he's hilarious. Especially when he's buzzed. Of course, when he's buzzed he likes to play the "Fuck With Tyler" game.

I don't engage. I just finish the stir-fry and pull out two plates. He takes one and chucks it into the wall like a Frisbee. It shatters.

"I only need one plate." He says this like he's kindly declining a refill at a restaurant.

I pour the entire contents of my dinner onto his plate and set the pan in the sink. I turn on the water and let it run over the hot pan, steaming up the window facing the backyard.

I can feel him watching me. I turn to get him a fork, figuring he's trying to show me how I'm his bitch and all that. "You're welcome," I say, setting the fork next to the delicious-smelling food that I paid for.

I've barely turned back to shut off the water when I feel my head being slammed toward the counter. But it's not the counter, it's the stove. I can feel the heat still rising off the burner. If I hadn't instinctively stopped my head from making contact, I'd be scraping my face off the still-hot burner. He pushes harder, and from my awkward angle, I can feel myself losing the battle.

He wants me to beg. I know it. He knows I know it. And he knows I won't do it. He's laughing and kicking at the back of my knee, trying to get me to lose balance.

I push back just as he hits my knee at the right angle to drop me. My ear meets the burner and it hurts like hell. He tries to hold my head so the burning sensation can really take its toll, but my adrenaline flares and I elbow him in the windpipe. He lets go. If he weren't coughing so damn hard, he'd be kicking the shit out of me. He holds his throat and glares.

I leave the water running and grab Captain and run to my room, locking it behind me just as I hear him plow into the door.

"You fucking asshole! I'll fucking kill you! You hear me? I'll fucking kill you! I'll kill you!" His screams become sobs and I can tell he's now lying on the floor right outside my door. "Why'd you do it, Sarah? I miss you so much. Why'd she do it? I'm sorry, Sarah. I'm sorry. I'm sorry, Tyler. I shouldn't be allowed to be a parent. Not without Sarah. I miss her, Tyler. It hurts so much. Sarah." He repeats her name over and over until I'm forced to blast the stereo just so I'm not tempted to try to help him. I can't. Not after what he just did. Not even when he's like this.

I punch and kick my bed until I feel my little toe snap.

I limp into Dr. Dave's office the next morning.

"What's with the gimp routine?" he asks as I take my usual seat. I just hope he doesn't notice the beginnings of a scab on my ear. Good thing I still haven't gotten the haircut I so desperately need.

"I think I broke my toe."

"How'd you manage that?"

"Kicking the shit out of my bed."

"For any particular reason, or you just didn't sleep well?" He grins.

"I was looking at the pictures of my mom again," I lie.

"We need to find you a healthier outlet."

"I think I'm projecting feelings for Jordyn because she's the only person who's nice to me. Besides you, of course." I hope he takes the bait. I have to change the subject.

"Well, wait a minute. Would it be so bad if your feelings for Jordyn were real?"

"No, it wouldn't. You see? That's the problem."

"I don't see a problem. It's only a problem if you act on it in typical Tyler fashion." He lowers his glasses to give me a mock-judgmental glare.

"But if my feelings for her are real, what if I screw it up? She's the only friend I have. I . . . need her."

"And that scares you?"

"Of course it scares me. What if— I mean, I don't want to need anyone, you know? They'll just end up leaving like Mom di—" The realization hits me like I stepped into a steaming hot shower to find it freezing cold. It takes my breath away.

"She's not going to leave you, Tyler," he says gently, nudging a box of tissues toward me on the coffee table even though I'm not crying.

"You don't know that."

"You're right. I don't. And you don't. But is it worth not living just in case she does? You plan on living your whole life like that? Never trusting anyone? Never loving anyone because they might leave you, or they might die? What about your dog?

Are you going to toss him aside because you'll likely outlive him?"

"It's not the same."

"Isn't it?" He watches me for what feels like forever. "Do you think Jordyn has feelings for you?" he finally asks.

"I don't know. I mean, she recently hooked up with her douchebag ex at a wedding shoot and he was kind of like the old me. And she sends me mixed messages, but I can't read her. This is new territory for me. I'm used to chicks being pretty straightforward. Remember the last one?"

"There aren't even words for that last one." He sighs. "Tyler, Jordyn isn't the same. She isn't just a cheap lay. You're having feelings. Surely you've had feelings for a girl before hooking up with her?"

"Not really."

"That's . . . sad."

"Doc, I was hoping you'd talk some sense into me and here you're telling me I should act on my urges toward Jordyn."

"I didn't tell you to act on your urges, I told you to act on your feelings. I hope for your sake you know the difference."

When I see Jordyn at work, she's still not wearing any makeup. And it's seriously messing with my head. I'm not entirely convinced she's not doing it for me. But then again, I've seen her actually talking to people at school for a change. I'm probably being an arrogant douchebag.

When she asks why I'm so weird today, I tell her I'm thinking about Mom not leaving a note. It works. She doesn't bring it up again. But I'll have to figure out how to put a lid on this shit, because that excuse will only work for so long. I notice her eyeing my ear, but she doesn't ask. Unlike the rest of the world, she knows I'll talk about it when I'm ready.

TWENTY-FOUR

As soon as I'm settled in at work the following Saturday, Jordyn saunters over and tosses a book on the counter in front of me.

Or Not to Be: A Collection of Suicide Notes by Marc Etkind.

"Thanks?" I say.

"I'm just saying . . . they're not all gems. It's kind of fascinating." She shifts her feet like she does when she's nervous. "Forget it. It's messed up." She reaches for the book, but I hang on.

We both hold the book and also intense eye contact. I think she might be waiting for me to kiss her, but if I'm wrong . . . Or she might just be trying to read me, trying to figure out if I'm actually offended that she bought me a book of suicide notes.

She bought me a book of suicide notes! I feel a smile creep onto my lips. I wonder if this is what Dr. Dave meant by feelings. Because I kind of love that she bought me a book of suicide notes. Who does that thinking it's thoughtful? And it *is* thoughtful. And she's so beautiful—she's got these dark brown, cat-like eyes with little flecks of gold, and this thick, glossy black hair that falls over her shoulder, just reaching the top of her breast. And the fullness of her bottom lip . . . it's the kind of lip you want to take between your teeth.

I'm not sure how long we've been holding on to the book. I've completely lost track of time. I brush my finger across the book until it meets hers. If she doesn't move her finger or let go, I'll take that as a sign.

She does move her finger, but only to brush my finger back. My breathing speeds up. That tiny little touch is enough to make my entire body throb with electricity. I pull on the book, drawing her closer, looking from her eyes to her lips and back again. She licks her bottom lip. I lean in slightly. My stomach feels like I've swallowed a hurricane.

I stare at her lips until I'm close enough to feel her breath against my face. I shut my eyes wanting to memorize every sensation. Our noses touch and my heart speeds up. I hear her lips part and I feel her tip her head up so her lips come closer to mine.

And then the phone rings. We jump apart like a couple of kids caught playing doctor. And it's damn good timing too. Just as Jordyn returns to her chair to answer the phone, Henry bounds in, whistling what sounds like that one song from the musical *Cats*.

Jordyn and I don't so much as acknowledge the almost kiss. We simply go about business as usual. But damn if I don't think about how much I want to try again every second of the rest of the day.

○ ○ ○

Henry's first in on Sunday, much to my disappointment. I was hoping for a replay of yesterday morning. And he keeps me busy helping him all day. I don't get a chance to even see Jordyn until after the final client leaves and the three of us sit at the counter, sighing.

"Welp, that was a day," Henry says, kicking his feet up on the counter.

Jordyn and I just nod, occasionally exchanging glances.

"Can you believe it's Thanksgiving already? What are your plans for the big day, Tyler?"

"I'll probably just hang out at home."

"No family close by?"

"No. And that's fine. My dad and I . . . we're not really Thanksgiving people."

Henry looks like he might faint. "That won't do. You'll come to our house." And that's that.

Jordyn smiles and I smile back.

Unfortunately, the three of us walk to our cars together. It's that weird Colorado kind of cold that's more refreshing than freezing. And it's started to snow. The first real snow of the year is always kind of magical. Jordyn smiles up at the sky, allowing flakes to melt on her face. I wish Henry would leave. I want to kiss her more than I've ever wanted to kiss anyone in my life.

I wonder if Henry knows my plan and that's why he's not leaving, but then I realize his car isn't here.

"At least let me in the car while you frolic in the snow like a crazy person," Henry grunts at Jordyn.

"I'm coming, I'm coming." She shrugs at me as if to say, "Sorry, I wanted it as much as you did." Or maybe that's just wishful thinking.

At school the next day, I'm nervous. How will Jordyn react? Will we pick up where we left off? Do I really want to make out with her at school? But I don't see her until after lunch when I'm on my way to Mrs. Hickenlooper's class. She's walking with that guy from my chem class and they're both holding cups from Burger King. I didn't realize they were actually friends; I just thought they were in a class together or some thing. Plus she always implies she doesn't have any friends. She doesn't even glance at me today. Ouch. And she's back to wearing that shit on her face.

I'm utterly confused.

I don't bother looking for her at lunch the next day. Or the day after.

Thanksgiving. I arrive at Henry's house at noon as instructed. I feel underdressed in jeans and a sweater, which is dumb, seeing as I know Henry will most likely be wearing his uniform of flannel and denim.

I stand there. Do I knock on the giant glass doors? Fortunately, Henry spots me from the back of the house.

"Come in," he bellows as he bounds toward me. "Where's your dad?"

"He, uh, had a work thing."

"Oh. Well, more for us, right?"

"Right." This house looks like the result of a castle and a log cabin gettin' it on. It's . . . *manly* is the only word I can come up with. I'm surprised there aren't mounted heads and rifles on every wall. The floors are dark distressed wood. Stone, slate, and dark wood paneling cover every other available surface. After passing an office that I can't imagine Henry using because it's far too organized, and a staircase that resembles a multi-story library with a twenty-foot window flanked by bookcases all the way up to the ceiling, we enter the great room. This is the family room/kitchen/dining room, and it's the size of a church, with ceilings almost as high.

In the kitchen at the far end of the enormous room, there's a huge granite counter with high-backed stools surrounding it. There's also a table in the center of the room that seats at least ten, and a smaller table off to the back that seats six in front of a door that leads to the back deck, where there is yet another table. Three people live in this house. How many places to eat do they need? And one of them only lives here part of the time. I can't even begin to imagine waking up in a place like this every day.

The side of the room that isn't designated for eating is dominated by a gargantuan slate fireplace. The thing is almost as wide as the whole room, and it runs all the way up the tall wall. A giant, three-sided leather sofa that could easily fit twenty people, I kid you not, faces the fire and a screen that rolls out from some kind of secret compartment. This is their TV. Jordyn's dad, I assume, as he is an appropriately aged man of Chinese-Malaysian descent, is alone on the sofa, and he's too busy shoveling pretzels and dip into his mouth while watching football to notice me gaping at the immensity of, well, everything. I only ever saw him in photographs when we were kids—he was always traveling. I know his name is Aslan—like the lion from Narnia. I remember thinking this was cool. I also remember Jordyn telling me how her grandfather changed their last name to Smith because Ng was impossible for anyone to figure out how to pronounce. It's pronounced *ing*, by the way.

Jordyn's in the kitchen with her mom, Henry, and another woman I think must be her stepmom. And they're all laughing and playing and teasing each other. I feel the sudden heat of jealousy pressing down on me, matched only by an oppressive sense that I shouldn't be in a place like this. On the big screen, some running back completes a fantastic play, scoring a touchdown. My stomach clenches. Aslan jumps up and whoops. And it's Thanksgiving and Mom's not here and all of a sudden I really want to go home.

I consider slinking back toward the door, but Jordyn finally notices me and waves me over. She's smiling like everything's back to normal. Like the almost kiss never happened. Like she didn't tactfully avoid me for the last three days. I've never been more confused in my life, and the part of me wanting to leave is losing a battle with the part of me that wants to stay just to figure out where the two of us stand.

She's completely makeup-free and has her hair in a ponytail, revealing a small streak of hair dyed fire engine red at the nape of her neck. I never noticed that before. She's also wearing something I didn't even know she owned . . . color: a burnt-orange thermal shirt with buttons halfway down the front. It's deliciously snug.

I realize I'm staring at her chest about halfway to the kitchen and correct myself, guiltily glancing around.

Jordyn shoves a plate of hors d'oeuvres at me, most of which are so fancy-looking, I can't even begin to imagine what they are. I don't want to be rude, so I take one that sort of looks like a mini pizza and search for a plate or napkin.

"Over there." Jordyn points to the other end of the counter without looking. She's at the sink doing something and I am now privy to a view of her ass in some tight-fitting jeans. All her shirts and flowy skirts usually cover it up, and for the life of me I can't understand why.

What the hell am I doing? Three of her parents are standing right there. I snap out of my perversion and head toward the little plates shaped like turkeys. The pizza thing is actually really good. I take another.

"You like the quiche, I see," says Jordyn's mom. This is when I realize I've not been properly introduced to everyone. Jordyn seems to realize it at the same time and jumps in.

"Mom, you remember Tyler Blackwell?"

Jordyn's mom wipes her hands on her green apron. She has long, silky brown hair and light brown eyes. She doesn't wear any makeup, but then she really doesn't need it. She's very pretty. Her smile is almost exactly the same as Jordyn's. Actually, Jordyn resembles her quite a bit, seeing them side by side. She reaches out her hand for me to shake. "Of course I do, but this is not Tyler Blackwell. Because if it is, then I must be a hundred and ten, and I'm not even in my thirties yet."

"God, Mom, that's just . . . lame," Jordyn says.

"My daughter may call me lame, but you may call me Kelly."

This is when a woman who looks very much like Kelly, only blond and a bit plastic, turns her attention from the stove. "Jordyn! Now, this is the kind of boy you need to bring around the house," the blonde says, eycing me like I'm the turkey. "Not that strange little Jeffrey kid. Patricia Henderson-Smith." She wipes her hand on her aggressively tight jeans and extends it to me like I'm supposed to kiss it. Unsure what to do, I awkwardly shake it.

"Mrs. Henderson-Smith," I say.

"Call me Patricia," she says with a wink, and then she turns back to the stove. This lady is what Sheila will grow up to be. The second wife. The wife that almost lives up to the first one who didn't want to keep the guy around and he never got over it. The one he screws while pretending she's the other.

"Dad!" Jordyn yells across the room. "You're being rude. We have a guest."

Her dad mutters something and pauses the game, walking over to gawk at me with the rest of the room.

"What's the score?" Henry asks him.

"Seventeen to twelve," he says, like he's just sure the team with the lower score can easily beat the team with the higher score.

"Who's playin'?" Henry asks, then he starts laughing just before Jordyn's dad opens his mouth. "You know I don't give a shit who's playin'. I'm just messin' with ya."

"This guy!" Jordyn's dad grabs the back of Henry's neck,

which he has to reach up pretty high to accomplish, and mock-punches Henry in the arm while making gruff manly noises.

"All right, all right." Henry shrugs him off with a chuckle. "Tyler, this ol' coot here is Aslan Smith."

"Mr. Smith." I extend my hand.

"Nah, bro. We do this." He holds his fist out. I look at Jordyn as I go to fist bump her father, and she closes her eyes like she's about to die of embarrassment. "Yeah, man. That's the shit! And seriously, call me Aslan. I hate all that formal ass-kissery unless I'm at work."

Is this guy for real? He's like a Ken Jeong character.

"So, Tyler, you play ball?" Aslan asks, looking me over.

"Not really," I say.

Jordyn gives me a look that clearly says "Good call."

"Seriously, bro? You look like you could throw a ball around. What's your sport?"

"Um, I like to run," I say.

Aslan places both hands on my biceps and begins to squeeze like there's nothing weird about this at all. I look to Jordyn, but she's doubled over, shaking violently until she finally snorts. When the others turn to see, they all start laughing too.

Patricia comes running over. "Oh, are we fondling the merchandise?" She ducks under Aslan's arms so she's between us and places her hands just beneath her husband's hands.

Holy shit. What did I get myself into?

"All right, all right. Enough o' that. Don't scare off my second-best employee." Henry pats Aslan on the back. Aslan releases his grip on my arms, but Patricia does not. Then she makes insane eye contact until Jordyn, still laughing, grabs my wrist and pulls me away.

"I'm going to show Tyler the rest of the house."

"I might need to start with the shower," I say under my breath. She starts laughing again. The sound of it makes my urge to escape evaporate.

Jordyn starts the tour with her parents' room, which is on the first floor on the other side of the giant fireplace, and then she shows me the spare rooms upstairs, and finally takes me down to the basement, where her room is. I guess we're just pretending the last few days never happened.

"A fellow basement dweller," I say, and then I see that her basement is more like a large luxury apartment. There's a full kitchen/bar, an overstuffed sofa facing a fireplace with a giant TV mounted above it, and there's a lounge area with a pool table and a dartboard next to the doors leading out back. "Um, never mind. This is nothing like any basement I've ever seen."

Then she takes me down a hall to a small gym, another guest room, and finally her room.

I expected some kind of gothic-themed bedroom with black walls and shit, but her room is surprisingly girly. Her furniture is all white, as are the bedding and curtains, and the walls are a very pale blue that reminds me of the sky just as the sun comes up. The best part of her room might be the little reading nook in the corner with a chair that would probably be comfortable to sleep in, and a lamp that looks like one of the lights in the photo studio. Next to that is a huge desk overflowing with pencils, brushes, drawings and paintings, and a bunch of photos in a heap of disarray. I try to take a closer look, but she steps between me and her work in progress.

"Okay, tour's over. I just heard the door. The cousins are probably here." She places her hands on my shoulders and pushes me back out of the room. I want to bring up the almost kiss, but then footsteps come pounding down the stairs. Six or seven kids, all boys, bound into the room and head right for the darts and pool table. Jordyn introduces me to everyone, but I'll never remember all their names.

Then we head upstairs to where Kelly's putting the finishing touches on the turkey.

I sit next to Jordyn toward the end of the long formal table where Henry and Kelly are.

"Kelly, this is seriously the best turkey I've ever had in my entire life. Hands down." I shovel another piece into my mouth not even caring that I'm already almost stuffed.

"Oh, please. I'm sure your mom's a great cook. What's she up to these days anyway?"

Jordyn practically chokes on her roll, erupting into a coughing fit. I slap her on the back and offer her water. "It's okay," I whisper to her. Looking back to Kelly, who's eagerly awaiting my response, I say, "She, uh, she died."

"Oh my god! Honey. I'm so sorry to hear that." She looks genuinely saddened by this. "She was such a great lady. I always meant to keep in touch with her after the move. I feel terrible."

"Don't worry about it," I say.

"Was it cancer?" Patricia says from the other side of the table with a hand on her heart.

216

"Um, no," I say.

"How's your book coming, Trish?" Henry interrupts. "Patricia's writing a self-help book."

Patricia brightens at the opportunity to talk about herself and she dominates the rest of the meal. Henry gives me a small nod as if to say "I've got your back." Jordyn places her hand on my leg and squeezes. I put my hand on hers and then we entwine our fingers and sit like that for the rest of the meal.

After dinner, Henry pulls out a guitar and we all sit around the fireplace drinking wine—the adults insisted, so I obliged, even though I usually avoid any and all alcohol-related beverages for fear I'll turn out like my dad—and everyone sings and tells stories well into the night. I didn't even know families could be like this. I really was dealt a shitty hand.

As the night winds down, the extended family packs up to leave. Soon it's just Jordyn's immediate family and me. Henry sings a love song to Kelly, who mouths all the words along with him because she's heard it a hundred times. Patricia sits on Aslan's lap with his arms wrapped around her, whispering in her ear and kissing her neck. Jordyn sits across from me on the floor with her back against the couch next to Henry's feet, eyes closed, completely lost in the words of Henry's song. Everyone's so damn happy. It's too much. I excuse myself, heading to the basement guest room. Kelly's insisted I stay because she won't have me drinking and driving.

I shut myself into the guest bathroom and stare at my reflection. All I can see right now is my mom. My stupid fucking coward mom. If she loved me as much as all those crazy people upstairs love Jordyn, she never would've killed herself.

I splash some cold water on my face hoping it'll calm me down, and then rest my hand on the doorknob, steadying myself for the goddamn love fest upstairs.

When I finally open the door, Jordyn's standing against the wall, waiting. A drip of water trails down the side of my face, but before I can wipe it away, she's doing it for me. She holds her cool hand against my cheek. Her eyes meet mine. My breathing picks up. Her hand brushes down my face and arm, and she takes my hand. I gently pull her to me. Her eyes momentarily flutter shut as I run my fingers down her cheek and then trace her lips with my thumb. I tip her face up to meet mine. Our noses brush and her lips part. I breathe her in; the heady, sweet smell of red wine on her breath mixes with the flowery scent of her shampoo. The wine didn't affect me nearly as much as the way she's looking at me does. I'm pretty sure we're both floating several inches off the ground. My lips softly brush against hers and my whole body is suddenly on fire.

I run my fingers through her hair, cupping my hand against the back of her neck. And then I pull her closer and kiss her with every last part of me. I need to feel every inch of her. She must feel it too because her hands are under my shirt, gripping my back, pulling me closer still. I run my hands over her clothes and she looks at me in a way that has me sliding my hand under her shirt and unfastening her bra. She moans against my mouth. I pull her legs up and around me, pressing her back into the wall. She moans deeper. My hands find their way back under her shirt and I groan as I cup her breast in my hand, rubbing my thumb over her hard nipple. Our clothes are really getting in the way. I begin to pull her shirt over her head when I hear footsteps on the stairs.

Jordyn stiffens and I quickly set her back down on the ground. She straightens her shirt, adjusting her unfastened bra just before Kelly appears at the bottom of the stairs. It's pretty obvious what we were doing, especially if she were to glance at my crotch for some reason, but Kelly says, "I wanted to make sure Tyler was all set in the guest room, and that you showed him where the towels were and gave him a spare toothbrush." I think maybe she's too tipsy to put two and two together. Thank god.

Once she's retreated up the stairs, I turn to Jordyn, hoping she'll suggest we pick up where we left off, but she's having a hard time looking at me for more than a second at a time. It's awkward and yet there's still a little bit of a sexual charge in the air. But when I take a step toward her and she backs up, the sexual tension evaporates. I wish her good night and close myself in the guest room.

I lie in the most comfortable bed I've ever felt and can't stop thinking about what would have happened if Kelly hadn't interrupted. And that makes me hard again. I grab the towel Kelly gave me and head to the shower.

TWENTY-FIVE

I'm awake before the sun is up, acutely aware that there's only a wall between Jordyn and me. I can still feel her hands gripping my back and her legs wrapped around me. Did that really happen? And is there any way to make it happen again? I think she was as into it as I was. But then why did she back away after her mom left?

Only one way to find out.

Opening the door to the hallway, I listen for any sound of life. All's quiet on the western front, so I sneak over to Jordyn's room. The door is unlocked. Had she been waiting for me to come over here last night? Or maybe she just leaves her door unlocked. It's not like she has anyone she needs to keep out.

Her breathing is deep and steady; she's obviously still asleep. I cautiously sit on the edge of the bed memorizing her peaceful face. My fingers want to touch her, so I do, cautiously. Her cheeks are soft. I run my fingers through her hair and she stirs.

"Mmm."

"Morning," I whisper.

She adjusts herself so she's looking up at me. Her smile is killing me. I want her more than I've wanted anything. Ever.

But then her smile vanishes and she leaps out of bed, pushing me aside, as she disappears into her giant closet. When she reappears, she's wearing a heavy robe and carrying some clothes. "You should have everything you need in the guest bathroom," she says as she stalks toward her bathroom, not even bothering to look at me before slamming the door.

What the hell just happened? I don't understand. I replay everything leading up to almost having sex in the hallway and realize . . . oh. I am a fucking idiot. It was out of pity. It had to have been. And . . . what? Now she's annoyed I didn't realize it? I mean, what else could it be?

The shower stops. I hear a hair dryer turn on. As much as I don't want to go home, I'm pretty sure Jordyn doesn't want me here. If I leave now, I can at least get out without another awkward encounter.

When I reach the top of the stairs, Kelly's in the kitchen. There's no way to sneak past her without seeming like a total dick.

"I'm making eggs, Tyler. Come, sit." She gestures to a stool at the counter. Her brown hair is pulled up into a twist.

I really want to be gone before Jordyn comes up, but I also don't want to be rude to the person who made me the best meal I've eaten since my mom died.

Kelly sets a plate and a fork in front of the stool. "Scrambled okay?"

I eye the front door. God, I want to leave, but the smell of

Kelly's cooking is probably *worth* more awkwardness with Jordyn, so I sit. "Absolutely."

Kelly pushes a glass pitcher of, I'm guessing, freshly squeezed orange juice toward me.

I pour her a glass, then one for myself. "I seriously don't know how to thank you for yesterday. That was by far the best Thanksgiving dinner I've ever had."

"Oh, you're sweet." Kelly scoops some eggs onto the plate in front of me. "Hash browns?"

"Yes, please."

She picks up the pan and scrapes some perfect golden-brown hash browns onto my plate and then onto hers, which she then scoots over to the place next to me.

It's a little awkward, it being just the two of us, and I find myself glancing back at the basement stairs.

"Jordyn's probably still sleeping," Kelly says.

I almost correct her.

After another few awkward bites, I feel Kelly watching me. I finally steal a glance at her. She turns her head and scratches her eye.

Now I don't care how awkward things are with Jordyn, I just want her to hurry the hell up so I don't have to sit here alone with her mom anymore. I eat faster.

Kelly takes a big gulp of her OJ. I can hear her swallow and for some reason it infuriates me. I set my fork down, my appetite completely gone. I'm pissed off and I don't even know why. All I know is I don't want to be here anymore. My leg has started fidgeting. That's it. I have to go. I wipe my mouth on my napkin, set it down, placing my hands on either side of the plate and ready myself to stand, but then Kelly laughs softly, stopping me.

"Do you remember when Sarah and I took you and Jordyn to Casa Bonita on the last day of third grade?"

It's so out of nowhere that I have absolutely no idea how to respond.

"You broke the piñata on the first swing and that one crazy mother got so mad that her little two-year-old didn't get a turn. And while she yelled at you, Sarah took the little girl and helped her get a ton of Tootsie Rolls. And then the crazy mom didn't even thank her!"

My chest hurts. My hands clench against the counter. I'm going to lose it. Because no, I don't remember, I don't remember that, and who does this woman think she is? Having memories of my own mother? She didn't even bother keeping in touch with her.

It's only when I feel my legs shake that I realize I'm standing. And then it all happens so fast. Kelly's holding me up and I'm sobbing into her hair like a baby. She's crying and rocking and telling me she's sorry, and I hate her and I need her. I hold on to her so hard.

And then I hear footsteps coming up from the basement and I abruptly head for the front door and jump in my car before there's a chance for anyone to follow.

A bout of exhaustion hits me after driving around for twenty minutes, trying to shake off whatever the hell that was. It's still early when I reach the driveway. Dad should be asleep. He doesn't have work, so I'll have to figure out a way to avoid him. Last night I'd fantasized that Jordyn and I would spend the day together talking and kissing, and when did I turn into such a girl?

Captain barks when I walk through the door. He's probably starving. I shush him unsuccessfully as I pour a scoop of food into his bowl. Then I head down to my room to change into running clothes.

"Where the fuck have you been?" Dad groans from the couch and I practically jump out of my skin. He must've passed out there and Captain woke him with his barking.

"Out," I say, hoping it doesn't look like I've been crying for the last twenty minutes.

"That's your answer? Show me some goddamn respect. I'm your father, for Christ's sake."

"If you acted like a father, I *might* respect you, but let's not kid ourselves." I can't help myself. Today already sucks.

Dad tries to pull himself off the couch, but his hand slips and he falls back. He's still drunk.

I shake my head and open the door to my room. "Pathetic."

I hear a bottle shatter against the door as I lock it. Then there's some swearing and another bottle crashes. Even drunk, the asshole still has great aim.

I crank my stereo up as high as it goes and I lie on my bed staring at the ceiling.

What kind of fucking life is this?

I bet that's what Mom thought. But she wasn't a minor. She could've left anytime. So what stopped her?

And why now? Why not wait until I graduated? Or why not sooner? Or why at all? I kick my mattress.

She hid what Dad did to her from me as much as she could, but I could usually tell when something had happened. He'd let up on the beating since the time he went off on Mom and I punched him so hard—and he didn't see it coming—that he lost his balance and fell, cracking his head against the kitchen table on the way down. I was almost sixteen. I thought I'd killed him. So did Mom. After he came to, she got mad at me for the whole thing. As much of an asshole as he was, she loved him. I think she held on to the hope that he would change. But I knew better. So what happened to make her realize what I always knew? And how did I miss it?

The book Jordyn bought me about suicide notes creeps into focus next to the football I've been staring at without really seeing. For lack of anything else to do, I start reading. It's interesting how some people leave perfectly coherent notes with instructions for how their loved ones should deal with their bodies and belongings, and others are obviously in so much pain that their brains are unable to properly convey why they can't take it anymore, but it's clear they can't take it, and this is the only solution they can see.

Mom was always insanely organized, so why didn't she leave instructions for me about what to do with her stuff or how to deal with Dad? If she was in such unbearable pain that she felt there was no way out, I wish she would have told me. Why did she hide it? If I'd known she was hurting, I might have helped. If I'd just gotten home five minutes earlier—

I slam the book shut, pick up the football, and hurl it against the wall as hard as I can. Then I pull out that notebook with the goddamn smiley face and a pen and I do something I never thought I'd do: I write. And write and write. About everything. About how pissed I am. About how Jordyn made me feel and then yanked the rug out from under me. About Dad, even, but I rip all those pages out and hide them in the metal box. I don't want Dr. Dave to read that, and if Dad found them, he might kill me.

Once I've purged all the thoughts in my head, I turn on the TV and pass out watching an *X-Men* marathon.

When I wake up, it's dark. The house is silent.

I venture upstairs to see if Dad's gone. He's not on the couch, but that doesn't mean he's not in his room.

Captain comes bounding through the doggie door. He's been rolling in the snow and now there are snow dreadlocks all along his belly. The sight of him lightens my mood.

"Look at you. Let's get you melted." I motion for him to head down to my room.

The second I turn on the bath water Captain jumps in, splashing me. He loves water. He starts biting at the faucet, which always cracks me up.

"You crazy dog. You're the best thing I've got," I say. To which Captain begins to dig at the spot where the running water hits the bottom of the tub.

I manage to shampoo him without completely soaking myself, not that it matters, because in the course of getting rinsed, he shakes violently, sending soapy water flying everywhere. Once he's fully rinsed, I drain the tub, but he refuses to get out until the last of the water is gone, pawing at it as if to say "No! Come back!"

After he's dry, he passes out on my bed. I'd love to be him, to find that kind of pure joy in something as simple as a bath.

I take in the damage left in Captain's wake. Every wall is dripping dog shampoo water. As I wipe things down, I spot something shiny behind the toilet. The razor blade. I thought I'd put it away after . . . It gives me the creeps and I want to call Jordyn. But that's not an option. I should have listened to Dr. Dave.

TWENTY-SIX

I have a thoroughly unhelpful session with Dr. Dave on Saturday. He doesn't even react to me doing his lame assignment. In all fairness, I don't tell him he was right about me fucking things up with Jordyn either, so I guess we're even. I spend most of the hour picking at my shoe.

And now I'm parked in front of the studio.

I don't want Jordyn to figure out how, you know, pissed I am. And I don't want her to be all awkward either. And I hope Kelly didn't tell her what happened before I ran out of there, or . . . God, what if Jordyn saw it for herself?

I should really find a new job.

I'm startled by a knock. It's Jordyn. She's waving and smiling through the passenger window like nothing happened. So that's how she's going to play it?

All that day, she's so good at pretending, I begin to wonder if I made the whole making-out thing up. She even flirts with a guy right in front of me. Maybe I should just stick with girls like Ali. At least there wouldn't be all these . . . feelings.

When Henry comes in and doesn't say anything about my awkward breakfast with Kelly, I think it's pretty safe to assume she didn't tell either of them. I somehow manage to make it through the day. Then I duck out before Henry or Jordyn are totally finished closing up, claiming I have to be somewhere. But the only place I have to be is away from them.

School is weird. It feels like everyone knows I have these, like, feelings now, and they're all pointing and staring.

I skip lunch to run around the track even though it's thirty-eight degrees out. I notice Coach watching me, but I ignore his impenetrable glare. I need to run. I need to get rid of this shit, this baggage. I still want Jordyn so badly. I can't help it. It's like she forced these feelings into me, then left me without instructions.

I repeat the whole running for lunch routine the next day, and the next. The less I see Jordyn, the faster the feelings will evaporate. Maybe I'll call Ali this weekend. As a bonus, Coach has even stopped blatantly glaring at me.

I'm heading up the hall after gym on Thursday when I see Jordyn for the first time this week. She's not wearing the usual makeup, and she's got on that burnt-orange thermal shirt—the one I vividly remember wanting to rip off her. She's standing in the middle of the hallway staring at me. There are tears streaming down her face. At first I don't understand, but then a large group passes out of the way and I see the whole scene.

Jordyn is cornered. There's Sheila, some of the other cheerleaders, Reece, the quarterback, and Brett. And they're laughing at her. Marcus is there too, but he's not really part of it. He's got his hand on Sheila's shoulder, trying to get her to leave, but then Brett spots me and pushes him out of the way before turning back to Jordyn.

"Where's your usual getup? I miss it. You know, because vampires suck so good," Brett hisses into the side of her neck. She tries to get away from him, but then Reece is there, holding her in place. The girls erupt in laughter. Sheila's distinct laugh rises above the others' and she looks directly at me. Brett grabs the bottom of Jordyn's shirt and starts yanking it up. "Here. We'll help you change back." Jordyn fights it, but she's not strong enough. Especially when Reece gives him a hand. They pull her shirt all the way over her face, trapping her arms over her head, completely exposing her breasts, which are covered by only a sheer lacy bra. The girls laugh harder.

Marcus pulls at Brett's shoulder, trying to make him let go. He says something I can't hear, but it's obvious Brett isn't listening.

I don't even remember the first hit. My hand is throbbing and Brett's on the ground, holding his nose, and Jordyn's on the ground pulling her shirt down, and Reece is beneath me on the ground, holding his jaw.

"You okay?" I ask Jordyn. But I don't hear what she says because Reece's fist meets my jaw. It barely hurts.

"Are you fucking this loser, Tyler?" Brett asks from somewhere behind me. "Way to downgrade, bro."

I run full speed at Brett, knocking him in the stomach with

my shoulder. Then I'm on top of him. Everything's calm around me, like the world's on pause and Brett and I are in slow motion. I slam my fist into his head. His jaw. His eye. Over, and over, and over until I realize he's stopped struggling. Hands are pulling at my arms, my shoulders, my hair. There's blood running down Brett's face and covering my hands. The cheerleaders are looking at me, mouths wide. Marcus and Jordyn look scared.

Next thing I know, I'm sitting in Principal Riggs's office with an icepack on my right hand, which is throbbing something fierce. I'm pretty sure my right ring finger is dislocated. It's hanging at a weird angle. But all I know is the rage I'm still feeling. Marcus is sitting next to me with an icepack on his eye. Apparently I elbowed him as he tried to pry me off of Brett.

My ears ring. I only make out about every other word Riggs says. I catch the gist, though. Something about suspension, something about me being lucky I'm not expelled, something about calling my dad. Fuck.

When Riggs opens the door, still barking at Marcus and me, I exit, keeping my head down. I can't afford to lose it on anyone else.

TWENTY-SEVEN

Jordyn's car is in front of my house when I get home. She's sitting on the front step. No doubt here to rip into me about, what? Take your pick. How I made her the focus of the evil cheerleaders and Brett? How I kicked the shit out of Brett like a total psychopath?

I finally get out of my car. As I get closer, I see that she's crying. "You okay?" I ask. Stupid fucking feelings.

"Honestly?" She won't meet my eyes. I get the sense that she's scared of me. Shit, I'd be scared of me too. "I don't know."

I keep my distance.

"You didn't have to . . . You . . . It totally freaked me out to see you—"

"What? Turn into my dad?"

"Shit. No, Tyler. That's not what I was going to say."

"Wasn't it?"

"Of course not!" She stands. Now she's looking at me. I can tell she wants to say something more.

She spots the icepack tied around my hand and takes a step toward me. Then another. And then she lifts my hand and kisses the tops of my fingers.

I fumble with my keys in my left hand, but she takes them from me and lets me into my house. Then she leads me to the kitchen and removes the icepack. She doesn't flinch when I reach out to wipe her tears, but she still only looks at my hand as she unwraps the bandage the school nurse attempted.

"Oh my god, your finger." She very lightly brushes the most swollen part of my hand. It feels like a truck is slowly rolling over it. "We should go to the emergency room."

I nod. But when she starts to lead me to the front door, I stop. "I can't," I say. "I can't afford it. I'll just . . ." I'll just what? I'll try to put it back into place myself?

"My mom and Henry will take care of it when they hear what you did for me. Not that I'm encouraging that. What you did. Just . . . shut up. Let's go." She looks me in the eyes. Her intensity scares me into submission, so I allow her to drive me to the ER.

Amazingly, I'm in and out in under two hours—X-ray, splint, and all. By some small miracle, nothing was broken. My first two fingers were pretty badly jammed, and the third finger was dislocated. The dislocated finger didn't even hurt that much compared to the pain when they popped the damn thing back in. Luckily they've prescribed a few days' worth of some serious painkillers. Jordyn makes me take them the second the bottle is in hand.

So I'm feeling pretty good when we pull up to my house. Also, a little loose-lipped.

"Dad's gonna beat the shit outta me for this. I'm just gonna have to go back to that nice doctor lady again later."

"What?" She looks alarmed. "Are you being serious, Tyler?"

"Abso-fucking-luteley," I say, struggling with the car door handle and my new splint.

"Tyler, you have to tell someone." She's clearly frustrated.

"I told you. He'll just get worse. Plus, you saw me back there. I can take care of myself."

She watches me, wanting to say something else. About how scared she was—is—of me? About how she's worried I'll kill my dad? But then her expression goes all stubborn and she says, "Well, then I'm staying until he gets here. I'll explain what happened. He can't blame you after he hears the truth."

This completely sobers me up. I turn to her. "You can't stay. I can't get you involved. It'll be fine. I'll avoid him. It's not even that bad. I'm just high from the codeine."

She leans across to open my door. "I'm staying. Let him try to touch one hair on your head without me calling the cops. Come on. You need sleep." She suddenly appears on my side of the car and takes my good hand, leading me into the house. She's still got my keys.

Captain's greeting is somewhat subdued, as if he knows something's wrong. I lean down to pet him. Jordyn gets down and gives him a proper scratch. She's thanked with lots of kisses on her chin.

"Hey, now, don't get frisky with her, Captain. I might lose my shit again."

"Not funny," Jordyn says. "Where's your room?"

I lead her down the stairs and point to the door. "I need you to open it for me. It's the second key from the car key."

"You lock your room?"

"He'd trash it if I didn't."

She puts her hand on my face and I can't stop myself from leaning into it. I close my eyes.

When I open them, she's still looking at me. I lean down to kiss her, half expecting her to pull away, but she kisses me back. It's slow and tentative, like we're both making sure of the other.

When we pull apart, she studies my face. I drop my eyes to the doorknob.

"Are you okay, Tyler?" she asks quietly, unlocking the door. "Like, you know? At Thanksgiving . . ."

I push the door open and motion for her to lead the way down the stairs. After locking it behind me, I take a deep breath and go in, joining her on the edge of the bed.

I take another breath. Then: "Kelly's perfect turkey," I say, "Henry's guitar playing, you . . . That was the best Thanksgiving I've ever had and I felt insanely guilty because, you know, it was the first one without her. I mean . . . God, you have no idea how lucky you are, Jordyn. Your mom and Henry and your dad and even his crazy wife, I think, love you so much, it . . . No one . . . It just hit me that no one will ever love me like that. I'm not even sure my mom ever *did* love me like that. Otherwise why'd she leave me, you know?"

"That's not true." Jordyn turns her whole body toward me and takes my hands. "Your mom loved you, Tyler. She really,

really loved you. I remember. And your dad, as fucked up as he might be, loves you in his own way."

A bitter laugh escapes my throat. "First of all, my dad actually hates me. He tells me on a regular basis, and I know it's not just words. He hates me." I stand. "And if my mom loved me as much as you say, she wouldn't have left me alone with my prick father and no explanation."

"Tyler," she begins, but I stop her with a kiss. Not a hot kind of kiss that would, under normal circumstances, lead to sex, but a kiss that lets her know how much I appreciate her, how much I care about her. I can see that she understands its meaning by the way she pulls me down next to her and looks at me. "Thank you for standing up for me," she whispers against my lips.

"It's you who . . ." I whisper back. "It's you."

We stay like that for a little while, just holding on.

"Why'd you freak out after . . . ?" I ask, somewhat embarrassed.

"Me? You're the one who ran away as fast as you could."

So Kelly didn't tell her about my breakdown. "Well, you basically threw me out. And then I thought maybe you thought it was just a drunken mistake and that you felt sorry for me. And then you ignored me and acted like nothing happened. That killed me, by the way. All this is new to me. I, like, got close to you. And you threw it in my face."

She closes her eyes and seems to shrink, like she knows. "I didn't mean to. I just panicked. I know your reputation and I know I'm so not your type. I guess I kind of went on the defensive before you could hurt me."

"I'll never hurt you," I breathe against her mouth. She kisses me, and it's all that's left in the world at that moment.

"I want to show you something." I lean down to the wood panel and pull out the metal box. Then I remove the key around my neck and hand it to her.

"I always wondered what this was for," she says as she places the key in the lock.

I stop her when she goes to open the lid. "I've never shown anyone this." I'm suddenly very nervous.

She places a hand over mine. A gesture that tells me to take my time, that she gets it.

I pull out the pictures and place them on the bed, side by side. She takes her time examining each one.

"She always seemed so happy," she finally says.

"I know. That's why it's so messed up."

"Tyler . . ."

"It's all I have left of her," I say. "Plus Captain. And this." I place the razor blade on the bed.

I feel her breathing pick up. When I look at her, she has tears in her eyes.

We don't say anything for a very long time. Until Captain whines from outside the room.

"He's probably hungry."

I'm scooping food into Captain's bowl when Jordyn hugs me from behind. I stand there, scoop in hand, and take it all in. Then I notice the clock. It's almost seven.

"You should go. I really don't want you to be here when he gets home."

"I'm staying, Tyler. I won't let him hurt you."

"What scares me more is . . . if he hurts you, I'll kill him."

She can tell I'm dead serious, but it's too late. Dad's footsteps hit the front steps and the door is flung open.

He stops short of screaming when he sees Jordyn. Then he lets out a sharp snort. "You would hide behind a girl."

"Dad—"

"Shut the fuck up. Two weeks? Suspended for two fucking weeks?"

"Dad!"

"Mr. Blackwell, he was—"

"Get. Out," Dad says to Jordyn, his voice barely a whisper, which is so much worse than his yell.

He stares at her and I tense up, preparing for the worst.

"I'm not leaving." She threads her arm through mine. "Tyler promised to help me with my calculus and I'm not going to fail that class because you're too goddamn stubborn to hear his side of the story," she says. Then she takes my good hand and pulls me down the stairs to my room, making sure to lock the door behind her.

I'm too stunned to speak.

I turn to face her and she about passes out in my arms. "Holy shit, he's scary!"

"You're crazy," I say. "And amazing." And brave. So much braver than I am. I should have been the one protecting her, not the other way around.

I kiss her deeply, hoping it'll lessen my shame, which only partially works, because when we part, I feel the hot threat of tears. "No one's ever stood up for me. Not even my mo—"

She kisses me.

Not even me. My shame thunders loudly. I can feel it in my throat, threatening to spill. How can she be so much stronger than I am? I shove my humiliation aside—it's like moving a physical mass—and I melt into her, forgetting about everything today, everything ever, until there's nothing but her.

She holds my head in her lap stroking my hair. We talk about nothing, everything, for hours, until all is quiet upstairs. She can't leave till he's passed out. I don't want her to leave ever.

"I really don't—"

"I'll be fine. I know how to avoid him," I say to Jordyn as I walk her to her car.

She sighs, stopping herself from saying more.

"What?" I tip her chin up so she looks at me.

"I feel like anything is better than living like this. Even a group home." Her eyes drop before she says "group home."

I breathe in, count to three, and let it out. "If that were to happen, my whole life, as fucked up as it may be, would be ripped away from me. And I don't know if I can handle that again. It's bad enough to lose her, but to lose Captain, my home"—I hesitate—"you."

She looks back up at me, frowning, still worried.

"It's only for a few more months. And I'm really good at avoiding him. I've survived seventeen years and eight months. I'll be fine. I promise."

She sighs again, resigned. "I'll let Henry know what happened with the fight and the suspension and the hospital, and tell him to take advantage of your . . . sabbatical, but you have to promise me you'll use your words next time. No fists. Okay?"

I nod.

"Henry and Mom'll be grateful you stood up for me. And I promise, no matter how much I might want to, and no matter how much it makes me feel like a total Lifetime movie girl-friend cliché, I won't tell them about your dad." She's holding my face in her hands again.

"What did I ever do to deserve you?" I say. Then laugh. "I mean, speaking of Lifetime movie clichés."

She smiles sadly. "You deserve everything, Tyler."

TWENTY-EIGHT

Henry calls right away. He tells me how grateful he is that I came to Jordyn's aid and that he'd have probably "killed that little shit." He's also glad to have my help every day of my forced absence. So, thanks to Henry, I'm able to avoid Dad for practically the entire two weeks. Because I'm a coward.

The Saturday before the official start of winter break, I come home from work to feed Captain before heading over to Jordyn's place, a regular thing now. Dad's not home, so I can shower in peace. But when I open my bathroom door, he's in my room, sitting on my bed, his shoulders slumped, staring at the wall.

Shit. I forgot to lock the door.

The music was turned up way too high and I didn't hear him.

I eye the disaster he's created—and it is definitely a disaster—trying not to be obvious when I glance over to the loose panel. But my hiding place is intact.

I towel off as I casually stroll over to the pile of clothes that used to be in my dresser. I can do this. I can face him. I can confront him. I pick out a pair of jeans and some boxers, pulling them on without bothering to shield my nakedness from him. I have a sneaking suspicion my dick is bigger than his.

Sure enough, he turns away, boosting my confidence.

"You want to tell me what the fuck you were looking for?" I say.

He just sits there. I don't even realize what I'm doing when I pull him up from the bed and shove him up against the wall. It's like it's happening to someone else. My forearm pins his neck and I can feel the pressure all the way up my arm. My injured hand should hurt when he tries to pull my arm away from his neck, but I'm too pissed to feel it. His face is red and now I see that he's crying. He refuses to look at me.

"You have no right!" It's like all the shame and fear has suddenly turned into rage. My face is hot and my head is light. "I stay out of your shit. I work hard for mine. It's about time *you* show *me* some fucking respect."

He chokes out a laugh, or maybe it's a sob.

"I hate you." My voice is an intense whisper. My eyes burn. "The wrong parent died. I wish you'd just kill yourself already. You know how many times I've fantasized about that. About coming home to your body swinging from the railing. Yeah, I always picture you hanging because I hear it's a slow, painful death. Once you kick the chair out you start to regret it but it's too late."

He still won't look at me. Which is just as well. I don't want him to think the tears I'm blinking back are anything other than pure rage.

"Now, get. The fuck. Out. Of. My. Room." I let him drop.

Coughing and rubbing his neck, which is an angry shade of pink, he stands and pulls himself together. "You're gonna regret that." His words are threatening but his voice is shaking and he still can't look at me. He grabs the bottle of Jack I hadn't even noticed off my desk and trudges up the stairs. I expect him to slam my door but I don't even hear it close.

I begin to straighten up my room, but I'm just too angry. What gives him the right to invade my space? We're both grieving. Who the hell does he think he is? I abandon my cleanup, pulling my shirt on. I've got to see Jordyn.

Just as my foot hits the bottom stair I hear the most awful yelp from the kitchen. I rush up just in time to witness Dad kicking the shit out of Captain. There's blood everywhere. I have no doubt he has every intention of killing him. The look in his eyes is terrifying. It's inhuman. I reach him as he lands a heavy stomp on Captain's rib cage. I hear snapping just before I throw Dad back into the counter. He makes a move to come at Captain again, but I backhand him with my good hand and he stumbles.

He laughs, spitting at Captain on his way past us up to his room. "You should probably just put that fucking thing out of its misery." His bedroom door slams and I'm left there staring, wondering how the hell this happened. Did I cause this? Captain's nose is bleeding pretty badly. And he's whimpering in pain. He looks like he's been hit by a car. I should've just kept my mouth shut. I'm not sure if there's anything that can be done for him, but I run down to my room and grab all my cash and a towel, lock my door, and then I scoop Captain up.

I have a hard time driving to Jordyn's, I'm shaking so hard. And I can barely breathe. If Captain dies, I swear to god I will kill my father. I honk frantically as I pull up to the house. Jordyn and Kelly come running out.

"What's going on? Did something happen? Are you hurt?" Kelly asks, pulling open the car door.

I manage to choke out, "Captain."

Jordyn understands and rushes to the back window. "Oh my god!" She gets in and cradles Captain's head in her lap.

"I'll meet you there," Kelly calls to Jordyn as she runs back to the house.

"Go!" Jordyn screams.

I do. She calls directions to me as I speed to the place where she volunteers.

"He did this, didn't he?" She's pissed.

I nod. "But it's my fault. I started it."

"It's not your fault. He's a fucking psycho."

"Please don't tell your mom and Henry, Jordyn. Please."

I can see how much she wants to ignore this. But she takes a deep breath. "We'll tell them he got hit by a car."

"Thank you."

The vet rushes Captain into the back and Jordyn follows, leaving me alone in the waiting room. Kelly and Henry run in a few minutes later.

"Are you okay?" Kelly asks, guiding me over to a row of seats.

I'm still shaking. "He got out and someone hit him." The fact that she's asking about me makes me wonder if Jordyn has said something to her. I begin to pull away, but then Kelly sits next to me, putting her arm around my shoulders, and I can't help myself; I turn toward her and let her hold me like my mom used to and I cry.

"Honey, I'm so sorry," she whispers, stroking my head.

"He was my mom's," I manage to get out.

She holds me tighter, rocking me, rubbing my back, and all her mothering suddenly makes me sadder than anything that's happened tonight. Henry sits on my other side and pats my back as I completely come undone.

Finally, after forever, Jordyn comes out. I jump to my feet, somehow finding the energy.

"He's going to be fine," she says, which makes me start crying again. "The X-ray showed six broken ribs and we were afraid his lungs might be punctured or his stomach ruptured because of the bloody nose, but, luckily, it's just a bloody nose. He's going to hurt for a while, but he's going to make it."

I pull her into me and hold her tight, still crying, because there's no more room in me for all the relief.

"I can't take Captain home. He'll kill him," I say as Jordyn drives my car back to her place. Which was a good call because, though I managed to pull myself together, I now feel like every ounce of energy has been drained out of me.

"I'll take care of Captain until you get the hell out of that house."

I look over at her, the red stoplight reflecting off her hair. "I really don't deserve you."

"I wish you'd stop saying that." She turns and kisses me.

I nod.

"You can't stay there tonight."

TWENTY-NINE

Kelly's made some kind of pot roast, and what little I manage to get down is delicious. I just don't feel like eating. At least I'm not wearing my blood-soaked clothes; Kelly insisted on washing them and gave me one of Henry's shirts and some sweatpants that look older than me.

"Can I get you anything else, Tyler?" she asks as she watches me pick at my meal.

"This is absolutely delicious, I promise. I'm just . . ."

"Well, I made plenty. I'll send some home with you for when your appetite returns."

"That's good 'cause Tyler's on his own for the next few weeks," Jordyn says.

I look at her curiously.

"Why's that?" Kelly asks me.

I have no clue.

"His dad's visiting some relatives for the holidays," Jordyn says. "Where'd he go again? Idaho was it?"

"Uh, yeah. Idaho. To see the brother he hasn't spoken to for years. That's why he didn't want me to come along. He's not even sure he'll be welcome. His sister-in-law set it up as a surprise," I ramble.

Jordyn nudges me with her leg under the table. I rest my hand on her knee.

"Maybe you should stay with us for a few weeks," Kelly offers. "I won't have you spending the holidays alone. Especially for your first Christmas . . ." Sounding a little choked up, she stops herself. It's the first time I haven't been annoyed with someone unable to finish that thought. It's like, it's not about not being able to say it because it's awkward, but because it hurts her the way it hurts me.

"I think that's a great idea," Henry says, laying a hand on her back.

"It's very nice of you to offer, but I don't want to intrude."

"I insist." Kelly blinks rapidly and looks down at her plate.

"You know we have four guest rooms, right?" Henry grins, lightening the mood.

"You can get your things tomorrow. But you're staying tonight. That way I won't have to worry about you driving in this mess." Kelly gestures toward the window. It's snowing pretty heavily. I hadn't even noticed.

I don't really have much of a choice. Kelly has made up her mind and that's that.

Jordyn squeezes my hand under the table. I squeeze back.

"Thank you," I say. To all of them.

"So it's settled." Kelly takes another bite of potato.

Part of me wonders if her insistence isn't necessarily because she buys the bullshit story, but because on some level she knows what's really going on, or that maybe Jordyn told her, but that's probably in my head.

After helping Kelly clean up—she tried to shoo me away, but I insisted—Jordyn and I head down to the basement to watch TV. I can't focus, though. What's going to happen when I have to see Dad? I keep replaying the way he looked when he was kicking Captain and wondering if that's how I looked with Brett, if—

"You okay?" Jordyn asks.

I shrug.

She takes my bad hand and kisses it. "He'll be fine. We can bring him here tomorrow. He'll need pain pills, but that's about it."

I nod. But now my mind isn't on Captain or my dad. There's a goddamn jewelry commercial on where the kids give their mom a necklace for the holidays and she cries and everyone is so fucking happy. I want to throw something.

Jordyn follows my gaze and gets it. She crawls closer and curls into me. She doesn't say anything. And I love her for it.

After another half hour of *A Christmas Story*, I finally speak. "I guess it didn't really hit me until your mom . . ." I trail off.

"At least you'll be with people who care about you. Your dad can screw himself."

I kiss her temple, and then she's kissing me, and nothing else matters.

Jordyn begged to come with me to get my stuff, but is she crazy? I don't want her anywhere near Dad after what he did to Captain. If he's realized he can get to me by hurting my dog, who's to say he won't move on to hurting the people I love? I can't chance it.

Of course, Jordyn didn't listen. I saw her following me about four turns back, and now she's parked several houses away. At least Dad's car isn't in the driveway.

I walk toward her and gesture for her to open the window.

"Don't come in, but if you see him come home, start honking." I turn away without waiting. This is how she can help me; hopefully it'll keep her out of the house.

I see Dad didn't bother cleaning up Captain's blood. There's a small, coagulated pool amidst a mass of dark red flecks next to the kitchen table. I hope it stains the tile grout like Mom's did.

When I round the corner to my room, I slow, seeing that my door's open and the lock looks like it's been blown apart by a mini stick of dynamite. My heart freezes in my chest. I run down the stairs. My hiding place is still intact, but I rush to open the metal box, making sure all the contents are still there.

They are. I sit back on my heels.

My things are all strewn around the room in even more chaos than before. What the hell is he looking for? Money? Drugs? Booze? As if I have any of those things.

I grab a duffel bag from the storage room and start shoving things into it. When I reach for some jeans atop a pile of clothes, the distinct stench of urine hits me. I drop the pants. Seriously? He *pissed* on my stuff? Who does that? I tear off a garbage bag and stuff the pee-soaked things into it. What a prick.

I pack everything I don't want ruined by Dad marking his territory again, then grab my metal box, and throw the duffel over my shoulder. With the garbage bag under my arm, I rush up the stairs. I have half a mind to retaliate. But *I'm* not a god-damn animal. I couldn't get myself to pee on someone else's stuff for anything.

I don't bother locking the front door, just stride quickly to my car. I hope someone breaks in and steals all his shit. Would serve him right.

Jordyn flips a bitch so she's right behind me the whole way back to her place.

"Open the trunk," she says as I pull my bag from the back-seat.

"Why? You worried I killed my dad and shoved his body in the trunk?"

"I'm offering to help you carry your stuff in, dumb-ass," she laughs.

"Funny story . . ." And I proceed to tell her about the state of my belongings in the trunk.

"Who does that?" she says as we step through the door.

"My dad. That's who."

"That's seriously messed up."

"Welcome to my world."

There's no way Kelly and Henry can know about my pee-soaked clothes. So after finally finding a Laundromat about twenty minutes away—no one would be caught dead in a Laundromat in our pristine little suburb—and washing my things twice for good measure, Jordyn insists on driving to pick up Captain, which is fine by me. I want to be able to hold him. He's still pretty drugged, but his tail thumps slowly against the ground when he sees me. My eyes get hot and I blink furiously.

The vet helps us load him into the backseat next to me, and then she hands Jordyn a bag of stuff—pills and bandages. She offers me a sympathetic smile before turning back to Jordyn. I hear her say it'll be a few more days until he's able to stand up on his own but he'll probably still hurt too much to move. Then she says something about the possibility that he could still go into shock and die and to check for white gums and I have to stop listening.

After dinner with Kelly and Henry, Jordyn flops down on my temporary bed and watches me unpack my stuff.

She brushes the metal box with the tips of her fingers. "May I?"

I abandon my task and join her on the bed. Unlocking the box with the key around my neck.

She lays the pictures side by side in front of her and studies them. "I love this one." She picks up the one of the two of us on the couch. "Look how happy you guys are. God, you look so much like her."

"That was only a week or so before."

She carefully picks up the razor and turns it over in her hands, searching my face. I can tell she wants to know everything. She wants to understand. That makes two of us. Still, I try.

"I was at football training," I say. "I mean, I was always at football—practice or camp or a game or hanging out with the guys or whatever. Football got me out of the house, away from my dad. But I was at training. It was so damn hot that week. Unusually hot for June. My socks were soaked through so bad, I could feel the sweat sloshing around in my shoes. I remember my knee was kind of acting up. Coach was pushing me extra hard.

"So I slipped out to head home and grab my knee brace and some fresh socks and Advil while I was at it. I was out of Advil, so I went up to my parents' bathroom to swipe some of theirs. I was so focused that I didn't see her at first. When I turned to leave, that's when I saw her in the tub. I immediately shielded my eyes because who wants to see their mom naked, but it was like I just knew something wasn't right and I had to look. My brain took forever to process what I was seeing. I didn't understand why she didn't wake up when I slammed the medicine cabinet. I didn't understand why the water was pink. I didn't understand why her skin was so white.

"When my brain finally figured out what was happening, I threw myself at her. I pulled her up out of the bath, slipping and falling. I was on the ground. She was on the ground, like half in the bath. I held her in my arms, trying to press my hands over the wounds and dial 911 all at the same time. But it was already too late."

Jordyn is completely still for a second, then she takes my hand and lightly touches her lips to the tops of my fingers.

"She was still warm. I wonder if I'd gone up to get the Advil first, if I'd have been able to help her. Or if I'd been home five minutes earlier, would I have been able to stop her?"

Jordyn brushes her cool hand across my cheek.

"I threw up. After I called 911, I vomited. My mom was dead in my arms and I vomited all over her," I say, my voice cracking. "What kind of reaction is that?"

She pulls me into her and wraps her arms around me.

We stay like that for a while.

Then all of a sudden my mouth is on hers. Her hands are under my shirt. Then my shirt's off. And then *her* shirt's off and my hands are on her smooth back. She's pulling me down on the bed, on top of her. And before I know it we're making love. I've always hated that term, "making love." I mean, it sounds gross, right? But there's no better way to accurately describe what we're doing. It's slow and it's intense and I'm reveling in every moment, every touch, every sound. I want to consume her. I can't touch or taste or feel her enough. My heart beats in rhythm to our rocking bodies. I focus on the sensation of her cheek brushing lightly against mine, the way her legs wrap around me, the taste of her neck on my tongue. And the connectedness—her eyes, the look in them. This isn't just physical; I mean, the physical is beyond anything I've experienced, but it's so much more than that.

It's not until after we finish that I realize the magnitude of what's occurred. I've just had sex with someone I'm pretty sure I'm in love with.

THIRTY

I wake up curled into Jordyn. Early morning sunlight streaks across the mess of Mom's photos on the floor. I pull myself out of Jordyn's arms and slip down to gather them up and place them back in their home with the razor. I pause as I'm about to lock the metal box. There's really no need to lock it or even hide it. In this house it's safe from anyone trying to destroy its secrets.

I stand next to the bed and look at Jordyn, the way the sheet's barely covering one of her perfect naked breasts and her shiny black hair is fanned out over the pillow. She looks so peaceful, so content. I, on the other hand, look awful, as I soon discover in the bathroom mirror. My eyes are sunken, my cheekbones sharp. I'm way too thin. I don't even look like me.

When I return from the bathroom, Jordyn's awake.

"Hey." She pats the bed next to her.

I sit down and she wraps her arms around my waist, curling into me. Her hair smells like jasmine. I breathe her in. This is the first time I've ever had sex with a girl and stuck around for any significant amount of time after, let alone the whole night. And yet it feels like the most comfortable thing in the world.

We both have to work at the studio today, so I don't get to enjoy it for very long. Or anything else that might come of sitting in bed naked together.

After work, Jordyn and I decide to grab something to eat—Jordyn's treat—to give Henry and Kelly some alone time. They're not around when we get home, though both of their cars are in the garage. I don't even want to think about what they're probably doing.

Jordyn seems to have the same thought, because as soon as we get down to the basement, she says, "Gross, right?"

I laugh.

We settle on the couch and flip through channels until I stop on an old episode of *Friday Night Lights*.

"So what's going on with Stanford? Have you checked or anything since—"

"What's the point?" I say, sighing.

She pulls herself out from under my arm and turns to face me. "The point, Tyler, is so you can make something of yourself and get as far away from your prick father as you can. I know you could do something amazing if you had half a mind to."

"How are you so sure? And anyway, I'm not playing this year—they've probably pulled my scholarship alre—"

"It's called financial aid. I mean, look at your grades. They can't *only* be interested in you because of football."

"Trust me, they can. And . . . I don't know. What's the point? What if I just end up giving up, like . . ." I trail off. I didn't mean to say that out loud.

She leans in so I'm forced to look her in the eyes. "You're not like her."

"You don't know that."

"Tyler, you're stronger than she is. You will get yourself out of a situation that makes you feel you don't have a choice before you ever get to that point."

I stare at the TV, not really seeing it.

She squeezes my leg. "You miss it, don't you?"

"What?" I practically whisper because I know.

"Football, stupid."

I'm not sure how, but she's managed to make me smile.

"Well?"

"I guess I do. Sometimes. But whatever. It kept me from her when she needed me."

"I get that. But you know it has nothing to do with what happened, right? I mean, you do know it wasn't your fault. Or football's. Don't you?"

I shrug.

"Tyler, look at me."

I do.

"It. Was *not*. Your. Fault."

I nod. But it still feels like it was partly my fault.

"I just can't understand why she thought it was the only way out," I say.

"I never understand why people think dying is a way out at

all. I mean, you're dead. There's nothing else. You're just dead. Why would anyone think that's better than . . . something else? *Anything* else? I don't understand how they're afraid, or whatever, of anything more than they're afraid of dying. Or maybe they're *not* afraid of dying, and I *really* don't understand that."

"'Cowards die many times before their deaths; the valiant never taste of death but once. Of all the wonders that I yet have heard, it seems to me most strange that men should fear; seeing that death, a necessary end, will come when it will come.'"

Jordyn stares at me.

"*Julius Caesar*," I say. "I don't know. Maybe my mom felt like a coward, dying every time my dad . . . And maybe that time— Maybe that was her valiant necessary end."

Jordyn leans over and kisses me hard. "But it's not *your* necessary end. You have options, Mr. Shakespeare-quoting-smarty-pants."

I crack a small smile.

"Maybe your mom didn't feel like she did, but you do."

Maybe I do have options. At least, more than this. For the first time since Mom died, I actually feel . . . hope. And it's scary as shit.

I'm in the middle of a dream that has something to do with playing a football game inside the school, like in the hallways, and Coach is yelling at me, and for some reason I can't remember how to run. And then Marcus hands me the ball and I *kiss* it, but now it's Jordyn.

It's only then that I realize the kissing is actually happening.

Jordyn has crawled into my bed and she's kissing me. Then she curls up into the crook of my arm. I run my fingers through her hair. The small red streak of hair is peeking out from underneath and I curl it around my finger. I love the way she feels. I love the way she smells. I love the way she looks at me.

"I love you," I say. I don't even register I've said it until she smiles wider than I ever thought her capable of. I want to take it back, but then I realize, no, I don't. I've never said those words out loud to anyone that I can remember. Not even Mom—well, except when I was really little—for some reason we just didn't say it. I've only ever spoken those words to Captain. It's terrifying. And exciting. And terrifying. I'm holding my breath.

"I love you too." She brushes her lips to mine and then rolls us so I'm on top of her and she reaches for a condom.

My heart has exploded inside my chest. I'm probably dying right this very second. I can feel the warmth radiating from the center of my rib cage. But I can't stop smiling. Who knew those four little words from her lips could actually kill me? I didn't know death could feel this good. I didn't know I could die from happiness.

"Tyler's going to Stanford," Jordyn announces over coffee and blueberry pancakes.

I drop my fork into my syrupy plate.

"That's great. Congratulations. You were always a smart kid, I just didn't realize you were *Stanford* smart," Kelly says as she raises a steaming cup to her lips.

My ears are as hot as the coffee in my cup.

"He's in all AP classes. What's your GPA again?" Jordyn asks.

"Um. Around four point three, I think." I lick the maple syrup off the end of my fork and dig back into the pancakes.

"Not bad. What'd you get on the SAT?" Henry asks. He suddenly seems very interested in this topic of conversation.

I haven't shared that score with anyone except Mom and Coach. Dr. Dave knows—he's seen my file. But we've never talked about it directly. It feels so braggy.

Jordyn nudges me under the table.

"Twenty-three forty," I say into my plate.

"Shut up!" Jordyn slaps my arm. "What about the ACT?"

"Thirty-four."

Henry and Kelly are staring at me like they've invited some strange creature to breakfast and they're only just figuring out it's not human.

"I knew you were smart, but . . ." Jordyn says with a look on her face not unlike her parents'.

"Stanford is lucky to have you, son." Henry raises his cup to me and then puts it to his lips. The disgusting slurping sound sort of ruins the effect, but I expect nothing less from Henry.

"And Jordyn's only just getting her applications ready," Kelly says. "I would blame Aslan for the procrastination gene, but I think we all know she gets it from me. Maybe you can help her out, Tyler."

Jordyn bats her eyelashes, making me love her even more.

o o o

By Christmas Eve my hand is completely back to normal and Captain is able to get around on his own. Now he gets to sleep on a giant plush bed Kelly bought for him that sits in the corner of my room. Which is good for when all the relatives come. Kids seem to have a short memory when it comes to instructions, and we don't want them hurting Captain or, worse, have him bite someone because he's being hurt. So he gets to spend Christmas in my temporary room. He doesn't seem to mind.

Christmas Eve dinner is nothing short of an event at the Smith-Franks's house. All the same people who were at Thanksgiving show up and most of them stay the night. The couches are littered with small children vying for sleeping space, while the adults take the guest rooms. The meal is every bit as delicious as Thanksgiving. And I don't even like ham. I don't know how Kelly does it. She should have her own restaurant or something.

After the big meal, we all gather by the giant fire and Henry plays the guitar again. And again Kelly forces wine on everyone, I think so she's not the only one getting sloshed. The main difference between Christmas and Thanksgiving is that Jordyn doesn't hide her affection for me. She sits on my lap and boldly kisses me in front of everyone. All the young cousins "ew" and all the adults tease us. They also give Henry and Kelly a hard time for letting me stay in the house. "I hope you're keeping an eye on Jordyn's door to make sure there's no funny business going on right under your nose," Patricia teases.

My face is the temperature of the fire and I'm sure it's much redder than Jordyn's is.

Henry and Kelly exchange a look that says they're completely aware that we're having sex right under their noses. Then they laugh and kiss.

What is even happening?

Jordyn snuggles up to my ear and whispers, "Mom knows, and I imagine she told Henry. They're fine as long as we're, you know, being safe. They'd rather we do it here than in the back of one of our cars or something."

I wish the floor would open up and swallow me. I can't look at Henry or Kelly ever again. I will have to find a new job now. I will have to move and change my name and start a new life as Stuart Longfellow. Somewhere Henry and Aslan—oh, god, Aslan. I can't even glance in his direction—can never find me.

Jordyn is giggling on my lap and I want to be like, "What is wrong with you?" but, thankfully, someone's changed the subject to one of the cousins starting private school.

"You're not mad, are you?" Jordyn says into my neck.

I turn to face her with a tight smile. "You're lucky I love you. Where's your dad right now? Is he looking at me?"

She laughs and kisses me again. "Don't worry. He's totally oblivious."

At least there's that. Not that I'm all that afraid of Aslan, but he strikes me as the kind of guy who has moves you don't expect, like castrating the daughter's boyfriend with one easy flick of his wrist.

The days after Christmas are spent helping Jordyn fill out forms and writing essays and organizing her portfolio. My favorite is how she uses photographs she's taken of things so close up they're unrecognizable and draws from the texture to paint something that incorporates the photo. It's unlike anything I've ever seen before, not that I'm so well-versed. Watching her get lost in a piece . . . it's like when an entire practice day felt like about ten minutes. I wonder if I'll ever have that again. And then I realize, like whiplash, why the hell can't I?

After working up the nerve for a few days, I finally run the idea by Jordyn of writing Stanford a letter explaining my situation, and when I do, she literally jumps up and down. At first I thought it was gross to play the sympathy card like that, but then I started writing and I realized I wasn't bullshitting. I want this. Like, really want it. It's like Jordyn said, I have choices. I choose to do something.

I hesitate before dropping the letter to Stanford in the mailbox, but Jordyn snatches it out of my hand and drops it in before I can change my mind. Then she kisses me deeply right there in front of the post office and I'm not even fazed by the public make-out.

And then the worst thing happens: Winter break comes to an end.

THIRTY-ONE

Jordyn helps me come up with a story that'll keep Captain at her house for the rest of the school year. I know she really wants me to tell her parents the truth. I know she hopes they'll offer to let me stay too. But if I stay much longer, Dad will figure things out, and he could do something to any of them.

"So we'll call the cops and he'll go to jail and then you'll be safe," Jordyn says, after I explain my reasoning for the four hundredth time.

"You don't get it," I snap. This conversation is wearing on my nerves. I know she means well, but she doesn't know my dad. I take a breath, calming down. "Sorry. I didn't mean to—"

"I know. And I know you're afraid—"

"Of course I'm afraid. He will *hurt* you."

"I think you're wrong."

"Look what he did to Captain!"

"That's my point exactly!" Jordyn's losing patience too.

"I can take care of myself. But if I have to worry about you or Kelly or Henry, even, I won't be able to function."

"How do you think *I* feel knowing he's going to hurt *you*?"

"That's different." I pace to the window, trying not to seriously lose it.

"How?"

Silence.

Jordyn sighs and I hear her lie back on her bed.

"What?" I say.

"I'm afraid to say anything else."

I shoot her a "spit it out" look.

She rolls onto her side, propping her head up with her hand. "What if my mom became, like, your legal guardian or something?"

"Jordyn, I—" I sigh, turning back to the window. "Can we please stop fighting about this?"

She doesn't want to let it go, I can tell, but she does. For now.

Our—well, Jordyn's cover story for Captain involves him having to climb down too many stairs to reach my backyard. It's not true, and if Kelly were to come over for any reason, she'd clearly see why, but it works for now. Kelly insists he stay with them. Also, she's home all day and loves having him to dote on. She's really getting attached. Sure, it makes me a little jealous when Captain occasionally runs to greet her before he greets me, but I know he's so much better off here.

As for me, I have to find an adequate lock to keep Dad out now that he's destroyed mine. Also, a new door. Jordyn and I scour the Internet trying to locate the best lock for the job. It's her treat. She's insisted. It's my Christmas present, even though all I was able to get her was a set of charcoals I saw her eyeing and then she got all distracted and forgot to buy them. She went crazy when she opened it. She was impressed that I remembered.

The lock and door are, like, two hundred times more expensive, but she has absolutely insisted on helping to keep me and the rest of my things safe.

We found the perfect lock and she's having it installed today along with a solid wood door. We're on our way to meet the guy. I just hope Dad didn't choose today to stay home from work.

Thankfully, his car is gone when we pull into the driveway, because there's a white van waiting out front.

Max, the guy Jordyn called to install the lock, strides over and gives Jordyn a hug.

"Max is one of Henry's fishing buddies. He did the locks at the studio," she says after introducing us.

Max wastes no time getting to work. He lets out a low whistle when he sees the damage done to my previous lock and door, but doesn't say a word.

Jordyn and I sit at the kitchen table and I mostly stare at the front door just in case Dad walks in for some reason. Well, that and the red-stained grout on the tile next to my foot.

"He's not going to tell Henry about this, is he?" I whisper.

"I told him you had a break-in and they only went for your room. I told him we think it was one of the guys you got into a fight with trying to retaliate."

I brush her hair behind her ear, caressing her cheek with my thumb. "Thank you."

Max is done in a little less than two hours. "Give me your phone." He holds out his palm.

Jordyn digs it out of my pocket and places it in his hand while I try to figure out why the hell he needs my phone. He tap-tap-taps and hands it back to me with a new icon on it.

"Tap there."

I do.

A screen comes up that reads: *User: One. Name: Tyler Blackwell. Access: Unlimited.*

"This shows that you are the only person able to access this lock. Ever. Now I'll just program a spare key in the event that you lose that one and be on my way."

I nod. He takes another key from the box the lock came in as well as my phone, then he taps around some more before handing both back to me.

"If anyone tries to jimmy it, you'll get an alert on your phone and the lock'll shut down, so it is virtually impossible to open without your master key. And this door should hold, good choice. It's not a steel door, but I think nothing short of an ax will go through this bad boy. You should be all set. I programmed my number in your phone so if anything happens, call me and I'll talk you through it." He hands me a thick manual.

"Thanks, Max." Jordyn throws her arms around his neck and kisses his cheek.

He laughs. "You got some girl here," he says to me.

"Don't I know it." I shake his hand. "Thanks, man."

"Let's celebrate." Jordyn takes my hand and suggestively pulls me down to my dungeon as soon as Max is on his way. But the mood is killed when she sees the damage Dad's done to my room. "Oh my god."

"It wasn't this bad before I left."

Along with all the contents of my shelves and drawers scattered all around the room, there are now two holes punched in the drywall above the paneling. And the paneling has been kicked and crushed in in several spots.

"Tyler . . ."

"It's all cosmetic. Don't worry about it." I can see the fright clear on her face. "I'll be fine. I promise. I just wish I knew what the hell he's looking for."

"So, what'd you get me?" Dad's on the couch when I get home from school the first day after winter break. His tone lacks its usual disdain. "Or did you not feel the need to get a Christmas present for your only parent."

I head to the fridge, ignoring him. Why is he home, anyway? Then he starts coughing violently and I realize he's sick again. Good. I hope he dies.

"Throw me a beer, wouldja?"

Of course, he's never sick enough not to drink.

When I throw him a beer he actually says "Thanks."

I pull out my phone and start texting Jordyn while I wait for the pan to heat up.

"Where'd that fancy door come from?" Dad sets the opened beer on the coffee table before slowly trudging up the stairs into the kitchen.

"It was a gift," I say, stuffing my phone back into my pocket. "Want me to make some soup?"

He launches into a coughing fit, not bothering to cover his mouth. "I don't need soup. I need whisky."

Yeah, that'll help.

He reaches out and gently pats me on the shoulder—the way Henry does—as he passes me to get to the cabinet above the fridge. It completely freaks me out. Did he actually miss me or something? I watch him struggle to get the bottle down, too stunned to say anything. I turn back to my cooking before he sees me staring.

"I'm short a bottle of vodka. You wouldn't know anything about that, would you?" He's standing right behind me at the stove. So close that when he coughs I feel something hot and wet hit my neck.

"I haven't exactly been here, not that you'd notice," I say under my breath.

"I noticed." He says this like it hurt his feelings or something. "So, that dog okay or what? I didn't mean to . . . I'm . . . I don't know how you're able to keep going like you do. Got that from her, I guess. Or, well, maybe not. Definitely didn't get it from me, though. Anyway, I like Captain, he's a good dog."

"Well, he died," I snap.

He's very still for a moment. I can't even hear him breathing. Then he puts his hand on my shoulder and starts crying.

"Shit. I'm . . . Shit, Tyler. I'm so . . . I'm—"

I can't do this. I turn the stove off and throw the pan in the sink, chicken and all.

I call Jordyn as soon as I get into my car. I tell her everything. I tell her how I made him feel guilty and how he sort of apologized and how it only made me angrier. She tells me to come to the studio until he's passed out. I pick up some burgers for us on the way. Then I spend the rest of the night hanging out with Jordyn and Henry. But instead of working, I do my homework.

"Are you , , , ?" Jordyn feels my forehead with the back of her hand. "Are you feeling okay? Because I'm pretty sure that's . . . homework. And you're, like, applying yourself."

I grin back at her. "What can I say? I actually found this assignment interesting."

She shoves my hand out of the way to further investigate. "Yep. Definitely sick. Nobody actually finds calc interesting."

"AP calc," I say, shoving her aside playfully. "And I do find it interesting."

"Freak." She kisses my cheek.

"Love you," I call out as she bounces through the curtain.

And I actually do find it interesting. In fact, I enjoy all of my classes this semester. I don't have Mrs. Hickenlooper anymore, so that in itself is a reason to enjoy school again.

Before long, I find myself falling back into my old groove. Almost like I was before I found Mom in the tub. Some of my teachers comment on it, but in a delicate way. And it doesn't even bother me. Not even when Mrs. Ortiz stops me in the hall to tell me she's so happy to see me smiling. And it makes me wonder . . . Shit, maybe she actually did want to help me and just didn't know how. Like Sheila.

How many other people did too?

THIRTY-TWO

Dr. Dave is speechless. And all I did was tell him what I did over break.

"So I guess I'm, like, cured or whatever?" I joke.

"I'm really impressed. I think I need to meet this Jordyn."

"I can't believe I'm in love. Like, honest-to-god in love, Doc."

He laughs. "So are you thinking again about going to Stanford?"

"If they still want me." I wipe my hands on my jeans.

"I think writing that letter to the admissions department was a really good call. I don't think you have any reason to be nervous."

"Jordyn really encouraged me with that, you know. I don't know that I would have actually been able to mail it if it weren't for her."

He leans forward in a mock-serious manner. "Are you sure she's a real person? Do other people see her, or does she only appear to you?"

"She's not a hallucination. And if she is, I don't wanna be cured."

Dr. Dave smiles. "We should all be so lucky. So what did your dad have to say about you spending the holidays away from him?"

"He didn't care. He actually broke into my locked room and destroyed it. Even pissed on some of my stuff in a drunken stupor."

Dr. Dave's eyes go wide and I realize I've slipped up. I swore I'd never let him know about Dad. Because then he has to report it. Shit.

"It wasn't that big a deal," I say, all casual. "He didn't really destroy it—he just went through my drawers. I think he was checking for drugs or something. And he only pissed on some clothes I left on the bathroom floor. He has bad aim when he's been drinking."

Dr. Dave's not buying it. "Is this typical behavior for him?"

"Not at all," I lie, rather convincingly, I think.

He scribbles something in his little book.

I crane my neck to see what. No luck. "In all fairness, I shouldn't say he didn't care I was gone for the holidays. He did kind of admit that he missed me. We even bonded over dinner that night." A slight exaggeration.

"You always keep your room locked?"

"I don't want him finding my porn stash." Not that I have a porn stash. I mean, who needs that with the Internet?

Dr. Dave scribbles something else down.

He's not buying a word I'm saying.

"Doc?" I ask, hoping he'll look up from his frantic writing. He doesn't.

"What aren't you telling me about your father, Tyler? I can't help you unless you're honest with—"

"Nothing. He's just a dick."

"Why do you really keep your door locked? Are you afraid of hi—"

"Of course not. I just want my own space. A place that isn't his or Mom's."

"Are you hiding something?"

"I told you about the pictures of Mom and what he'd do if he found them." I'm getting angry. I really don't want to talk about this. How the hell did I screw up like that?

"You're positive that's all it is?"

"Yes!" I snap.

"Okay." He holds his hands up.

I seriously need to change the subject. I take a deep breath before speaking again. "I'm thinking about asking Coach for advice on the whole Stanford thing. You think that's a good idea? I mean, I think he's probably still mad, but I kind of miss football and I'd like to apologize to him for leaving the team in the lurch."

This does the trick. Dr. Dave eyes me warily, but then he sees I'm not bullshitting. "I think that's a very good idea."

"Yeah? I wasn't sure. I mean . . ." I trail off, stopping myself.

Dr. Dave can tell I'm on the verge of letting him in. He's trying so hard not to push me—I can see it all over his face—that I even kind of want to.

"I didn't realize I missed football so much, but I do. I really do. And I was thinking the other day . . . Well . . . I can't keep blaming football for keeping me from being there for my mom. She probably would've killed herself either way, right?" I'm not asking him to confirm.

He sets his notebook down and leans forward until I look at him. His smile is a mixture of elation and pride.

I have to look away. "It wasn't because of football that I missed the signs. That was all on me. It was my fault for pulling away. For not wanting to see what was happening. What it was doing to her."

"No, Tyler."

I look up. The smile's gone from his face.

"It was! I, of all people, knew how helpless and hopeless he could make you feel. I knew she was in pain. I knew she hated him and she was afraid of him and she loved him and she blamed herself for the way he . . . I knew all that. I just didn't want to deal."

"Tyler, look at me," Dr. Daye says in a way that makes me do it. "It wasn't your fault. Not one bit of it. You understand? You should never have been put in a situation that made you feel responsible for either one of your parents. They are your *parents*. They are not your responsibility. *You* are *theirs*. Okay?"

I nod because I think that's what he wants me to do.

"Good," he says, sliding a box of Kleenex my way even though I'm not crying. "Now, when you say she was afraid of him and that you knew how that felt . . ."

Shit. I tune out the rest of his question, desperately searching for a way off of this topic. "Look, my dad is a master manipulator," I finally say. It's not a lie.

"Meaning?"

"He knows how to word things in a way that will cause the most harm. He hits below the belt. He likes to remind you that you are not better than him," I say. "That's why I don't talk about him. I don't want to give him any more thought than is absolutely necessary."

"Does he—"

"I'm done talking about him." I sit up taller, making it absolutely clear that I will leave.

"Okay," he says, conceding.

It's tense in here now. I eye the door while Dr. Dave arranges his notebook on the coffee table, aligning it just so with the edge of the wood. Finally, he speaks.

"I'm proud of you for writing that letter to Stanford. They'd be crazy not to have you. I mean that, Tyler."

He does mean it too. And it feels so good that he believes that about me that I stop hating him and breathe a sigh of relief. That was too close.

Coach is completely caught off guard when I wander into his office.

"Blackwell. What do you want?" He makes himself busy even though I know he was probably just playing online poker.

"Do you have a minute?" I ask, gesturing to the empty chair across from him.

He grunts. I take that as a yes and sit.

"First of all, I'd like to apologize. For everything. For abandoning the team, for fighting with Brett. And Reece. And just being an all-around asshole this year."

He's stopped pretending to be busy and is now completely focused, taking his reading glasses off to stare at me. I can see the wheels turning. When he settles back into his chair, I take that as a sign to continue.

"This is kind of hard for me." I clear my throat. "I've been talking to a therapist since . . ."

He nods.

"Well, I guess I kind of blamed myself and football and, well, you by proxy, for keeping me from being there to help my mom. Not just on that day. On all the days. Like, I was using football to . . . to hide from her, from the situation, and had been for a while. I know it's not rational, but there you go. It took me a very long time to realize she would have found a way whether I was at training or not. It took me even longer to realize how much I missed playing."

Coach nods again.

"I don't know how much Marcus told you about my financial situation, but—"

"He said your dad was making you work."

"He wasn't making me work. He just wasn't paying for anything for me anymore. And that included shoes, clothes, my phone bill. I really didn't have a choice. But yeah, I used it as an excuse to keep my distance too."

"I wish you would've come to me. I might've been able to

help." He's dropped his usually gruff front. I find it discon-
certing.

"I appreciate that. But I just wasn't ready. I'm sorry if I
fucked up your record by not playing this year."

"Language."

"Sorry."

"And apology accepted." He extends his hand over the desk.

I have to get up to reach it. I sit back down. "I know I'm not
in any position to ask a favor, but . . ."

"Ask away."

I pull out a copy of the letter I sent to Stanford and set it on
top of the papers that cover his desk. "I sent this to Mr. Barker
at Stanford. I haven't heard anything from them about what's
going to happen now that I missed playing this year. I was hoping"—I take a deep breath—"I was hoping you might be able
to make a call for me?"

He takes the letter and shushes me as he searches for his
glasses, which have managed to somehow bury themselves
under the mess in the two seconds he's had them off. Then he
leans back in his chair and reads.

I start to leave, thinking we're done, but he snaps his fingers
at me and I sit back in my seat. It's so awkward, having him
read something so personal right in front of me. He flips the
page. I stare at all the stuff he has hanging haphazardly all over
his walls. Mostly inspirational quotes from various famous
players over a photo of them mid-game. Plays scratched on
papers with frayed edges. Photos of the team from the past ten
or so years. I study the ones I'm in. When I was a freshman—

so scrawny and cocky, I have to laugh to myself. I look like a complete tool. The sophomore picture isn't much better. But the picture from last year is pretty decent. I've lost the chip on my shoulder; I'm even smiling. If I didn't know myself, I'd say that kid loves football.

Coach clears his throat. I bet he's at the part in the letter where I explain how I felt responsible for Mom's death. It got Henry too.

He finishes a few minutes later and sets the letter back on the desk.

After a very long pause he finally looks at me. "Tyler, I think I owe you an apology. I had no idea any of this was going on in that head of yours. I should have tried harder to get through to you."

I wave him off.

"No, really, I knew what a great kid you were and I feel like I've failed you."

"You didn't fail me. Even if you'd offered to help, I wouldn't have let you."

"You know . . . your mom . . . Uh, you know it wasn't your fault, right?" He's having a hard time looking at me now.

"I do now. I mean, I'm getting there."

He pulls himself up from his desk and lopes over to me. Grabbing my shoulders, he pulls me up into an intense bear hug. I pat his back.

"I'm going to call Barker first thing tomorrow morning. If they don't take you after that letter, fuck 'em. We'll find you a college that will."

"Language." I laugh as he pounds my back hard enough to leave a red handprint.

"Sometimes there's just not a better word."

Coach checks in with me every day. He hasn't been able to reach Mr. Barker at Stanford yet, but it is now his mission in life. And it takes close to a month for him to complete it. I'm in the middle of a creative writing exercise when Mrs. Ortiz pokes her head in. She waves a yellow slip of paper at Mr. Craig and says, "I need Tyler Blackwell."

I follow her out into the hall and she hands me the slip. "Coach Millikan wants to see you."

I snatch the yellow hall pass from her and sprint toward the gym and Coach's office.

I brace myself for bad news.

I knock.

Nothing.

I try the handle. It's open, but Coach isn't here. I decide to wait, but I'm too nervous to sit, so I pace the length of the room, stepping around piles of books and papers. Someone should really help this guy get organized.

"Well, Blackwell," he says, showing up in the doorway behind me, and trying to play coy but failing miserably.

I throw myself at him and hug him as tight as I've ever hugged another man. I even pick him up off the floor for good measure.

"Are you serious?" I ask.

He nods proudly. I go back in for another hug.

Once we've both collected ourselves, he tells me that Barker got my letter and was extremely impressed with my honesty and they'd be glad to have me. And that the scholarship is still on the table.

"They're even considering starting you for starting running back."

Now I'm speechless.

"You're going to have to start hitting some weights. Get some meat back on you."

I nod, because I'm unable to find words. A freshman in any starting position is rare, but a freshman who didn't play his senior year of high school?

"Now get back to class. If those fast legs of yours still work, that is."

Oh, my legs still work all right, but I have no intention of going back to class just yet. I bound up the stairs to the art and photography rooms.

I spot Jordyn in her classroom and I gesture all crazy. She starts laughing when she sees me. Then I hear the door open and find her teacher glaring and at a loss for words.

"I'm in! They loved the letter!" I yell maniacally, then I run before the teacher can do anything. Laughter follows me down the hall and I can clearly pick out Jordyn's. God, I love her.

I'm on such a high that I manage to complete the writing assignment before class even ends. And that was less than ten minutes. Mr. Craig eyes me suspiciously when I throw it on his desk. Then I stare at the clock until the bell rings. I'm out the door before Mr. Craig officially dismisses us, but what do I care? I'm going to freaking Stanford!

Jordyn's out of breath when she meets me at lunch. I pick her up and kiss her, spinning her dramatically right there in the middle of the hall.

"You're practically vibrating," she says as we wait in line for pizza.

"Speaking of vibrating." I pull out my phone expecting to see another text from Coach congratulating me.

And that's all it takes to kill the mood. I've almost reached the hall by the time Jordyn even realizes I'm gone. She runs to catch me, grabbing my arm. I shake her off and push a few people out of my way. I'm trying to move fast, but I'm going against the sea of students. Jordyn manages to get out in front of me in the hallway and I end up pushing her and two other kids into the wall. Her face drops and I feel like a total asshole, but I'm too pissed to stop.

I'm halfway home without even seeing the road. I'm speeding and plowing through stop signs and all I see is my dad's stupid fucking face.

I throw the front door open. It hits the wall and bounces back hard enough to slam shut. I'm down the stairs in one swift step and there it is, my door busted open, the frame and some of the drywall completely destroyed. The crowbar and sledgehammer he used to break it down are staring up at me from the floor. So much for impenetrable. I stalk down into my room and see Dad kicking at the paneling. He's dangerously close to finding my hiding place.

I grab him by the shoulders and spin him around. "What the fuck are you looking for?" I scream into his face.

"You have no goddamn right to lock your door. This is my house!" He shoves me as hard as he can, catching me off balance. I stumble over a drawer that's been thrown to the floor. The bottom is no longer attached. The second I hit the ground, I feel a sharp pain in my side. Then another. The third time he hauls back to kick, I grab his foot and pull it out from under him. He falls but lands mostly on the bed. It gives me enough time to get up and get in his face. He wears an expression of pure unadulterated murder in his eyes. I'm pretty sure mine is the same.

"You can't keep me out of part of my own goddamn house. You don't pay the bills, I do!" He's right up in my face, so close he spits on me with each word.

"I am not required by law to pay rent in my own parent's house!" I'm concentrating very hard on keeping my hands at my sides. If I lose any of the control I still have, I will kill him. I'm sure of it.

"That gives you no goddamn right to hide shit from me! I know you have it!"

"What? What do I fucking have, Dad?"

"Her letter!" He swings wide and I'm easily able to maneuver out of the way of his fist.

That's what this is about? That's what he's been looking for?

"There is no letter, Dad. Don't you get it? She didn't leave us any goddamn explanation."

He stares at me, taking in my words. Then he shakes his head. "You shut the fuck up."

I almost feel sorry for him. "It's fucked up, but that's what she did. And we have to stop blaming each other and move on with—"

He uses his fists to shut me up. The first lands across the side of my head. The second hits me square in the stomach, knocking the wind out of me. It takes a second to catch my breath, and in that time he's landed another punch to my jaw. The sour, metallic taste of blood fills my mouth. It makes me think of Brett and the homecoming game. And that makes me think of all the times I hid away at football, hiding from what was going on here. I should have been there for her. I should have stopped him from slowly killing her will to live. I feel an eerie calmness come over me. I deserve this.

He lands another punch to my stomach. I double over. I feel the crack of his knee meeting my face and black spots appear in front of my eyes. But it doesn't hurt, it feels right. I deserve this. I steady myself, my hand to the wall, and wait for the next blow. The room fades in and out of focus. So does Dad. I reach out to grab hold of his shoulder for balance, but he's farther away than I expect and I start falling forward, but I'm turned upright as his arm pins me to the wall by my throat. I struggle to breathe, clawing at his forearm.

The black spots appear again in front of my eyes, but this time they grow bigger and bigger, fighting to overtake me until finally he releases his hold and I fall forward again. I reach out to catch myself on the bed, thinking he's done, but he lands another fist in my rib cage. And another. And another, then he rolls me over so I'm face-up on the bed. I feel the pressure of my face being hit and hit and hit but I no longer feel any pain. I can't see at all, but each time his fist meets my flesh, I hear the loud, satisfying sound of penance.

He shouts, "Fight back, you fucking pussy!" It sounds like it's echoing from somewhere down a long empty hallway.

He yells it again. And again. And each time it's farther away. I hear screaming and something that sounds like orders being shouted, and there's a high-pitched noise that slowly fades into complete silence.

THIRTY-THREE

The high-pitched noise has returned, but this time it's in a steady, rhythmic *beep beep beep*. I struggle to open my eyes. The small sliver of light is like a blade and I groan and squeeze them shut again. This causes even more pain.

"Tyler? Tyler?" I hear Jordyn's voice, but it's like I'm underwater.

I reach my hand out to find her—a sharp pain in my left side stops me. Then her hand is in mine and I squeeze it. I try to open my eyes again. The left one doesn't cooperate, but I manage to open the right. The light feels like the sun is singeing my brain.

Jordyn's hand slips out of mine and I see her outline retreating through a doorway. She's saying something, but I can't hear what.

I close my eye again and the burning stops. Now I feel a slow, steady throbbing ache throughout my face. Especially in my left eye.

Jordyn's hand takes mine again and I feel her lean over me,

close enough to smell that she's chewing mint gum. I breathe in the spicy scent mixed with the sweet jasmine of her hair.

"How are you feeling, Tyler?" a man's voice says from my other side.

I try to say something, but no sound comes out. I clear my throat—it feels like someone has stabbed me in the side. "Pain" is all I manage.

"I hear that. I'll just go ahead and up your pain meds," the weirdly cheerful guy says.

I hear two low beeping sounds and in a second I'm awash in lightness. My head is spinning and I feel like my body's twisting into positions that are physically impossible. I'm pretty sure my arms are on backward. But at least there's no more pain.

Jordyn strokes my hand and I try to open my eyes again. I still only manage to open the right one. The side she's on.

She looks like she hasn't slept for days. Her eyes are so swollen, I wonder just how long she's been up, how long I've been out.

"Hey," I say. My voice doesn't even sound like my voice. And my throat is on fire.

A cup is placed to my mouth from my blind side and a hand helps me to take a drink of water. I turn my head so I'm able to see the nurse. I didn't realize he was still here. He's a slim black man with a kind smile. The water cools my throat and I feel much better. I turn back to Jordyn and try again. "Hey."

"Hey." She smiles and a tear streaks down her cheek. I try to raise my hand to wipe it away but my side pinches so painfully, I stop.

"The pain meds are only good for so much. Try not to move a lot," the man says. "I'll see if I can find the doctor for you." He pats my shoulder gently and then leaves the room. I want him to come back. He makes me feel better.

Jordyn kisses the top of my hand.

"I'm so sorry I shoved you," I say.

She leans down so her lips are barely touching mine. "Shhh," she says against my mouth.

"Did you follow me?"

"Of course. Then I heard him attacking you from outside and I called the police. I ran in, not really sure what I planned to do, and I saw him beating the shit out of you. I thought he was going to kill you, Tyler." Her voice cracks.

"You saw?"

She nods.

I look around the room and she seems to understand what I'm looking for.

"He's in jail."

Part of me is happy and relieved, but then there's the other part that knows he needs help, and jail isn't where he's going to find it. What happens now? My birthday isn't for another month and a half.

Jordyn lets my hand drop. "I shouldn't have listened to you. I should have told my mom or Henry. This shouldn't have happened."

"Hey." I reach out, taking her hand back. But I can't think of what to say. Because she's right. I mean, shit. What if he'd hurt her when she came in after me? Or *killed* her? All my shit about a stupid fucking group home, and I risked her life. How big of an asshole am I?

She wipes her face on her sleeve.

"Tyler, this is Dr. Meyer." The nice nurse returns followed by a woman with curly, bouncy brown hair and a kind, round face.

"You suffered a ruptured spleen. We didn't have to remove it, but you'll have to remain here for another few days so we can monitor it. The rest of your injuries are superficial. Your eye socket was cracked, but there's not much we can do about that, it'll heal on its own. You might have bone fragments that will need to be removed at a later date. Just try not to move too much if possible and we'll have you out of here in no time." Her words aren't harsh, but her voice is. It's nothing like her face. Plus she's already out of the room before I can process what she's said.

"Doctors," the nurse says. "I'm Damon, by the way. Dr. Meyer may not have the best bedside manner, but she's really good. You're in excellent hands, my friend."

"Thanks, Damon," I say.

"Can I get you anything?" He's pouring me another cup of water before I even realize that I'm still parched. He holds it to my lips and helps me drink. Being babied by another man should probably be really emasculating, but all I feel is grateful.

Before I know it, it's dark out. I hear Jordyn protesting, but Kelly's insisting she needs to sleep, that she's already missed a day and a half of school and she has to go tomorrow.

A day and a half? It's been that long?

Kelly sees me watching them and turns to me, smiling. It's a sad smile. "You just missed Henry. He went to get the car. How are you doing, honey?"

"I've been better."

"I shouldn't have let you go back there." Her eyes get glossy, and she blinks quickly. "I always suspected. Your mom was good at covering, but I always thought something was off. I should have done something. Then. Now. I'm so sorry, Tyler."

"There was—" I grunt, clear my throat. "There was nothing you could do. She would have stood up for him."

She puts her hand on my knee. "This should never have happened."

"This was inevitable," I say.

"Don't say that." Jordyn is standing next to Kelly, frowning, angry.

I reach for her hand. "You were right. I'm sorry. I should've listened to you. I should have told someone. We could have—"

A mousy redhead pokes her head into the room. "I'm so sorry to interrupt, but visiting hours are over."

"Come on, sweetie. We'll be back tomorrow. After school," Kelly says.

Jordyn's grip on my hand tightens. "You really should go to school tomorrow," I tell her.

She looks at me like I'm crazy.

"I'll be okay. I've got Damon to keep me company. Just come after, like your mom says."

Kelly pats my foot and smiles, then puts her arm around Jordyn to lead her out. Jordyn leans over and kisses me, brushing her hand across my cheek. "I love you."

"I know." I attempt a smirk.

She smiles back at me.

"I love you too. Go."

She does.

My side starts to burn again, so I push the button for Damon.

A woman with a large tattoo peeking out of the top of her scrubs comes in.

"What can I do for you?" she asks.

"Where's Damon?"

"His shift ended. I'm Martha. Now, what's the matter, darlin'?"

"My side burns."

Martha messes with a few cords and buttons and then a wave of peace washes over me.

My arms are on backward again and then I feel a hand cup my chin followed by two cups meeting my lips: the first with a pill, the second with water.

"That'll help you sleep. If you need me again, you know what to do. Night." She flips off my light and shuts the door behind her.

When I open my good eye the next morning, my other eye opens a crack too, but not enough to see anything.

"I finally understand why you never wanted to talk about your dad."

"Doc?"

The screech of a chair against linoleum makes me cringe and my side burns.

"Imagine my surprise when someone called me asking if you were one of mine." He settles into the chair. He doesn't look happy. The crease between his eyebrows is more like a canyon today. "Tyler, I could have helped. It didn't have to go this far. Shit. I should've seen it."

"I . . ."

"You didn't want to end up in a home, right?" He sounds pissed. At me? At himself?

I nod, feeling like an asshole.

"I know how your mind works by now. Sort of. But there were other options. If you'd told me everything, we could've figured something out."

"So I guess we need to discuss those options now?"

His angry expression morphs into confusion. "You haven't talked to Kelly."

"I have. Why?"

"I take it she didn't tell you. She and Henry offered to take you in."

"Like I'm a stray fucking dog. Great." I stare past him out the window. "It's too much to ask of them."

"Trust me, they're happy to help. Lovely people. And Jordyn . . . That girl is head over heels for you."

I should feel grateful that Henry and Kelly are helping me. But all I feel is ashamed.

"Oh, uh . . ." He sets my cell phone on the table next to me. "Your dad's been calling you all morning from jail."

"He probably expects me to post bail," I mutter. "He almost killed my dog."

"He almost killed *you*. Goddammit, you should've told me everything."

"He needs help. With his drinking. With his depression, with dealing with Mom."

He shakes his head and sighs. "You're a good guy, Tyler."

"Doc?" I hesitate. "I didn't—I didn't fight back."

He leans forward and nods, taking in what I've said. I can tell he understands. "What happened with your mother wasn't your fault, Tyler."

"I know. I mean, I know that. But I feel like I deserved to feel a little of the pain she felt. For not seeing how much she hurt. For not being there for her when she needed someone."

"I don't know if that's what she would have expected of you, I didn't know her, but I do know that you have to stop blaming yourself. Think your mom would have wanted to see you like this?"

I shake my head. He's right. This was stupid.

"Stop being so hard on yourself, Tyler. I wish you'd see what everyone else sees. You deserve good things."

As soon as Dr. Meyer clears me to talk to the cops, a tall thin woman and a taller stocky man, both uniformed, question me for about four hours. Okay, maybe it's only forty-five minutes, but it feels like a freaking lifetime. And they have no interest in my suggestions for getting Dad help.

They finally decide on first-degree assault, and felony child abuse charges, since I'm still a minor. Both could mean sentences of up to twenty-four years. So Dad's basically fucked.

And he probably won't get any real help. If I'd told Dr. Dave everything, Dad would've probably been forced to get help before doing something that would keep him from ever getting it. Once again my selfishness fucks someone else over.

Jordyn comes to visit with Kelly and Henry right after school, as promised. They've brought me some amazing, gourmet chicken soup that Kelly made. I don't even have words for how grateful I am.

Henry isn't able to stay long –he has to get back to the studio, and Kelly leaves with him. My side is really bothering me. I was about to ask Damon for an extra dose of the pain meds right before Jordyn and everyone came, and then I sort of forgot.

"So my mom and Henry are talking about—" Jordyn stops. "You don't look so good." She sits on the side of my bed, laying her hand on mine.

"My side's bugging me. It's not a big deal." I reach for the button that summons Damon and wince as a sharp pain stabs through my torso.

Jordyn marches out into the hall and returns with a very concerned-looking Damon.

"Again?" he asks, lifting my shirt. Jordyn gasps when she sees the eggplant-colored bruising that covers pretty much the entire left side of my rib cage.

Damon carefully presses against the bruising and then shakes his head. "I have to get Dr. Meyer in here. This is the third time. I'm starting to worry."

As soon as he's out the door, Jordyn, who looks horrified, gently sits on the bed again.

I reach up to brush her hair back. "It's probably nothing," I say. But I'm scared shitless.

THIRTY-FOUR

It seems like a year before Dr. Meyer finally strolls into the room. I hate that she looks so nice, that she doesn't act how she looks.

She pokes and prods much harder than Damon and I want to die from the pain. I'm trying to hold my shit together because Jordyn is in the corner seriously losing hers and I can't stand it.

I'm pretty sure Dr. Meyer likes to speak medical jargon so I won't know what the hell's going on. I wish she'd just hurry it up.

"It's not a big deal," Damon explains after she leaves. "Dr. Meyer just wants to run a few tests to make sure everything's healing as it should be."

"I'm going to need surgery, aren't I? They're going to have to take out my spleen, aren't they?"

"Probably not, but we just need to be absolutely sure. It's not a big deal even if we do." He says the last part to Jordyn, who's now shaking, she's crying so hard. I wish I could hug her as much for my sake as for hers, but even the thought makes me wince.

"If I need surgery . . . ?"

"One of your guardians will be able to sign off on it," he says. It's awesome how he's able to anticipate my worries like that. He's really good at his job.

Another nurse comes in, and she and Damon work together to unplug and unhook things so that I'm mobile. Then they wheel me out of the room and Jordyn's left there in that sad little mauve chair, alone. As they push me down the hallway, Damon assures me that he'll go back to check on her just as soon as I'm situated.

It's dark when I wake up back in my hospital room. Damon's shift is long over, so I'm shocked to see him sitting with Jordyn.

"How are you feeling?" he asks.

"Enh" is all I can manage. He explains that something started bleeding again and they thought they might need to take out my spleen, but it turns out they just had to cauterize a pesky blood vessel. It required a "non-invasive" procedure. Non-invasive my ass. They still had to cut into me in a bunch of places and stick a camera and some tools in my side. That seems pretty damn invasive to me.

I'm still kind of out of it, but I can't feel anything. So in that way I'm doing pretty damn good.

"Visiting hours are technically over, but . . ." He shrugs.

I try to say thank you but it comes out as an incoherent drool/moan.

"You have twenty minutes, sweetie," he tells Jordyn as he leaves the room.

She nods. The top of her green shirt is wet, but she's not crying now. Somehow I manage a small nod, gesturing for her to come over.

She does.

I lift the side of my blankets and she climbs in, resting her head on the good side of my chest. My eyes are seriously heavy. I stroke the top of her arm and breathe in her jasmine shampoo and drift off to sleep.

Jordyn's gone when I wake up and part of me is missing. That's what it feels like.

Damon comes in carrying an IV bag. "Sleep well?"

It's only then that I realize it's morning.

I nod. "So, when can I get out of here? Not that I'm not enjoying your company."

"That's good, 'cause you'll have it for a few more days."

The door creaks and I expect Jordyn, but it's Kelly and Henry. Damon greets them as he squeezes by on his way out.

"How are you doing?" Kelly sits in the chair next to my bed.

"I'm ready to get out of here. I'll never be able to pay for all of this."

"It's all taken care of." Henry stands behind Kelly, placing his hands on the chair back.

"You can't— You really don't have to do all this, you know," I say, my voice cracking. My eyes sting. I have to close them.

"We know." Kelly rests her hand on my shoulder. "We want to." She reaches up for Henry's hand.

"You should have told us how bad things were before it got so outta hand, Tyler," Henry says to me. "We would've gladly gotten you the hell out of there."

I stare out the window, not seeing anything in particular. I can't look at them.

And then Jordyn comes in carrying a camera? She can't be serious. Though I am glad for the interruption—things were getting a little real there.

"What? Not feeling like your beautiful self today?" She holds it up. "Smile."

"All right." Henry reaches out and Jordyn hands the camera over. He holds it up like he's giving a toast. "Better run. Can't keep the Bryson wedding waiting. Don't worry about anything but healing, kiddo, understand?"

I nod because there are no words.

Kelly pats my shoulder. "I should go too. Captain's probably ready for a walk."

Before the door has even closed, Jordyn climbs into bed next to me, nuzzling her head into the crook of my neck. I kiss her forehead and lay my head back. My eyes are hot, and now my chest hurts nearly as much as my side. I'm one lucky unlucky shit.

THIRTY-FIVE

Five days later, I'm released from the hospital.

"I'm kind of like your brother now," I say to Jordyn as we lie on the basement couch watching the fire. Her head rests on the good side of my chest and her hair fans out across my shirt. I run my fingers through it until I find the little red strip.

"Well, you know what they say. Incest is best," she says, reaching her hand to where a sister should never touch.

"Watch it. I'm not allowed to exert myself for another two weeks." I curl the red hair around my first two fingers

"Mmmm," she moans. "Too bad."

"Dinner's about ready," Henry calls down to us.

"I'm going to need you to stop that or I will be extremely inappropriate at the dinner table."

Jordyn lifts herself so she's hovering over me, then she carefully straddles and kisses me. The kiss grows deeper and deeper and my body reacts.

"You're mean," I say against her mouth.

She laughs and then hops up, offering me a hand. "Let's go, *brother*."

I glance down at my rather conspicuous erection. "Not. Cool."

She laughs again and then bounds up the steps.

I'm alone at the studio with Henry, and it's a fairly busy Saturday. I don't have to work anymore—Henry and Kelly are taking care of everything—but I like it, so I keep the job. My injuries are almost completely healed. It's been about a month. Time is flying, especially now that I don't have to worry about going home to a ticking time bomb. Dad took a plea. He's still facing a minimum of ten years, though. His sentencing isn't for another few months. I might not even be here to see his disgraced face as the judge doles out what's coming to him. It all depends on when football training starts up.

"So . . . the big one-eight." Henry grins as he dismantles one of the lighting rigs. "Jordyn's still got till June. You better watch it, or you'll be in a cell next to your dear ol' dad." He laughs, then winces, like maybe he crossed a line.

I barely notice. My face is on fire. I know they know we have sex, but actually talking about it makes me want to die a little. Does he have conversations like this with Jordyn?

"I'm just messing with you. I know you love Jordyn like I love Jordyn."

"I hope not, otherwise *you'll* end up in a cell next to dear old Dad."

He laughs heartily. "Maybe it's best we change the subject."

"Couldn't agree more." I set the last of the equipment in the closet and shut the door.

Once the studio is in good shape, Henry and I head home. It's not even weird to think of it like that anymore—home. I fight the urge to call out "Honey, I'm home!" every time I enter the house and Jordyn's already there. Like today.

Before the door's even closed behind me, Jordyn runs up and grabs my hand. She practically pushes me down the stairs.

"What's going on?"

She lets out a sound that can only be described as a squeal and she pulls me to her room. She heads straight for her desk, where she retrieves a large envelope.

I snatch it from her hands. "You got in?" I pull out the contents to see the confirmation for myself. She got in to her dream school: Rhode Island School of Design.

"I never doubted for a minute. Especially with that weird and oddly terrifying bicycle drawing," I say, pulling her to me. I cup her face and she leans into my hand. God, I love that. It kills me every time. I brush my lips against hers. She does the same. And then I can't control myself anymore. I grab her and we tumble to the bed. We're practically at the point when clothes start to come off when we hear a throat clearing just outside the now-open door.

We jump apart so fast I almost fall off the bed.

Kelly starts laughing. "Trust me, this is just as awkward for me as it is for you."

I seriously doubt that.

Jordyn's face is practically glowing. I'm sure mine is a similar shade of fuchsia. I bet Kelly's also blushing, but I can't bring myself to look anywhere near her.

"I just wanted to see if you told Tyler the big news, and from all *this,* I gather you have." She sounds like she's trying to hold back another laugh. "Anyway, I'll just . . ." She turns to leave, closing the door behind her. But just before it's closed, she stops herself and pushes it back open. "I'm, um, not sure . . . but, uh . . . I think maybe the door should stay open, though."

I want to die.

Once Kelly's footsteps have retreated all the way back upstairs, I look at Jordyn. The second we make eye contact, we burst into laughter.

When I've managed to regain my composure, I tell Jordyn about my awkward conversation with Henry earlier.

"Twice in one day? You poor thing." She scoots across the bed and straddles me. It has absolutely no effect, though. I can't even think about sex after that. Well, I *can,* but it's easy to keep from acting on it.

Captain comes galloping through the door and jumps up on the bed. Kelly is madly in love with him. I'll probably leave him with her when I head off to Stanford. I can't exactly have him in the dorms, and I can't afford to get an apartment. And that's when it hits me.

"Rhode Island," I mumble, petting Captain.

Jordyn rolls over so she's using Captain like a pillow. She reaches out to brush her fingertips over my lips. "California," she says.

"Could we have picked schools farther apart?"

"I know." She closes her eyes. I watch her for several seconds until she opens her eyes and pops up. "Let's not dwell on it now. We have a celebration to attend," she says, throwing her arm out. She yanks me up from the bed and pulls me upstairs. Captain follows at our heels.

Henry and Kelly are taking us to some fancy steakhouse for my birthday and to celebrate Jordyn's good news. Thankfully, Kelly doesn't bring up that she walked in on me dry-humping her daughter. When the subject of Rhode Island comes up, I try my best not to let it bring me down. Jordyn knows. She holds my hand tightly under the table.

THIRTY-SIX

The end of the school year is approaching fast, and the understanding that we're all about to start the rest of our lives has made even the vilest people somewhat standable.

With the Stanford stuff in play, I've agreed to take Coach up on his offer to run drills with me. And when the underclassmen start training for the new season, I train right alongside them. Thankfully Brett and most of the other seniors have decided it's beneath them.

"Hey, man," Marcus says as I'm changing out of my practice clothes in the locker room one afternoon.

It's been a while since we've even spoken—not since the big fight that got me suspended before winter break. I didn't make much of an effort, honestly, and Sheila and Marcus are practically inseparable. Probably why he hasn't tried either.

"Hey." I take a seat on the bench to put my shoes on.

"You're looking good out there."

"Thanks."

"Coach tells me you're still on track for Stanford."

"Yep." I stuff my things into my bag and close the locker.

I can tell from the look on Marcus's face that he's feeling as awkward as I am.

"I just wanted to say congrats, bro." He pats me on the back sort of sideways.

"Thanks."

"I better . . ." He trails off as he heads for the door. "See ya, man."

I watch him go, feeling weirdly sad, like that's the last conversation we might ever have.

The old funeral suit—which almost fits perfectly again now—gets another outing when Henry books a big wedding gig. Kelly joins us because she and Henry are going to Vail for the weekend before the snow starts to melt. The venue is this old lodge in the foothills overlooking the entire city. We had a little spring snowstorm today, so everything's white, but it's still not that cold. Which is good because the bride was not about to let her wedding get moved indoors.

The best part about the wedding is that when it's over, Jordyn and I will have the house to ourselves.

She's smiling at me in that way that makes me practically lose my footing as we walk through the door. I desperately need to undo my top button or I might pass out.

When we reach her room, she unbuttons it for me. Then she slowly moves to the next. And the next. Never losing eye contact. It's so hot. Once the whole shirt is unbuttoned, she brushes her hands up my chest and pushes the shirt off my shoulders. She kisses my neck, then my shoulder, then my chest, then my stomach. Her lips are soft and hot where they brush my skin. I can feel them long after they've already moved on to the next spot. She kisses her way back up my chest while her hands unfasten my belt.

When my pants hit the floor, I take her hands and place them at her sides, and then I slide my hands up her arms, skimming her skin with the tips of my fingers. One hand comes to rest behind her neck and with the other I brush my thumb across her lips. Her eyes drift shut. I lean in and kiss her just next to her mouth. I brush my lips right beneath her ear. I kiss her neck, pushing her hair out of the way of her zipper. My lips linger on that spot under her ear that drives her crazy, and I very, very slowly unzip her dress.

Her breathing picks up.

I trace my fingertips up her back, following the line of the zipper—she's not wearing a bra and I almost forget to pace myself—and then I pull the straps down over her shoulders and the dress falls to the floor.

I sweep her onto the bed and my lips trace her jawline. She tastes like the faintest hint of salt, and the spicy scent of her perfume tricks my senses into thinking she also tastes like cloves and vanilla. I slowly kiss every inch of her neck, working my way to her mouth.

I want to screen-capture this moment and live in it forever. No retouching necessary.

When my lips finally meet hers, she moans against my

mouth. It's such a turn-on that I can affect her this way.

She curls her hands in my hair and our kissing deepens. I take it all in— the arch of her back, the smoothness of her skin, the taste and urgency of her lips, the cadence of her breathing. I savor everything.

I'm drifting off to sleep, wondering what's going to happen when an entire country separates us.

"What's wrong?" she asks, her breath hot against my chest.

"I thought you were asleep."

She shakes her head and reaches for my hand, entwining our fingers. "What's wrong?" she asks again.

"I don't know how I'm going to live without you."

She lifts her head so she can make eye contact. "Let's not think about it yet." She smiles, but there's a sadness in it. I pull her close and she rests her head back down on my chest.

Everything changed after that night.

The Stanford coach called me up and asked me to join the summer football camp they offer for high schoolers looking to get a leg up before applying next year. He wants me to be on top of my game by the time training starts up in August. He told Coach he's really hoping to start me. Of course I said yes. The downside, and it's a major downside, is that I'll have to leave about a week after graduation. Needless to say, Jordyn wasn't happy about it, but we agreed that it was the right thing for me to do.

Jordyn's been busy working on her mixed-media art projects. She's trying out all sorts of new techniques before she gets to her dream school.

When we *are* together, I sort of feel like she's always somewhere else. I think I probably come across that way too, like we're trying to slowly adjust to being apart while we're still together. And the thing is, and this makes me sad. . . . it feels right.

After that night I thought being away from her would be the end of my world, but I'm starting to realize there's so much more out there that I'm going to discover. Even if we try to stay together, with texting and FaceTime and everything, by the time we actually see each other in person again, we'll be different people. And maybe those two new people won't be such a perfect fit for each other. Or maybe they will. I don't know. The idea of ever falling out of love with her appeals to me about as much as being locked in a room alone with my dad.

Is it better to acknowledge what we have now and let it stay perfect in our memories? Or push it and risk it all falling apart? I don't know. I really don't. All I know is that when I see her again, I want to be happy about it.

THIRTY-SEVEN

The hum of the stadium crowd fills me with that certain thrill—the one I used to feel before a big game. Of course, it's the same stadium we played in, so that might have a little to do with it. I think about the last real game I played here, Mom screaming from the stands.

"You ready for this?" Jordyn takes my hand.

"Absolutely," I say.

"You thinking about your mom?"

"How do you do that?" I smile at her. She's got her graduation cap pinned at a jaunty angle, eyes shining. "What am I going to do when—"

She cuts me off with a kiss. Nothing inappropriate, but it's slow and wonderful. My heart thumps heavily in my chest.

We're interrupted when Mrs. Ortiz announces that it's time to line up alphabetically.

I'm smashed between Philip Black and Fernanda Blades. The sun is scorching and the black gowns aren't exactly helping things. By the time we take our seats, I'm sweating my balls off. Philip Black—at least I think it's Philip, though in all fairness it might be Fernanda—forgot deodorant this morning.

When it comes time for my row to make the crawl up to the stage, I find myself wondering about Dad. I hate the bastard, but it feels so damn lonely not to have family when each time a name is announced, the family of that kid cheers wildly. Not that Dad would have ever come to this, and if he had, he would most definitely not have cheered. But . . .

"Tyler Nathaniel Blackwell," the announcer calls right as my foot hits the stage.

Jordyn screams so loud she'll probably be hoarse later. But her cheers aren't alone. I search the crowd and see Henry, Kelly, Aslan, Patricia, and, I think, Dr. Dave applauding wildly. Patricia's standing and doing this kind of inappropriate dance. Just behind her I swear I see my mom, but then my eyes adjust and I remember that she's dead all over again.

I'm blinking back tears when the principal shakes my hand. He says something, but I have no idea what. Maybe she is watching. Somewhere. Not that I necessarily believe in any of that. I don't.

I follow the line of my fellow graduates back to our row and Jordyn jumps up from her seat and throws herself into my arms, wrapping her legs around my waist. One of the nearby teachers—oh, god, it's Mrs. Hickenlooper—leaps into action, peeling her off of me. But Jordyn gets in a good, long kiss first.

o o o

After the ceremony, which was about twelve hours long, we head to the house, where all of Jordyn's family is waiting to shower her with graduation gifts.

I sit back at the fire pit, watching Jordyn hug and thank various relatives. I've never had that, and while part of me thinks that that much family could be a hassle, another part considers how different things might have been if I did have extended family. If Mom had had someone she could turn to when Dad made things unbearable. If she had a sister or a brother or a close cousin she could've confided in.

Aslan's laugh erupts from across the lawn as he chats with one of Kelly's brothers. He notices me and strides over. "You kidder. Kelly tells me you're going to Stanford on a *football* scholarship. I'm hurt you didn't tell me you played. We could have seriously bonded, bro." He punches me on the arm.

"I wasn't exactly thinking straight this year."

"Yeah, I heard. You dealing okay now? You need anything?"

I almost laugh at his serious face. It looks like a bad put-on, but I know it's not. It's just the way he looks. "I'm good now. Jordyn helped."

"Whatever she did, you know she gets that from me, right?"

I manage a laugh. "Sure?"

"Well, you come back and visit us, okay? We gotta do some football bonding. Maybe at Thanksgiving."

"Maybe," I say. He hears his name being bellowed by his wife and leaves me with a hearty fist bump.

I scan the crowd for Jordyn, but she might have gone inside.

So I lean back and stare past the flames, taking in the Colorado beauty. The purple mountain majesties with their brilliant orange halo seem to have made themselves even more spectacular, as if they know I'll be leaving them for good and are trying to seduce me into staying.

Captain nudges my hand with his cold nose, forcing me to pet him, then he rests his chin on my leg and closes his eyes blissfully. My heart twists.

"He'll be here when you come home for Thanksgiving." Henry hands me a Coke and sits down next to me. Captain doesn't move from his head-petting.

I'm unable to look at Henry. If I look at him, or anyone else that I care about, I'll probably lose it, so I stare into the bright orange and yellow flames.

Henry doesn't say anything for a long time. Neither do I.

"You're always welcome here, you know." He takes a long swig of his beer. I haven't so much as sipped my Coke.

My eyes burn, and not from staring into the fire. First Aslan, now Henry. I swallow hard, unable to put into words how much his invitation means to me. And how much it hurts that I won't take him up on it. And just like that, I know that I won't. I can't. It's suddenly clear. I have to move on. I have to evolve. I can't linger in the past. And this place has too much of that. This—all of it—it'll soon be a bunch of memories, beautiful and tragic and significant, but it's not my future.

"Henry, I don't know how I can possibly—"

Henry cuts me off with the clank of his bottle against mine, and one of his *Henry* looks that says more than any number of words could. Then he gets up and heads inside. I'm not sure, but I feel like he understands. I know his invitation is very real, and who knows, maybe I'll take him up on it one day. But for right now, there are too many ghosts in this city.

THIRTY-EIGHT

I spend the next week putting on a brave face. Kelly seems oblivious, but I find Henry watching me with . . . I don't know, maybe a sad kind of admiration? Or maybe I'd just like to think that. Jordyn has been acting "normal," and by that I mean not normal at all. She's been way too happy and excited. It's out of character, but then I'm doing the same thing, aren't I?

The day before the day, I wake up, finishing any and all last-minute packing, which, let's face it, there's not much of. Then I head out to my last session with Dr. Dave.

I saw him after graduation—yes, it was him in the crowd with a view of Patricia's ass—and he told me that I didn't have to come, but I insisted.

His face is a mash of emotion when he greets me.

"Hey, Doc, don't go getting all mushy on me. I'm barely hanging on as it is." I throw myself onto the couch and kick my feet up.

Dr. Dave chuckles as he joins me. "What can I say, Tyler, I'll miss you."

"Yeah, yeah, yeah. I'm . . ." I can't finish because a piece of feeling has gone and gotten stuck in my throat.

"It's okay, I know." Dr. Dave scoots that goddamn Kleenex box toward me on the table. When I glare at him, I find him holding in a laugh.

"Yeah, laugh at the poor messed-up kid. That's really cool." I take the box and toss it at him.

He laughs out loud, and I do too.

"Did you think about what I said? About continuing our meetings via FaceTime?"

I nod. "Yeah. I can't really afford it, though. Henry and Kelly have been awesome about helping me continue coming since my birthday, but I can't ask that of them once I'm gone." Social Services decided that on my eighteenth birthday, whether my treatment was over or not, I was done. I was an adult and if I wanted to follow in my mother's footsteps, I was no longer their problem.

"Here's what I want to do, then." He leans forward and rests his elbows on his knees. "You have my number and my e-mail. Use them. I would like you to check in whenever you feel like you need to talk. Or even if you just *want* to talk. I expect to hear how Stanford is all you hoped it would be and all that clichéd crap."

I crack a smile. "Doc, I hope you know what a can of worms you're opening. You might seriously reconsider when I start drunk-dialing you."

"I'm okay with the occasional drunk-dial."

"Occasional? We'll see about that." I want to tell him how much his offer means to me, but I just can't. He knows. I know he knows.

"And you'll be back for the holidays. We can work something out."

I return my focus to the coffee table.

"Oh." He gets it. "Do Kelly and Henry know?"

"I think Henry suspects. Kelly, no, I don't think so."

"And Jordyn?"

I swallow. "I can't really tell."

"You haven't talked about it with her? Has she brought it up?"

I shake my head. "You think I'm an idiot for not having discussed it with her, don't you?"

"I think you're chicken-shit. And human."

"I can live with that." I smile and nod. "Do you think I'm being stupid about . . . ?"

He shakes his head. "Not at all. It's understandable to want to put some distance between you and this place with all these memories. Healthy even."

"I don't know. Maybe I'll change my mind. Maybe I'll actually miss it here."

"Maybe. And you know what? That's okay too."

It's a slow weekend, so Henry gives Jordyn and me the day off. When I get back from Dr. Dave's, I pack a cooler and wait with Captain on the front steps for her to get back from the mall with Kelly.

"What's this?" she asks.

"We're going for a run." I smile.

"Cool. Let me change." She disappears for a few minutes and reappears in shorts and a sports bra.

I place the cooler in the trunk. "You're seriously going to run?"

"I'm probably going to die, but I'm going to try my best."

I laugh as I get into the car. "You know I'd never make you run. Unless you wanted to."

"I know. Figured I'd just play along. So where are we really going?"

I drive us to my favorite running path in the foothills near Red Rocks. The path I used to hike with Mom. The path with the perfect little picnic spot.

"Maybe if you carry the cooler, I'd be able to jog. For a bit anyway," Jordyn says, letting Captain out of the backseat.

"Doubt it."

She smacks me on the arm.

Poor Captain keeps doubling back as we hike, trying to get us to move faster. I would normally love to push myself on my favorite path one last time, but today slow feels right.

At just past the halfway point, we reach the long, flat rock, next to the single tree. The sun's even cooperated, remaining behind the tree so we have some shade. I pull out a container of leftovers from Kelly's amazing dinner last night, a couple Cokes, some silverware. Then I pull out the water dish and a treat for Captain.

"It's so beautiful," she says, admiring the side-swept rock formations about fifty yards away.

"It is," I say, admiring her.

"I can see why you like it here. You going to miss it?"

"More than you know." I'm not talking about the trail.

I shift my focus to the view just as she turns to face me. I'm not sure whether or not she understood that little exchange. She doesn't acknowledge anything other than our meal. And a fine meal it is. Kelly made one of her signatures last night: steak salad. How is a steak salad so special? I have no idea. But I swear to god it's life-changing.

"It's awfully claustrophobic for being outdoors," Jordyn says, running her fingers through Captain's fur.

I meet her eyes. She looks sad.

"I think we've avoided the elephant for long enough, don't you?" she says softly.

I nod.

"Neither one of us is stupid enough to think we could actually make a long-distance relationship work." She squints up at me, eyes shiny.

"I know." I scoot over so I'm close enough to touch her. "I love you more than . . ." I give up.

She's crying now, and so am I.

"I mean it."

She nods. "I love you, Tyler. I'll always love you."

I brush my lips to hers, closing my eyes. I whisper "I love you" against her mouth.

Nothing else needs to be said.

○ ○ ○

When we get back to the house, Henry and Kelly aren't there.
There's a note on the fridge and a wrapped box on the counter.
Jordyn hands me the note without a word.
It's addressed to me in an elegant, loopy scrawl.

Dearest Tyler,

It's been such a pleasure having you in our lives this year.
We're sorry about the circumstances that brought you to
us, but we are beyond words about how you've changed us
for the better. And the way our beautiful Jordyn lights up
when you enter the room, well, there just aren't words for
how that makes us feel. You've truly been like a son to us.
And we are very, very serious when we tell you that you
are always welcome here. No matter what. We love you,
Tyler. Which is why we're unable to be here to see you off.
As much as we'd love to spend your last night here with
you, we know that you and Jordyn probably want to have
your good byes in private. We know you'll be tempted to
graciously decline our gift, but please don't. It's the least
we could do. Henry and I love you and we know you'll do
well in everything that you set out to accomplish. Please
keep in touch.

Love,
Kelly and Henry

My hands shake as I attempt to open the gift. Jordyn has to steady me once I've managed to unwrap it.

"It's too much," I choke out.

Sitting on the counter in front of me is a seriously expensive Mac laptop. And I don't even have to turn it on to know that it's filled to the brim with software.

"For school," Jordyn says, and she smiles.

I'm shaking my head and swallowing hard as Jordyn rubs circles against my back. My breathing hitches.

I simply can't fathom someone doing something like this for someone who isn't their family. Even though I pretty much feel like they are my family. They're more my family than my dad ever was.

Jordyn pulls away slightly so she's able to look me in the eyes. I kiss her gently on the forehead and then I hug her tightly.

How can I leave this? How can I survive without this? Maybe we could try the long-distance thing. Maybe we could make it work. Maybe.

She takes my hand in hers and leads me to the basement. "I have something for you too."

"Jordyn—" I begin to protest.

"I don't want to hear it. I got you a present and you will accept it and you will love it and that's all there is to it."

I actually manage to laugh.

When we reach my room, she sits me on the bed and orders me to close my eyes. "And don't even think about opening them."

"Yes, sir."

She kisses me quickly and then I hear her run out of the room.

Her footsteps are slower when she returns and it takes every ounce of self-control not to peek.

After shuffling around for a minute, she sits next to me on the bed and takes my hand in both of hers. "Okay. Open them."

If the laptop is the most generous gift I've ever received, this is the most thoughtful—probably the most thoughtful, most meaningful gift I'll ever receive in my life.

A large framed piece of art that Jordyn had somehow managed to keep hidden from me leans against the dresser.

All five pictures of my mom have been blown up and converted into black-and-white and placed throughout the canvas, with beautiful watercolors of mountains overlapping them and a remarkable pencil-drawn resemblance of Captain. It's absolutely perfect.

I'm completely and utterly speechless.

Jordyn climbs onto my lap and I hold on to her, burying myself in her jasmine hair. She adjusts herself so her lips can reach mine. We kiss gently and then more deeply until I feel like not kissing her would be like dying, like I would flatline without her kisses to shock me back to life.

There is absolutely no doubt that this is it. This is good-bye.

THIRTY-NINE

She doesn't stay with me that night. I heard her crying as she left the room early this morning. I could've stopped her, I know it, but it was too much for me too. My heart is heavy when I wake up to the realization that that was the last time I will ever be with her, will ever touch her, will ever make love to her.

When I head toward the kitchen, I see that her bedroom door is still closed. I wonder if she plans to avoid a good-bye like Kelly and Henry have. God, I hope not. But by the time I've finished eating breakfast, and washing the dishes, and loading the remaining items into my car, and she hasn't emerged, I understand that that's exactly what she plans to do.

My heart breaks. I don't have any right to be angry with her. I'm the one leaving after all, but I thought I'd get to say good-bye. One last kiss. Some parting words. I don't know. Something.

The computer and her beautiful gift are the last things I

load, and then I head back to the house for Captain. At least he won't cheat me out of a good-bye.

I plop down on the living room floor and he immediately throws himself on my lap. His tail is wagging and he's licking my face, completely oblivious that this is the last time he'll see me for a very long time, maybe ever. I'll try to come back for him as soon as I'm able to get a place that allows dogs, but who knows when that'll be. Hopefully next year. And even then, maybe he'd be better off with someone like Kelly, who'll actually have the time to give him the attention he deserves. I can't think about logistics right now.

I hug my dog to me and he whines in excitement. "I really wish I could take you with me, buddy."

He licks at my chin, lapping up a few stray tears.

After a good fifteen minutes, I finally pull myself up. It's time.

As I pass the basement stairs, I pause. I could just go down and force her to see me. I take two steps down the stairs and then I stop myself. Maybe it's better this way. Maybe it's like ripping off a bandage. I hesitate for a second longer. Then I turn back up the stairs. I hug Captain one more time. "You take care of these amazing people, Captain. You'll have a wonderful life here. I love you, you crazy dog." I kiss the top of his head and then I head for the door.

When I reach the driveway, I hear the front door fly open. I've barely managed to turn around when Jordyn throws herself at me. I gather her up. She holds me tighter, her hands gripping my shirt.

We stay like that for god knows how long—however long it is, it's not long enough. When we finally pull apart, I try to speak. "Jordyn, you are the best thing that's ever happened—" My voice breaks and I fight to regain my composure. "I can't thank you enough. For everything."

She cranes her neck until her lips meet mine. And there's so much in that one kiss.

She buries her face in my shirt again, her shoulders shaking. When she looks up, it's like she's memorizing me. I'm doing the same, running my fingers over her eyelids, her eyebrows, her lips, her jaw, memorizing everything about her.

Then I lean down and kiss her one last time. It's slow and lingering and filled with . . . everything. And this time when we break apart, it's for good. I step back and she drops her hands to her sides. I take another step away, memorizing the slope of her shoulders and the elegance of her stance. And another, memorizing the exact black of her hair, with just a hint of blue when the sun hits it the right way. And another, memorizing every detail of her face, from the shape of her eyebrows to the golden brown of her eyes to the perfect almost-pout of her lips. Until I reach the car door. And then I pause one more minute before I get in. A small smile manages to spread across that perfect mouth, and she raises her hand to wave.

"I love you," I say.

"I know."

Then I get in the car and back down the driveway. She follows me all the way to the street. Captain must've pushed his way out the door, because he has now joined her in the driveway. I shift the car into drive and offer them one last wave. And then I hit the gas.

It takes everything in me, but I don't look back. I can't. Not after everything.

ACKNOWLEDGMENTS

I am forever indebted to all the many people who helped shape this story into a book.

Writers dream about working with a rock star dream agent, and you, Laura Bradford, are the kindest, smartest rock star dream agent a writer could hope for. Thank you so much for believing in me. I absolutely treasure your guidance and advice. And a big thanks to Taryn Fagerness, my foreign rights agent. Wow, do I have an amazing team.

Jessica Garrison, what can I say? You made this whole experience beyond awesome. I couldn't have been matched with a better editor. I swear you're in my head. Your suggestions were exactly what I meant to write in the first place. Without your brilliant insight this book wouldn't be what it is.

Nancy Conescu, I can't thank you enough for making all of this happen. Your edits started me in the right direction and I was so sad to see you go, but you left me in excellent hands with Jess. I hope Australia is treating you well.

And I'd like to thank everyone else at Dial and the Penguin Group who helped make my dreams come true, especially my copy editor Regina Castillo for her keen eye, and Jessie Sayward Bright, who's responsible for this awesome cover.

To all my Fearless Fifteeners: How would I have made it through these past two years without you guys? Especially my fellow Fearless Angelinos: Mary McCoy, Charlotte Huang, Nicola Yoon, and honorary members Nicole Maggi, Kerry Kletter, and Anna Shinoda!

Amazing critique partners are precious commodities. Thank you, Andrea Hannah, for juggling writing, teaching, and kids, and still having time to give me amazing notes. You're a superstar!

Big thanks to the Studio City Fiction Writers Group people who gave me invaluable notes way back when this book was just a baby manuscript. Beth Shady, Amy Ball, Jim Sullivan, Eric Dzinski, Ari Jarvis, and Jess Place, you made me love Mondays. And an especially big thanks to Lindsay Champion for starting the group in the first place, and remaining an awesome critique partner after moving across the country!

I have some seriously amazing friends. Jessica Brody (my unofficial mentor), Jennifer Bosworth, and Gretchen McNeill, your sage advice has kept me sane. Thanks for holding my hand through this crazy journey. Kristen Keller, you've been my biggest cheerleader for twenty-plus years. You are the reason I discovered my love of YA. Here's to many more years of book discussions! Sara Docksey, Kristen may have introduced me to YA, but you certainly helped fan the flame. And Elisha

Gruer, who also happens to be the best casting partner in the world, your encouragement means the world to me.

I have to thank my family again. Mom and Dad, you don't know how grateful I am that you always encouraged creativity. I wouldn't be who I am without that. I love you guys. Billie, the best niece in the whole world, thanks for always keeping my spirits up. I love you so much. You're not allowed to read this book for a few more years, though. Seriously. Why are you still reading this? And to Audrey Jilka and Craig Rosenbaum: Thank you for blessing me with creative genes.

And finally, a special, huge thank you to Michael Levy. Without an oversharing (sometimes past the point of awkward) brother like you, I would never have been able to write like a dude. Love you!